ROHIT CHANANA

DIL SE DOST

Celebrating gratitude, building dosti, inspiring resilience, curiosity to grow...

First Edition: February 2025
Printed in India

Printed at Gapmeta Ventures Private Limited, Navi Mumbai
Typeset in Adobe Garamond Pro

ISBN : 978-93-6070-262-5

Cover Design: Prajakta Sawant & Rohit Chanana

Cover Ideation: Poonam Chanana & Ishani Chanana

Picture Credit: Manav Chugh

STORYMIRROR
Stories that reflect you

Publisher:	StoryMirror Infotech Pvt. Ltd. Unit No-F/705, 7th Floor, Kailas Corporate Lounge, Veer Savarkar Road, Vikhroli Park Site, Vikhroli West, Mumbai-400079, Maharashtra.
Web:	storymirror.com
Facebook:	@storymirror
Instagram:	@storymirror
Twitter:	@story_mirror
Contact Us:	marketing@storymirror.com

Disclaimer

This book is a reflection of the author's present recollection of his personal journey, perceptions, and interpretations gathered over decades of experience. The opinions expressed herein are solely those of the author and do not necessarily represent the views, positions, or policies of any companies, organizations, or individuals whether explicitly mentioned or otherwise associated with the author past or present.

While the author has endeavored to present facts and events accurately, given the passage of time and limitations of the reliance on memory, there may be instances where certain details are inadvertently misstated or incomplete. In addition, for privacy and storytelling purposes some names, locations and timelines may have been altered. The reader should not consider this book anything other than a work of literature. If any factual discrepancies are found, readers are requested to view them as unintentional oversights rather than deliberate inaccuracies.

The purpose of this book is to share author's experiences and learnings in good faith, with the hope that they may inspire and provide value to others. The author sincerely appreciates the reader's understanding and open-mindedness as the reader engage with this story. The author and publisher disclaim any liability for any loss or damage direct or indirect, arising from use or reliance of any information contained in this book. This includes, but is not limited to, emotional distress, financial loss or reputational harm. By reading this book, readers acknowledge the subjective nature of this memoir and understand that the author and publisher cannot be held responsible for individual interpretations or actions taken as a result of its contents.

Foreword - Ishani

It is with immense pride and a heart overflowing with gratitude that I pen this foreword for my father's remarkable journey. He could have chosen anyone to write these words, yet he entrusted me with this honor, a profound testament to the deep respect and unwavering trust he has in me as both his daughter and his investment partner at Sarcha Advisors.

As you delve into this book, I invite you to uncover not just the story of a man who has achieved extraordinary success but also the essence of who he truly is. In every sense of the word, he is my Hero. He is not just my father; he is my role model, my mentor, and my Guru. His values, principles, and unwavering dedication have shaped not only my life but also the lives of countless others who have been fortunate enough to know him.

If I were to encapsulate my father's journey in a single word, it would be "heroic." His life is a tapestry woven with heroic experiences, wisdom, and a profound commitment to his values. Through his highs and lows, he has exemplified resilience, integrity, humility and compassion, qualities that I strive to embody every day. Each challenge he faced became a lesson, not just for him, but for all of us who have had the privilege to witness his journey.

In the context of this book, I play three significant roles: a reader eager to learn from his experiences, a daughter filled with admiration, and an investment partner who has closely collaborated with him to shape this narrative. Together, we spent countless hours discussing what to include, sharing insights about his journey, and meticulously editing the text to ensure his story resonates with authenticity and depth. As you read this book, I hope you feel the love and passion he poured into every page. I've watched him dedicate countless hours to refining his thoughts and sharing his journey, ensuring that his story is not merely a narrative of achievements but a heartfelt reflection of his experiences and the invaluable lessons he has learned. His dedication to sharing this journey with you is a true testament to his belief in the transformative power of storytelling.

My hope is that you connect with this narrative "Dil-Se." May it inspire you, challenge you, and resonate with your own experiences. I encourage you to embark on this journey with my father; in doing so, I believe you will find not only inspiration but also a deep sense of gratitude for the moments that shape our lives.

Thank you for taking the time to join us on this incredible journey. I truly believe that you will find as much joy in reading it as he has found in writing it.

Ishani Chanana
Daughter

Foreword - Rohan

I vividly remember that day when I joined my dad at the breakfast table, and the first thing he said was that he wanted me to write the foreword for his book—a book that encapsulates his lifelong learnings. I must admit, I was both excited and nervous. It's an incredible honor and privilege to write a foreword for someone you've grown up admiring.

As his son, I've had the unique privilege of knowing the person behind the accolades and professional titles. Beneath the aura of success is a man driven by humility, curiosity, and a relentless hunger for learning. One of my fondest memories goes back to when I was around 13 or 14 years old. My dad would invite me to role-play with him before his important meetings. I'd play the role of his boss, asking tough questions and sharing feedback on his responses. Looking back, it amazes me how he treated my views with genuine respect and proof of his belief that everyone, regardless of age or status, has something valuable to offer.

This hunger for knowledge and his respect for others are perfectly captured in the title of his book, *"DilSe Dost." DilSe* means "from the heart," and *dost* means "friend." And that's who he is at his core, someone who speaks from the heart and treats everyone as a friend.

One anecdote that stands out is from my wedding reception. As guests from his professional circle came up to congratulate me, nearly every one of them said the same thing: *"Your dad is not just a colleague or a leader—he's a friend."* These were people from all walks of life, some older and more experienced, others just starting out in their careers. Yet, regardless of their position, they all saw my dad not just as a mentor but as someone they could genuinely count on.

This book takes you through his remarkable journey from humble beginnings to becoming a respected name in India's startup ecosystem. It's a story of sheer determination, hard work, bold risk-taking, and an unwavering belief in Goddess Durga, a symbol of strength and resilience. For those who enjoy Bollywood stories, you'll find this to be a real-life version of the "rags to riches" narrative: a young boy with nothing but dreams and the support of his life partner, building something extraordinary from scratch.

But this isn't just a story of success, it's also a practical guide. My dad has shared his philosophies and frameworks in these pages, along with short, relatable stories that will resonate with you. As you read, you may find yourself thinking, *"If he could do it, why can't I?"* That's the magic of this book, it reminds you that you already have the ingredients to succeed. The key is learning how to make the most of your potential.

Seeing this book come to life fills me with immense pride. This isn't just a book, it's a life lesson on dreaming big, staying grounded, and striving to become the best version of yourself. I hope you find these pages as inspiring as I have and that they motivate you to pursue your dreams with courage and heart.

Or, as my dad would say in his signature style: *Happy reading, dost!*

Rohan Chanana
Son

Preface

Hi ***Dost,***

You might be wondering why I am addressing you as "***Dost.***" For me, "***Dost***" (friend) evokes an immediate emotional bond, a sense of warmth, and a heartfelt welcome in my interactions with people from all walks of life. Calling someone "***Dost***" creates a "***Dil Se***" (straight from the heart) connection, nurturing relationships that endure the test of time. This term has become a cherished part of my vocabulary, and it's heartwarming to see others embrace it when they address me.

This book is far more than a recounting of my journey; it is a tribute to the belief that each of us has the power to shape our destiny, regardless of where we begin. At its core, it celebrates the values that have defined my life: gratitude, Dil Se Dosti, resilience, and an unwavering commitment to growth. Through these values, I hope to inspire others to discover their inner strength and carve their own paths, no matter the socio-economic challenges or obstacles they may face.

On a personal level, this book holds special meaning for me. My daughter, Ishani, encouraged me to share my stories in the form of a book, seeing it as a way to leave behind a lasting legacy. By documenting my life's journey, I aim to pass on not just the lessons I've learned but also the values I deeply cherish, ensuring they resonate with and guide future generations. This book is my way of offering a piece of myself to anyone searching for — insights, inspiration, and reflections on a life dedicated to creating meaning and impact.

Moreover, many of my dosts and over 500 founders I've had the privilege of meeting, have often expressed their desire for me to share my learnings in a tangible form. This book is also my way of repaying my Rishi Rin, fulfilling a karmic obligation to share knowledge and experiences that may serve as a guide or inspiration to others. Through this effort, I seek to contribute back to the world that has given me so much, creating a sense of balance, fulfillment, and purpose in my life.

This book aims to distill 66 years of living life to the fullest, with gratitude and literally no regrets. I feel incredibly blessed to have a life brimming with fun, happiness, and joy. While there are many paths to achieving bliss, I aim to share insights and experiences that shaped who I am today, especially as I promote entrepreneurship and exponential thinking.

Condensing 66 years—or six hundred thousand hours—into a 260 page book is a daunting task that will barely scratch the surface. Nevertheless, I will try to share meaningful lessons through short stories based on my experiences and interactions. I hope that this book garners your love and interest and that in turn will encourage me to write a second volume, sharing more stories and insights in the future.

I want to make an honest confession: this is my first foray into writing a book. Even after dedicating over 500 hours of focused effort, countless moments of subconscious reflection, and deeply heartfelt engagement over the course of a year, I humbly hope to at least meet, if not exceed, your expectations. This journey has felt much like building a startup—creating something new with the sincere hope of making a meaningful impact on people's lives.

Starting from humble beginnings, I was recently recognized as one of India's top angel investors by both Forbes India and Fortune India. This book captures over 40 years of professional experiences intended to inspire people to connect with their passions and pursue their paths as intrapreneurs, entrepreneurs, angel investors, professionals…all while staying true to their values and living the Purpose.

Every journey, like mine, begins with conveying gratitude to those who have subconsciously or consciously dedicated their time, efforts, love, and compassion to help me evolve into the best version of myself. With that in mind, I extend my gratitude to all well-wishers including my family and friends, their love and kindness have enabled me to befriend anyone and everyone I meet, spreading positivity, joy, love and happiness. My deep reverence to Goddess Durga for blessing me with opportunities and challenges that have helped me grow. Through this journey, I've cultivated values of gratitude, kindness, resilience, and humility, shifting my focus from myself to giving back and positively impacting others.

If you are reading this book, *Dost,* I first want to express my heartfelt gratitude. I hope that this book helps unlock your potential and guides you towards your vision in life. We can become what we aspire to be because we are the authors of our destiny. With strong faith in ourselves and our dreams, we can navigate life's challenges.

As social beings, the company we keep profoundly impacts our well-being. Had I not surrounded myself with positive influences, my story might have unfolded very differently. Trust your heart; it knows who is right for you. Embracing a "*Dil Se* Connect" fosters meaningful relationships and elevates everyone, allowing us to share the beauty of life's journey together.

I spent 37 enriching years working in three of the best-managed family-run businesses—Escorts, Ranbaxy, and Hero. During this time, I delivered outstanding results to all stakeholders while learning invaluable lessons along the way.

In early 2019, at the age of 61, I decided to embark on my Version 2.0, transitioning from an intrapreneur to a founder and entrepreneur. This new chapter has seen me evolve into an angel investor and a *Dost*, driven by a higher purpose: to be happy and spread happiness. As a passionate promoter of entrepreneurship, I've had the privilege of funding and supporting over 60 entrepreneurs, each of whom has contributed to shaping my journey. These experiences have honed my strategic decision-making skills, strengthened relationships, and deepened the essence of *Dosti* in my life.

I find immense joy in being a lifelong student—curious and eager to learn, like a 21-year-old—delving into psychology, philosophy, and digital technologies. I plan to continue this journey until I turn 100, after which I'll step into Version 3.0, a chapter that I envision lasting another 50 years while continuing to impact many more lives.

In writing this book, I aim to share the journey of becoming Rohit Chanana—the person behind the business persona. Drawing on over four decades of hands-on experience, I recount my rise from a young boy from a low-middle-class background to a Chartered Accountant, CEO, and angel investor. Along the way, I've had the privilege of working with extraordinary minds such as Late Shri Brijmohan Munjal Ji, Late Shri OP Munjal Ji, Mr. Sunil Munjal, Late Dr. Parvinder Singh, Mr. D.S. Brar, Late Mr. Vinay Kaul, Mr. Arun Maira, Mr. Deep Prakash Bhatt, and many more. These mentors supported me, fostered open dialogue, and shaped my perspective.

Similarly my family—my wife, love and partner, Poonam; our wonderful children, Rohan and Ishani, and their spouses, Upasana and Sirav; and my four-year-old grandson, Rihaan—have been pivotal in shaping who I am today.

Through this journey, I've learned valuable lessons from influential figures and my family whose guidance has inspired me to pay it forward, embrace failure as a teacher, and cultivate win-win relationships. At the heart of it all, I've strived to maintain gratitude, *sabr* (patience), curiosity, and humility—values that have guided me throughout my life.

Remember, in my mind, I am forever 21! This mindset keeps me open to lifelong learning from people of all ages and enables me to connect with anyone as a *Dost*.

This book is more than a reflection on my professional life; it offers a deeply personal account of my journey. It begins with my parents' migration from Pakistan to India during the Partition and their early struggles to rebuild their lives. It provides a glimpse into my childhood, adolescence, and the challenges I faced while navigating my education—from school to college—culminating in earning my Chartered Accountant qualification. These formative experiences, along with the professional journey that shaped who I am today, are woven together to intertwine the personal and professional threads of my life.

In Part 2 of this book, I delve into the timeless wisdom, values, philosophies, and frameworks that have shaped my life and guided my decisions. These principles have been instrumental in helping me achieve both personal and professional success, serving as a compass through moments of triumph and challenge.

Each of these lessons, gathered over the course of more than six decades, carries its own unique story—moments of learning, reflection, and growth that have left a lasting impact on my journey. These experiences are not just milestones but valuable guideposts that have helped me find clarity, purpose, and a deeper connection to life.

This journey of learning and evolving is far from over. As life continues to unfold, new experiences will inevitably bring fresh perspectives, shaping and refining my philosophies further. Life, after all, is a continuous process of discovery and growth, and I embrace the opportunity to keep adding new lessons and insights to this ever-evolving tapestry.

Through this part of the book, I hope to offer you insights and ideas that have illuminated my path, with the intention that they might inspire and resonate with you as you navigate your own journey. Whether you are seeking personal fulfillment, professional clarity, or simply a fresh perspective, these reflections are shared with the hope that they can spark meaningful thought and action in your life—and that you, too, will continue to evolve and refine your own philosophies as life's experiences shape you.

These philosophies have a *Dil Se Connect*—they come straight from the heart, born from a life of curiosity, reflection, and purpose. Not all philosophies may align with you, and that's fine. The philosophies shared here are summarized, but quite a few of them may deserve deeper exploration—perhaps even a chapter of their own. My hope is that you will take from this book what resonates with you and use it to shape your own journey.

I believe these reflections will not only inspire you but also help you write your own destiny, empowering you to shape a life that resonates with your values and aspirations. This is not just my story; it is an invitation for you to explore your own and embrace the journey with purpose, gratitude, and an open heart.

Remember, Dost, you have the power to embrace your destiny, find joy, and live each moment to the fullest.

Thank you. God bless you.

Rohit Chanana

Acknowledgement and Gratitude

I extend my heartfelt gratitude to all those who have shaped my journey and contributed immensely to my personal growth, values, and purpose.

To my parents, late Sarla Devi and late Sardari Lal, whose unwavering love and sacrifices laid the foundation for my life. Their hard work, frugal living, and deep commitment ensured I received the best education and remained grounded in values. Their trust in me gave me the courage to follow my dreams, and their example of resilience and integrity continues to guide me every day.

To my Maama, (Nani's Sister), who gave us shelter when my parents were homeless and instilled core values in my early years, helping shape the person I am today, she was my first guiding light and mentor in life.

To my second role model, Raghunath Mama Ji, who is known for his humility, grounded nature, and unwavering commitment to values.

To my wife, Poonam, my pillar of strength and constant source of inspiration. Your unwavering support, boundless energy, and dedication to our family—caring for my parents and our children selflessly—have empowered me to deliver my best. Through moments of joy and success, as well as challenges and tough times, you have been my rock. I feel truly blessed to have you as my partner, the cornerstone of our family's joy and harmony.

To my Gurus—Mr. Rakesh Chopra, Late Dr. Parvinder Singh, Mr. D.S. Brar, Late Mr. Vinay Kaul, Late Mr. Brijmohan Munjal, Late Mr. O.P. Munjal, Mr. Arun Maira, and Mr. Deep Prakash Bhat—thank you for imparting wisdom, values, and guidance. Each of you has left an indelible mark on my life, and I am forever grateful for your influence.

To our son Rohan, my dost during his formative years, whose energy and connection bring light to our family. Your advise in some of the major decisions has been great. Your sense of humor and wit always brighten the mood and remind us to find joy in every moment.

To my daughter Ishani, she has been our lucky charm. She is now my partner and dost at Sarcha Advisors and plays a pivotal role in decision-making. You have stood by me during tough times even when this journey was far from the cakewalk I had imagined. You inspire me every day with your strength, vision, and compassion. You have brought immense joy to our lives and encouraged me to document my personal stories, leaving behind a legacy in the form of this book.

To the new members of our family—Rohan's wife, Upasana, and Ishani's husband, Sirav—and to our beloved grandson, Rihaan. You all have brought life, love, and laughter to our family, enriching it in ways I could never have imagined. Rihaan, our little prince, has brought unending joy and fun into our lives.

To the founders I've had the privilege to work alongside—you've kept my curiosity alive and vibrant, helping me remain a 21-year-old at heart while striving to be a dost to you.

To my teams at various organizations, whose dedication and collaboration helped us achieve extraordinary outcomes together. Your trust and hard work have been integral to my journey, and I will forever cherish our shared successes.

To my dosts, Rajeev, Anil, and so many others who have walked alongside me with friendship, loyalty, and unwavering trust. Your companionship has been a source of immense strength and joy.

To my friends and well-wishers who believed in me and encouraged me to share my journey through this book—your faith and encouragement have been instrumental in this endeavor.

Above all, I bow in gratitude to Maa Durga, Mahalakshmi Maa, Saraswati Maa and Ganesh ji, (The Higher Power/The Supreme Being) whose divine guidance, inspiration, and blessings have lit my path. Their grace has enabled me to make a positive impact on the lives of others and remain steadfast in my purpose.

Finally, a special thank you to the team at StoryMirror, led by my founder friend Bibhu and Sneha, for their invaluable support and efforts in bringing this book to life.

Contents

Part I

Part II

Part – I

Chapter 1

The Sowing of a Seed

The story of life often starts not with one's birth, but with the roots that run deep into past generations—an inheritance shaped by tradition, culture, and historical events beyond one's control. It is not just about personal beginnings, but about the legacy passed down through the triumphs and trials of those who came before. For many, this legacy is a blend of prosperity and upheaval, resilience and reinvention. *Families do not merely endure change; they are often defined by how they rise from it, carrying forward the values, sacrifices, and dreams of ancestors who faced the unthinkable.* In such stories, the past is never truly gone; it is a living force that shapes the present and influences the path forward.

The story of my life began long before I took my first breath, deeply rooted in the legacy of an affluent and respected family in Pakistan. My lineage is one of honor and prosperity, where my grandparents stood as esteemed pillars of their community, their lives marked by both wealth and reverence. But in 1947, the winds of change swept through, uprooting our lives and scattering us across the uncharted landscape of a newly partitioned India. Our migration, though not uncommon, is etched with unique scars and memories that have shaped our journey and defined our resilience.

As my family crossed the border, our rich background was a mere thing of the past. We arrived in India with nothing but clothes and a relentless will to survive. My parents, once esteemed individuals, suddenly found themselves in a strange place with hope as their only asset. Luckily, it was my Nani's sister, (whom we fondly referred to as Maama, a compassionate and strong woman) who extended a lifeline to us. Actively involved in the Arya Samaj, a socio-religious reform movement, she played a pivotal role in a healthcare system governed by the municipal corporation of Delhi, where she managed a family welfare clinic. Her support offered not just shelter but a robust foundation to rebuild our lives.

Families do not merely endure change; they are often defined by how they rise from it, carrying forward the values, sacrifices, and dreams of ancestors who faced the unthinkable.

Maama's home—though modest—turned into a sanctuary. It was here that I formed a lasting bond with her. She served as a caregiver and a beautiful source of warmth and wisdom during my early years. My parents devoted themselves tirelessly to our future, often working from dawn until long after dusk. My father's day began at 7 AM and stretched until night, leaving little time for rest, while my mother, equally diligent, became a smallpox vaccinator traveling door-to-door to bring health and care to those in need. She was often seen by some as a doctor, a trusted figure whose work showcased her immense dedication to community welfare.

Maama became an ever-present companion in our lives, weaving the threads of spirituality and discipline into our daily routine through her deep association with the Arya Samaj. Each morning, she performed Havans—sacred rituals that were believed to cleanse the mind and soul. The Havan always began with the chanting of the Gayatri Mantra three times—a powerful, universal prayer believed to foster personal transformation through the illumination of intellect and the pursuit of a life aligned with righteousness and higher purpose. The daily Havans, with their rhythmic chants and the fragrant offerings of sacred herbs, became my first tangible connection to a higher power. Maama, a devoted follower of Arya Samaj, wove these spiritual teachings into the very fabric of our lives. In those sacred moments, I wasn't merely witnessing rituals; I was being embraced by the profound teachings of my first Guru, discovering the essence of wisdom and spirituality at a tender age, even as a toddler. Her gentle chants and the soothing aromas of burning offerings created an atmosphere of deep reverence, teaching me invaluable lessons in humility and egolessness. Maama's teachings extended far beyond the rituals themselves; they embodied a profound respect for all beings, modesty in facing life's challenges, and a deep sense of gratitude. She treated everyone with great respect, regardless of their background, and she instilled in me the importance of doing the same. These early lessons in humility and respect became the very foundation of my character, guiding me through the many winding paths of life.

Though she was only 4 feet 8 inches tall and slightly hunched, Maama was a formidable presence, radiating energy and positivity. She would say "Namaste" to every passerby, and expressing gratitude was second nature to her. Known for her brisk pace, she often outpaced others, regardless of her age and physical condition. Her dedication to our family's well-being left an indelible mark on me. In her professional life, Maama was a highly respected figure in the community, particularly for her role in assisting childbirth—a crucial responsibility at a time when caesarean sections were rare. Even at the age of 82, she insisted on making her own chapatis and washing her own clothes, refusing to let anyone else take over her chores.

Our family was large, a blend of both joy and sorrow. I had three sisters, all much older than me—12, 10, and 7 years my senior. The eldest sister was married when I was just 7 years old. My parents had long prayed for a son to support them in their old age, and their prayers were answered when I was born. My mother was a source of great strength and inspiration. She worked as a smallpox vaccinator, a role that demanded courage and compassion. In all kinds of weather, she traveled long distances to serve those in need. Her work was more than a job; it was a mission imbued with a deep sense of community welfare. People began calling her "doctor," a title she wore with quiet pride and humility. The stories she shared with us from her daily rounds were filled with the struggles and triumphs of the people she served, leaving a lasting impression on me. *Her dedication to her work, without ever expecting anything in return, taught me the true meaning of service and the dignity found in every task, no matter how humble.*

Reflecting on these formative years, I see them as the sowing of seeds—each experience embedding values and lessons that would later flourish and shape who I would become. Our family's migration from the comforts of Pakistan to the complex streets of Delhi was marked by loss, yet, it was simultaneously filled with love, resilience, and an unbreakable commitment to one another. which became the foundation of our new beginning. Fortunately, both my parents had completed their schooling until class X, which significantly aided them in securing jobs as they navigated their new lives.

Maama's wisdom, my parents' strength, and shared experiences with my siblings allowed me to learn gratitude, humbleness, strength, compassion, and empathy. The early lessons sown through these experiences became integral pieces of the character that guided me through life's many challenges and twists. Now, as I look back, I feel immense gratitude for the seeds planted so long ago—seeds that have blossomed into my life's attributes I hold until now.

However, any journey in life is not without its struggles. My mother faced significant challenges in her role as a smallpox vaccinator. I remember her sharing tales of knocking on doors, only to face ignorance or hostility sometimes. Worn out by exhaustion but undeterred, she still pressed on. Reminiscing, I remember the days she would return home fatigued, her spirit tested by the weight of responsibility. Yet, amid these grueling challenges were moments of triumph, where her persistence convinced families of the importance of vaccination, potentially saving lives. These hardships etched strength deep into her character—qualities she would impart to me through her words and actions.

My father secured a job as a Development Officer at the Life Insurance Corporation of India (LIC), once he recovered from bouts of sciatica, offering some stability to our family's precarious financial situation. Even with his quiet nature, my father took immense pride in his work, consistently putting in long hours and effort to ensure our family was well supported. His calm demeanor inspired me, teaching me the value of perseverance and diligent effort.

As time passed, and Maama retired from her active role in the Municipal Corporation, we transitioned to a compact apartment in Amar Colony. This new home—a two-room dwelling with a living room of 10 by 10 feet and a bedroom of 10 by 12 feet, along with a shared bathroom—symbolized a fresh start for our family. Since there were no coolers, we used to sleep in the open area under the beautiful skies during April-October and always prayed that it shouldn't rain. Though the conditions were modest and space was limited, this home fostered a sense of belonging and community spirit. Despite the challenges of our confined living quarters - love, and strength prevailed - and we continued our journey to rebuild our lives with unwavering determination.

Acknowledging my mother's burdens, my father became increasingly involved in helping at home, with the household chores, even taking on the role of cooking for our family. We were happy eating either a vegetable or lentils, and that habit to an extent has stayed with me even today. The supporting role of my father lightened my mother's load, allowing her to focus on her work and it truly reflected on the importance of teamwork and mutual support within our family.

My mother's efforts extended beyond work; she chose to walk 2-3 kilometers to save money on the bus fare, intending to invest those savings into my education. She saved 10 paisa each day by walking 3 kilometers and 3 paisa by even sacrificing to drink a glass of water. When she would come back home, her feet would be swollen because of long walks. *Every little bit saved for my schooling symbolized her firm belief in the transformative power of education.*

My formal education began at a local Hindi medium school in Kashmere Gate, Delhi. The school, though modest and unassuming, provided the foundational learning that would set the stage for my future success.

Regardless of the financial challenges, my family, on both my paternal and maternal sides, was celebrated for their hearty laughter. A trait that continued until my mother's health began to decline, ten years before she passed away due to a heart condition in 2008, at the age of 85.

Even as life shifted around us, the spirit of joy remained an indelible part of our family's fabric. Laughter continued to weave through our stories, a gentle reminder of the love that bound us together. It was in those moments of joy that made me re-live my, vacations in Saharanpur, where my mother's infectious joy illuminated every gathering. My childhood vacations in Saharanpur were some of the happiest times of my life, all thanks to my mother's big heart and the warmth of my Raghunath Mama Ji. Mama Ji was a man of great stature, both physically and in the immense respect he commanded in the community. He was so well-known that letters addressed simply to "Ch. Raghunath Chawla, Court Road, Saharanpur" would find their way to him—he was incredibly humble. He had a grand house in Saharanpur, where 20-25 of us children would gather during the summer vacations. Those days were filled with pure joy—playing on the swing in the courtyard, endless games of cards, relishing the taste of golgappas, and sometimes going to the movies in a cinema hall owned by one of Mama Ji's friends. We would dance, sing, and laugh, filling the house with the sounds of our happiness.

The journey to Saharanpur itself was an adventure. We traveled by train, pulled by a steam engine, a memory that still evokes the nostalgia of a bygone era. Upon reaching, the first thing we'd do was take a bath, washing away the dust and grime from the journey. Sometimes, we'd take a rickshaw to Mama Ji's home, and on special occasions, he would come to pick us up in his car. Although Mama Ji lived a grand life in Saharanpur, he would often visit and stay with us in our modest home in Amar Colony, Delhi. He never minded our low-key living conditions—one toilet and one bathroom for seven people to share. He would sleep in the living room, never once making us feel that our small space was anything less than sufficient. His love and respect for my mother were evident in these gestures, and their bond was a cornerstone of my early life. It's a relationship I cherish deeply, symbolized by the simplicity and humility they both embodied, despite the stark differences in their circumstances. He was my role model.

Back in those days, acquiring something as basic as a new phone, a car, or even an LPG gas connection took years. The 1970s was a time when patience was a necessary virtue, as the wait for these everyday conveniences could stretch on for what felt like an eternity. We got our first two-wheeler in 1968, our first car and TV set in 1986 and landline phone in 1987 post my marriage. I used to watch TV while standing outside of the windows of one of our neighbours until 1975 and thereafter we could watch at one of my best friends Rajan Sharma's house until we got our own TV. The means of communication was an inland letter or a postcard costing 20 paise and 10 paise respectively, and if you wanted a message to be sent urgently it was through a telegram which would normally reach between 6-24 hours, most of the time it was for sad news and rarely good news. For outstation phone calls, one had to book through a telephone operator, and the waiting time ranged from 2 to 12 hours, depending on the amount one was willing to pay.

Our parents are always with us—in every breath we take, in every aspect of our lives.

Reflecting on those early years, I cannot help but feel the weight of certain regrets. Among them is the lingering belief that I could have done more for my parents, even though most considered me an ideal son. This guilt stayed with me long after they passed, driving me to seek forgiveness from Maa Durga. Then one day, a close friend, Manoj Kohli, former CEO of Airtel, sent me a video of Amitabh Bachchan reciting a poignant piece of poetry that profoundly impacted me. His words reminded me that *our parents are always with us—in every breath we take, in every aspect of our lives.* This revelation transformed my understanding of regret. I began to sense my parents' presence once more, and with that, I made a vow to honor their legacy, ensuring that their names would always be a part of me.

In their memory, I named the firm in my Version 2.0 "Sarcha," a heartfelt blend of the first three letters of my parents' names—Sardari and Sarla—and the first three letters of our surname, Chanana. Rohan and Upasana played a role in crafting the name Sarcha and Ishani designed the logo of Sarcha Advisors. As I grew older, I found myself referring to them by their first names—Sardari and Sarla—a shift that symbolized the evolution of our relationship into a deeper, more meaningful friendship. In this new dynamic, they became not just my parents, but my cherished *Dosts*.

True wealth isn't measured by material possessions, but by the depth of one's character, the richness of relationships, and the ability to withstand adversity, and leaving a legacy.

The seeds sown during those early years, nurtured by my family's love and sacrifices, have since blossomed into a profound appreciation for education, resilience, and humility. These values, shaped by both trials and triumphs, continue to guide me through the twists and turns of life. As I look back on this journey, I realize that *true wealth isn't measured by material possessions, but by the depth of one's character, the richness of relationships, and the ability to withstand adversity, and leaving a legacy.* These enduring lessons stand as a testament to the power of love, sacrifice, and perseverance, and they remind me—and hopefully you—that the *real treasures in life are found in the bonds we forge and the strength we gain from overcoming life's challenges.*

The story of my family's migration from Pakistan to India and the struggles we faced taught me invaluable lessons that I hope will inspire the youth of today. It is important to note that role models, guru and family are instrumental in shaping our character; hard work and sacrifices are necessary to achieve the higher goal; cherishing childhood memories and making spirituality a way of life keeps us grounded and brings necessary values and gratitude in our life.

Real treasures in life are found in the bonds we forge and the strength we gain from overcoming life's challenges.

The seeds sown by my family's struggles and teachings began to take root, preparing me for the trials that lay ahead. As I embarked on my journey of education, these lessons became the compass guiding me through hardship and driving me toward success. In the next chapter, I will take you through the challenges and triumphs of this journey—a story of resilience, learning, and the pursuit of excellence against all odds.

Chapter 2

School Days: Learning, Laughter, and Lifelong Bonds

Hardship often demands not just strength of character, but also a vision that transcends the present struggles. In the face of necessity, even the simplest choices become monumental decisions, as each one holds the potential to shape a better future. This phrase encapsulates the human ability to adapt and make meaningful decisions, no matter how overwhelming the circumstances, because necessity sharpens our focus and forces us to recognize the value and impact of even the smallest actions.

Hardship often demands not just strength of character, but also a vision that transcends the present struggles.

For many families, *the pursuit of education becomes a crucial focus, fueled by the belief that it is not merely a path to success, but a gateway to transformation.* It is in these circumstances that the power of sacrifice is most evident—parents denying themselves comforts, carefully weighing every rupee, and enduring long, exhausting days to create opportunities that were beyond their reach.

This kind of dedication is not only about survival; it is an act of defiance against the constraints of adversity, a deliberate attempt to break the cycle of hardship through education and aspiration. The path is rarely straightforward, often fraught with barriers and setbacks. But, it is a journey defined by hope, relentless effort, and a commitment to a future that promises something greater.

The pursuit of education becomes a crucial focus, fueled by the belief that it is not merely a path to success, but a gateway to transformation.

Our family's financial situation was modest, with my father earning around Rs.600 a month and my mother contributing another Rs.200. This combined income of Rs.800 was essential and carefully allocated to cover our basic needs and essentials. My mother was committed to ensure a sound education for me and recognizing its significance, she diligently sought out top schools in Delhi—St. Xavier's, Columbus, Modern School, and Delhi Public School (DPS). Her dedication led to my enrolment in DPS, a prestigious institution with a reputation for academic excellence. However, the transition was fraught with challenges. Coming from a Hindi medium school, I needed to pass a special entrance test to prove my readiness. My uncle, a respected figure in the community, utilized his influence to facilitate this process. The school administrators were initially hesitant to accept someone from such a disparate academic background.

To bridge the gap between my previous schooling and DPS's rigorous demands, I turned to pocketbooks, which were easy-to-use guides that helped me understand various topics—friends, festivals like Diwali, vacations, and outings—which aided my grasp of English. The principal recognised the influence of my uncle and ultimately agreed to my admission. Through the initial challenges, I gradually found my footing at DPS.

My mother was my constant source of motivation during school. She dreamed of providing me with an English-medium education, often sacrificing to make this vision a reality. Despite our limited means, she worked tirelessly to ensure I had the resources needed for my education. Her sacrifices were numerous; she often worked double shifts, balancing her job and household responsibilities, leaving her exhausted yet resolute.

Walking onto the Delhi Public School (DPS) campus for the first time was like stepping into a whole new world—one that was both exhilarating and intimidating. The sprawling grounds, meticulously maintained with lush greenery, felt like a realm of endless possibilities. Every corner of the campus whispered stories of the countless students who had walked its paths, their aspirations nurtured within these walls. The main building, with its imposing columns and grand staircases, stood as a testament to the school's long-standing reputation for excellence. For a boy who had come from a modest Hindi medium background, being at DPS was nothing short of living out. It was as if I had stepped into an era of unending opportunities, and honestly, it felt pretty magical.

Having my uncle's influence and a cousin who also attended the school made a world of difference in what initially felt like an overwhelming new environment. My uncle's support, coupled with the presence of my cousin, eased my transition into this prestigious institution. DPS was like a dream come true—a chance for the kind of education my family had always hoped for. The campus, buzzing with life and energy, quickly became a place where I could start to picture a future full of possibilities.

However, my initial days at DPS were not without their challenges. The first few weeks were marked by a series of tests and assessments designed to gauge my academic readiness. I vividly remember scoring a mere 3 out of 20 on my first test—a performance that prompted the school to reach out to my parents and uncle, expressing concerns about my suitability for such an esteemed institution. The disappointment was palpable, but it was during this low point that my uncle's wisdom and calm demeanor became my anchor.

In a meeting with the school principal, my uncle acknowledged the struggles I faced but insisted that I be given the opportunity to prove my worth. He spoke passionately about our family's resilience, the sacrifices my parents had made, and the deep faith he had in my potential. His reassuring demeanor calmed the principal and rekindled my determination. My parents stood by me, their faith in me strong despite my early setback. That moment was a turning point—it was the push I needed to transform my approach to education and, ultimately, my life.

Renewed by their trust, I was motivated to prove my worth. The path from the bottom of the class to the top was neither swift nor smooth. The academic rigor at DPS was intense, and there were times when I felt utterly overwhelmed by the sheer volume of material I was expected to master. Yet, slowly but surely, I began to rise through the ranks—from being 39th out of 43 students (though I found some solace in knowing there were still four behind me) to 16th, eventually securing a consistent spot among the top ten.

I soon discovered that my strengths lay in Mathematics and Physics—subjects that fascinated me with their logical structures and the thrill of solving complex problems. However, English proved to be a significant challenge. Creative tasks, particularly essay writing, felt like insurmountable obstacles. English wasn't my native language, and my thoughts naturally flowed in Hindi, which I would then painstakingly translate into English.

This language barrier made every English assignment a test of endurance and creativity.

Improving my English wasn't just about meeting academic expectations; it was about proving to myself that I could overcome my limitations. The role of peer pressure to stay ahead also served as a constant motivator, pushing me to strive harder and achieve more. It became a personal journey of will power, perseverance, and the unshakeable belief that with enough determination, I could conquer any weakness. These traits, honed during my years at DPS, would shape every aspect of my life.

Even today, I find comfort in expressing myself in a mix of Hindi and English—Hinglish. While I've grown more confident over the years, those early struggles with language were a significant hurdle that ultimately helped shape who I am.

Despite the challenges, I gradually found my footing at DPS. My eventual success in ranking among the top students was not just a personal triumph; it was evidence of the support I received from my family and friends.

Life at DPS was not solely defined by academic pursuits. The school was a microcosm of life itself, where we were encouraged to explore our interests and passions beyond the classroom. The friendships I formed during these years were essential to my transformation. Among my closest companions during this time were Rajeev Gupta and Anil Khanna, two individuals who became integral to my journey. We were bound not merely by our classes but by a shared sense of adventure, love and compassion. Their friendship provided me with a sense of belonging and camaraderie that made the tough times more bearable. Rajeev was a force of nature—full of energy, mischief, and an unyielding zest for life. He was the kind of friend who would drag you into adventures you never imagined, and though he often got us into trouble, those were the moments that made our school days unforgettable. Rajeev's playful nickname for me was "Mote" (fatty) owing to my chubby belly and short stature of 5 feet 2 inches. and while it might have stung at first, it became a term of endearment that I eventually wore like a badge of honor.

Rajeev's father worked at Burmah Shell, a connection that provided us with an unusual advantage among our teachers. As I shared earlier, securing a gas connection in those days was no small feat, and Rajeev was clever enough to leverage this connection for our benefit. Whenever we found ourselves in trouble—which was often the case—Rajeev would subtly remind our teachers of the gas connections he had provided. This clever approach often allowed us to escape with only a reprimand or, at worst, a yellow or red card—a demerit in our school. The yellow cards were a form of public shaming, where we stood facing the assembly instead of the podium while the principal made announcements. It felt like a badge of honor—a sign of our spirited youth and rebellious nature.

One particularly close call came when Rajeev was stuck with my answer book during a final exam as we had shared our sheets with each other. We were sure we were about to face severe consequences, but luck favoured us and the teacher left the room momentarily, allowing us to exchange answer sheets on time and evade punishment. It was a narrow escape, but it was also a reminder of how close we always seemed to be to the edge of trouble.

Our mischief only strengthened the affinity we shared, creating cherished memories. Together, we developed a sense of unity—an understanding that these moments significantly shaped our lives. Rajeev lent an air of excitement to the ordinary, encouraging us to embrace each day with boldness, even if it meant occasional recklessness. There were a couple of teachers who hated Rajeev for his connections with most other teachers and Rajeev was not the one to take it lying low, he would still take a panga with them, and manage his way out sometimes without any consequences.

Anil Khanna, on the other hand, was the yin to Rajeev's yang. Where Rajeev was impulsive and daring, Anil was calm, thoughtful, and wise beyond his years. He had a way of grounding us when things got too wild, and his quiet confidence was a stabilizing force in our group. Anil's friendship was marked by a deep sense of love and loyalty, and he was someone I could always count on, no matter what.

One of the treasured memories is when we were in class 10. We went to see the film "Bobby" which had become the talk of the town and a cultural phenomenon of its time. The movie's love story, brimming with youthful passion and rebellion, was a magnet for us—three boys on the cusp of adolescence, eager to dive into a world that felt both foreign and thrilling.

As the weekend approached, we buzzed with excitement, counting down the hours until we could see it. Anil, ever the generous friend, quietly took the lead, surprising us by purchasing balcony tickets. Until that day, my cinema outings had always been a front-row affair—neck craned, eyes squinting, but full of joy nonetheless.

Stepping into the theater that day, everything felt different. The plush red seats of the balcony, the elevated view of the grand silver screen, and the sense of privilege were exciting. We felt like we'd been granted access to a world reserved for the fortunate few. As the lights dimmed and the film began, we were transported—not just by the story unfolding before us but by the shared experience of something special.

The movie was a whirlwind of emotions—laughter, tears, and the quiet understanding that we were witnessing something memorable. But more than the film itself, it was the camaraderie, the shared glances, and the whispered comments that turned that day into a lasting memory. We weren't just watching a movie; we were etching a moment in time, a moment that would forever be a symbol of our unbreakable bond. Watching the film in the packed theater, surrounded by the laughter, gasps, and cheers of the audience, made the experience even more exhilarating. The innocence of that outing, mixed with the excitement of exploring something new, remains etched in my memory as one of the defining moment of our carefree school days.

These friendships, with Rajeev and Anil, were the bedrock of my experience at DPS. They taught me the value of friendship, togetherness, the importance of shared experiences, and the joy that comes from being part of something bigger than yourself. Our adventures, both inside and outside the classroom, were the threads that wove together the fabric of my school years, creating a tapestry of memories that I would carry with me for the rest of my life.

Life at school was not solely defined by academic pursuits. We engaged in our fair share of mischief, often testing the limits of our teachers' patience. Whether it was playing pranks, singing, or dancing in class, we frequently found ourselves on the edge of controlled rebellion. Our teachers, understanding and compassionate, often let our antics slide, recognizing these moments as part of our growth. We could do all this as we were the only class during grade 9-11 where we were 19 boys and there were no girls. Even in class 9, I used to carry my books in a school bag made from a repurposed sofa cover, and it was so large that it hung down to my knees, I used to carry my lunch from home, and some of the hostellers would often barter with me, offering to buy canteen food for me in exchange for my home-cooked meals. These playful episodes taught us valuable lessons about boundaries, responsibilities, and maintaining a healthy balance between studies and play.

Another particularly fond memory from those carefree days was the first time Anil took me to the Taj Mahal Hotel—a place that, to me, epitomized luxury and sophistication. It was a world far removed from our usual haunts, and I remember the day with vivid clarity. As we approached the grand entrance of the hotel, my heart raced with excitement and a touch of nervousness. I had heard tales of the opulence that lay beyond those doors, but nothing could have prepared me for the experience of stepping into a five-star establishment for the very first time.

Anil, always cool and confident, led the way as he belonged there, his presence putting me at ease. We made our way to the hotel's coffee shop, Machan, where the aroma of freshly brewed coffee mingled with the soft murmur of sophisticated conversations. The ambiance was a revelation—plush seating, elegant décor, and an air of understated luxury that made everything feel special.

Anil ordered a simple Milanese minestrone soup served with breads. I could not even pronounce the name of the soup but I followed suit, still marveling at the fact that we were dining in such a place. It was only once the soup was served that I realised that it was a full meal in itself. The soup cost five rupees, a sum that seemed princely to me, but it wasn't the cost that left an impression. It was the moment—the quiet joy of sitting together in this grand setting, savoring a simple meal that made us feel like we were on top of the world.

I had grown up with a habit of simple living, simple clothes and simple food, we could eat our meals with one vegetable or dal, and the eating habit has remained the same even now. That day, in the heart of luxury, I realized that it wasn't the grandeur of the surroundings that made the experience unforgettable. It was the shared laughter, the sense of adventure, and the feeling of being part of something special with a friend who had always been there for me. It is these memorable moments that deepened our bond and remain etched in my memory as a testimony to the simple joys that define true friendship.

During these academic struggles, there were also moments of great joy. I became a maternal uncle at the age of 12. My eldest sister was blessed with a baby boy Rajan. Even to this date, he has a soft corner for me, both of us have mutual respect and love for each other. Now, he is 54 years old but to me, he is still a baby. Neera, my middle sister, was amongst the most privileged siblings as she started living with our Massi, who was the principal of Lady Shri Ram College. Neera stayed with her for six years before her wedding, almost like an adopted daughter. I greatly admired my Massi, not just for her role as an educationist but for the way she cared for Neera. Massi was the principal of Lady Shri Ram College for twenty years, a position of great respect, and Neera thrived under her guidance.

In 1973, Neera got married in Allahabad. It was a grand affair, with all our relatives staying in a Dharamshala. After the wedding, I began spending my vacations in Allahabad until 1978. Neera was incredibly generous, always giving me clothes and money whenever I went to stay with her. I remember crying every time I was to travel back home after spending vacation for two months. Another cherished memory is of my first vacation to Shimla with Neera and her in-laws and their extended family, we were almost 30 of us. Neera's in-laws and the extended family were fairly well to do and we stayed in some good hotels. I have fond memories of playing the Tambola, going for long walks on ridge road, visiting the skating rink, and the famous songs from the movie "Kabhi Kabhi", that would be playing at the skating rink. We also went to Anandpur Sahib Gurdwara and a few picnic spots. We would hire a bus and end up enjoying the journey - singing and cracking jokes. As time passed, Neera was blessed with three children - (Shitu, Shweta, and Tushar) all are married and have children. Neera is now a grandmother of 5 kids.

Coming back to school days, we were encouraged to participate in extracurricular activities, and I took full advantage of these opportunities. Whether it was joining the music class, participating in science fairs, or playing sports, I dived all in. These activities allowed me to discover new talents and passions. While I never made it to the school teams in any of the extracurricular activities, just participation itself was great fun. There used to be inter-school sports competitions and rivalry with Modern school was immense, whenever there used to be a match either in their school or our school, a few buses would go with students to the other's school to cheer our teams. The joy of winning was exuberating.

From a young age, I found joy in both simple grounded and more sophisticated activities, always approaching life with an open heart. I never felt the need to put on airs; instead, I eagerly joined my friends in games of Gilli Danda, marbles, and kite flying on our sun-soaked streets. While many from my school didn't play these games, to me, we were all just kids sharing our lives and this aspect became a part of my journey leading to elimination of class difference. I cherished the long walks to the Yamuna River, four kilometers of adventure that led to the refreshing coolness of its waters. Sundays were special, filled with the promise of adventure as we trekked to Kalka Temple, navigating hilly terrains that only added to the thrill of our journey. In the evenings, we would visit the nearby gurudwaras as one of my friends had taken a vow to visit regularly. Monsoons brought unique magic; the rain transformed our world into a playground, and we would joyfully splash in puddles, crafting paper boats that sailed on the surface. Celebrating Janmashtami filled us with excitement as we went door to door, collecting coins for our festivities. Yet, it always seemed the rain would pour down, washing away our decorations and reminding us of life's impermanence. But amid the laughter and soaked clothes, we discovered that *true celebration lies in our connections, in the love and joy shared together, no matter the circumstances.*

Most of you may be unaware of this but we used to chew sugarcane stalks to extract the sweet juice. This is often done by biting into the stalk, chewing to release the juice, and then spitting out the fibrous remains.

We also used to buy some stuff from roadside vendors—particularly enjoying local, seasonal, and traditional snacks like mooli (radish), kamrak (starfruit), aam papad (mango leather), and phalse (Indian berries) amongst other —is a beloved part of Indian culture. I have seen these vendors completely vanish from the localities that I live in now, and some consider it unhealthy to buy such fruits from roadside.

True celebration lies in our connections, in the love and joy shared together, no matter the circumstances.

The experience of throwing stones to gather shahtoot (mulberries), jamun (Indian blackberries), and amrood (guavas) from trees is a nostalgic and cherished part of my childhood. It reflects the joy of foraging fresh, seasonal fruits directly from nature, often shared with friends under the shade of the trees.

As the carefree days of childhood gradually gave way to the realities of adolescence, I found myself at a crossroads. Once I moved into my later years at DPS, I began to think more seriously about my future. The pressure to succeed academically was ever-present, but so was the desire to enjoy my remaining time at school. It was a delicate balance, one that required careful time management and a clear sense of priorities.

When I entered ninth grade, my academic performance improved consistently, and by the time I reached class 11th, I would often rank among the top three students in my class. This achievement was a source of pride not only for me but for my parents as well. It was also a testament to the support I had received from my family, friends, and teachers. My journey at DPS had been a challenging one, but it had also been incredibly rewarding.

A significant influence during my time at DPS were my senior school teachers. They weren't just there to teach—they were real mentors who genuinely cared about our growth. Their dedication to our education really stuck with me. They weren't just about books and exams; they were there to help us through the rollercoaster of adolescence, always ready with advice or just a listening ear. By embracing responsibility and creating an open, friendly atmosphere, they gave us the space to thrive.

The bonds I forged during these years—especially with Rajeev and Anil—became a cornerstone of my school experience, rich with shared adventures and laughter. Rajeev and Anil were not just friends; they were confidants whom I could rely on during times of challenge. Our friendship extended beyond the school, often resulting in outings that enriched our lives. One such memorable outing was when we decided to celebrate our journey at school, which was slowly coming to an end, and it was during this time that I tasted beer for the first time. I remember taking just a few spoonful, yet I somehow convinced myself I had become high, a psychological effect that made the moment all the more amusing. These were the simple joys of adolescence—moments of innocent adventure, camaraderie, and the thrill of trying something new, that left behind memories that would make me smile for years to come.

I recently formed a WhatsApp group three years ago with my classmates, I could connect with 15 of the 19 students. *Surprisingly, the love and bond that we shared during school days, still continue to be a thing of the present, even though we have rarely met.* As I navigated those formative years at DPS, every challenge I tackled, every friendship I formed, and every lesson I learned became a piece of the puzzle that makes me who I am today. Those experiences were like the building blocks of my future, giving me the confidence, skills, and values I needed to handle the craziness of adult life.

Even now, when I look back, those memories are still fresh, reminding me of the power of sticking with our beliefs, the importance of true friendship, and the endless value of learning. Those years at DPS didn't just prepare me to learn the subjects; they paved the way for everything that's come since.

My high school years at Delhi Public School (DPS) were not just about academics; they were about the invaluable lessons I learned through relationships and personal growth, learning to balance fun and responsibility.

As I reflect on those years at DPS, I realize how they shaped the foundation for my journey ahead. The friendships, the struggles, and the lessons from every corner of school life all came together to prepare me for what lay beyond the gates. In the next chapter, I'll dive into the experience of stepping into college life and journey of CA —an exciting yet overwhelming phase of self-discovery and decision-making. It was a time when I was faced with critical choices about my career, my future, and who I truly wanted to be.

Chapter 3

College Life: Freedom, Exploration, and Career Choices

College is often described as an important chapter in one's life—a bridge between adolescence and adulthood, where youthful ambition meets the harsh reality of future responsibilities. It is a time marked by exploration, new-found freedom, and the pressure to carve out a path toward a promising career. But it is also a period fraught with uncertainty, as choices about education and career begin to hold real consequences. *For many students, college symbolizes both opportunity and expectation, with each decision shaping not only their professional journey but also their identity and aspirations.*

In an era where career options were both revered and rigid, the expectations surrounding college were clear-cut but overwhelming. The options were largely limited to a handful of professions that commanded social respect: becoming a Doctor, Engineer, IAS, MBA, or Probationary Officer in a Public Sector Bank. I could not have become a Doctor since I did not study Biology, however, the other choices were also tougher and were still a distant possibility. Each path required both academic excellence and immense dedication, making the transition from school to college feel daunting for many. For those whose grades fell short of the competitive cutoffs, the weight of familial hopes and societal norms was compounded by the realization that their chosen path might not align with the opportunities available to them. This was not just a challenge but a defining moment, where dreams often had to be recalibrated to meet reality.

For many students, college symbolizes both opportunity and expectation, with each decision shaping not only their professional journey but also their identity and aspirations.

The monsoon of 1975 brought with it not just rain but a flood of expectations and realities that I wasn't quite prepared for. My parents, like many of their generation, had dreams that I would one day walk the prestigious halls of an engineering institute like BHU, IIT, or BITS Pilani. They envisioned me donning the mantle of an engineer, a title that symbolized success and respect in society. But as I stared at my report card, with a meager 66% staring back at me, those dreams seemed to wash away with the rain. The marks weren't enough to get into BITS, let alone the more competitive IITs. It was a devastating blow, one that left me feeling like I had let everyone down, including myself.

The days that followed were marked by a deep sense of failure. I remember sitting alone in my room, with the turmoil inside me, as I cried for hours. My classmates were securing their futures, and gaining admission to top engineering colleges, while I was left to grapple with the harsh reality that my path was no longer clear. My parents, though supportive, couldn't hide their disappointment. I could see it in their eyes—a reflection of the hopes they had for me, hopes that now seemed out of reach. It was a period of intense self-doubt, but also one of crucial decision-making.

As I was trying to sort out my educational journey, there was a moment of joy as we moved to our own house in Janak Puri DDA flats. It was a two-bedroom house with a living room and a balcony, a huge upgrade from our house in Amar Colony. The fact that we had permanent shelter was a huge relief and a reason to be happy, so this was God's way to balance the disappointment of my not-so-good marks. A couple of setbacks during this period was that my father met with a few accidents but could recover faster because of his will power, as he knew, I was still 7 years away from getting my first pay check.

With engineering no longer an option, I was at crossroads. I could either wallow in self-pity or chart a new course. Hindu College in Delhi, known for its excellence in commerce, became my lifeline. Having no background in commerce, as I had been a science student all my life, I chose to enroll in the B.Com (Hons) program. The transition wasn't just academic; it was a leap into an entirely different world. The first day at Hindu College was overwhelming. The campus buzzed with energy, and while others seemed to thrive in this environment, I felt like an outsider. There was some ragging by the seniors, but it was mostly harmless and less intense for day scholars like me, compared to those who joined as freshers but lived in the hostel.

My daily routine revolved around taking the University Special bus from Janakpuri at 8 AM. Depending on my class schedule, I would either return home by the 1:30 PM bus or the later one at 3:30 PM. The college fee was a modest Rs.15 per month, a sharp contrast to the Rs.100 we paid during our school years. We were entitled to a monthly bus pass for just Rs.12.50, allowing us to ride any DTC bus. However, the experience was often less than pleasant. Summers were sweltering, while winters could be biting cold, especially since many bus windows were perpetually broken.

Once I adjusted to the rhythm of college life, I quickly realized that the transition from school was more than just a change in routine; it was a significant shift in my academic focus. While I embraced the independence of higher education, the new challenges loomed large, particularly the leap from science to commerce. The academic shift from science to commerce was a struggle. My classmates, many of whom had a background in commerce, seemed to grasp concepts with ease, while I fumbled through unfamiliar territory. The textbooks might as well have been in a foreign language, and the subjects felt alien. Yet, amid this confusion, I found a small victory in my Accounting class, where I managed to score the highest marks—34 out of 50. It wasn't much, but it was a glimmer of hope that perhaps I could survive in this new environment.

This small success aside, my overall performance was merely average. I ended the year with a final score of 54% in the first year at college, a far cry from what was expected of me by my parents. The pressure to succeed was immense, and I found myself resorting to less-than-honest means to maintain my parents' trust. I convinced them that my internal marks were much higher than my final score suggested, and they believed me without question. My parents, who had not studied beyond the 10th grade, took my words at face value, not realizing that I was playing the system. Understanding that internal marks held little weight in the final tally, I began skipping internal exams altogether from 2nd year onwards. Instead, I spent my time at the college canteen or at nearby dhabas, sipping tea, smoking cigarettes, and indulging in Chinese food at a hawker van outside the Delhi School of Economics or visiting Shri Ram College of Commerce where quite a few of my friends were studying. During my second year, I gained 7 inches in height from a short guy of 5 ft 2 inches to 5 ft 9 inches.

This period also marked the beginning of my smoking habit—a habit that quickly escalated to 7-10 cigarettes a day, which cost approx Rs.3. My group of friends, some of whom were more carefree than academically inclined, became my partners in these rebellious escapades. We would go out at least once a fortnight for evening dinner or ride motorcycles to Connaught Place or gather at the Tibetan dhaba, serving Chinese food, near Kashmere Gate (both 25 km away from our place). One plate of chowmein would cost just Rs. 3. I was not allowed to drive the two wheeler as it was not considered safe, so my friends used to drive.

This phase of life introduced me to new experiences and friendships that shaped my routine. Occasionally, we would watch movies. Sundays would be spent playing cricket with a tennis ball, be it hot or cold. We could play for 4-6 hours at a stretch, and I used to play badminton in the evening.

It was a time of youthful rebellion, where the thrill of breaking the rules outweighed the consequences. In my second year, I managed to scrape through with 54%, but my internal marks were 0 out of 400—which was not a surprise given that I hadn't bothered to appear for any internal exams. My parents were confused when they saw the marksheet, but I shrugged it off, telling them that these marks didn't matter. Once again, they believed me, their trust in me unshaken despite the growing gap between their expectations and my reality.

As I was finishing my graduation, two significant events took place in 1977. First, my youngest sister got married, and for that, my parents had to sell a piece of land that had been gifted by Maama. That sale wiped out our savings. The second event was my father's retirement from LIC. Both of these changes brought us back to square one, although we now had our own house. My father started working with a friend of my brother-in-law for one-third of his previous salary, and the working conditions were much tougher-he had to travel to Jaipur for the first few years until he got a job in Delhi and used to work even harder at less than 40% of the salary. A couple of years later, my mother also retired, but since I was still a few years away from earning, she took on menial jobs to help make ends meet -she worked much harder to earn 30% of the salary. They both continued to work for the next ten years until I finally started earning, allowing us to live a somewhat more comfortable life.

With graduation on the horizon, the pressure to choose a career path intensified. My parents, still hopeful for a prestigious career, encouraged me to pursue an MBA guided by Massi, principal of Lady Shri Ram college. However, the entrance exams for IIM and FMS proved too challenging, and I failed to secure admission. With no other options left, I turned to Chartered Accountancy (CA)—a field I had once dismissed as uninteresting. The decision was born more out of necessity than passion, but it was a practical choice. With 54% in my B.Com, I barely met the requirement for CA, and I knew I had to make the most of this opportunity.

Feeling the weight of academic pressures, I was eager for a change of pace and a chance to explore the world beyond my studies. In a time when traveling by air was much more difficult and travel routes were limited, I took my first vacation by air, flying with Anil in 1978 to meet Rajeev in Bombay, right after finishing college. We planned to go to Goa from there by taking an overnight luxury bus, which took us 18 hours. While Anil was fairly well-off, we still opted for a room at a lodge that cost us Rs. 40 per night. However, as we reached Goa, it started to rain heavily, and we realized we had been traveling at the wrong time. We had to return by road on a bus with straight seats and broken windows, making it nearly impossible to sit comfortably. By the time we landed in Bombay, our clothes were extremely dirty, and we were utterly exhausted—proof that every great adventure comes with its fair share of misadventures!

The next few years were filled with adventure and discovery. I joined Prasad Azad & Co., a modest firm in Paharganj, through a family connection. It wasn't a top-tier firm, but it offered me a foot in the door. The work was intense, but it was here that I discovered a newfound passion for accounting and auditing. The last year of CA training was with GS Mathur and company. Unlike my earlier years of rote learning, I began to understand the logic behind the numbers, and the patterns that made sense of the chaos. My ability to devour a 600-page accounts or statistics book in a matter of hours became my greatest strength, a God-given talent that set me apart from my peers.

During my CA articleship (trainees), I was fortunate to be mentored by Ashok Batra, who would later become a leading authority on GST in India. At the time, he was more than just a mentor—he was my protector at Prasad Azad & Co., giving me the freedom to learn, grow, and make mistakes without fear of judgment. His guidance helped me navigate the complexities of accounting and auditing with a newfound confidence. Our monthly remuneration as an article clerk was Rs.60 per month in the first year, Rs.100 in the second, and Rs.150 in the third year. We were reimbursed for bus charges for traveling to clients' places in Delhi. I made good friends with the accounts team of each client, sharing jokes and laughter. This camaraderie allowed me to adopt a more relaxed schedule, often working from 11 AM to 5 PM instead of the official hours of 10 AM to 6 PM. It was all about having fun and enjoying the journey.-

My time during my CA articleship also included two significant audit assignments—one at Hindustan Zinc Ltd. in Udaipur and another at Hindustan Insecticides in Panvel, near Bombay. These trips were more than just work assignments; they were life-changing adventures. At Hindustan Zinc, due to the flexibility given to me by Ashok made the intense work bearable. We bonded over shared challenges, sometimes late-night audit sessions, and the occasional victory when the numbers finally added up. I would go to the office in the afternoon and return by 6 PM, after which we would enjoy evening tea, take leisurely walks, and share jokes before dinner at 9 PM. I even played bridge with senior professionals from other companies staying at the guesthouse. One of them, a professor from BITS Pilani who also practiced astrology, shared some incredible insights about my past and confidently suggested I would find more success as a professional drummer than as a CA. I wondered if perhaps my true calling was to keep the beat—after all, life is just a series of rhythms, and I was still figuring out how to dance to my own!

The experience at Hindustan Insecticides was altogether different, as the guesthouse felt more like flats. The excitement was heightened by its proximity—just 40 km from Bombay—where my friend Rajeev Gupta lived. Every Friday, I would be dropped off by a company car and picked up on Monday to go to the office. The colony where Rajeev stayed was a beautifully maintained oasis, surrounded by lush greenery and home to just 24 residences for senior executives of Burma Shell, which later became Bharat Petroleum. This microcosm of luxury was complete with a club, a billiards table, a swimming pool, and serene walking paths. The area was so picturesque that it occasionally served as a backdrop for Bollywood films, adding a touch of glamour to our otherwise quiet lives.

Despite being in our early twenties as Article clerk, we were treated with an unexpected level of respect by the senior officials of the companies that we used to go for audits. We stayed in the best guesthouses and had cars at our disposal, a stark contrast to the more humble lodgings when we had to travel on our own.

It was during these trips that I also picked up new hobbies, most notably playing bridge. The game became a way to unwind after long days of auditing, and I found that it sharpened my strategic thinking in ways that complimented my studies. The friendships I formed during these trips were invaluable, and the life lessons I learned—about discipline, hard work, and the importance of balance—stayed with me long after the audits were completed.

Another memorable audit was at the Sangam Picture Hall, where I spent more time sitting in a private Box watching the movie than actually working in the office. I must have watched the same film, Suhaag 36 times, enjoying burgers and Coca-Cola as I shirked my responsibilities. It was a stark contrast to the disciplined approach I had developed in other areas of my CA journey, a reminder that I was still very much a young man navigating the temptations of freedom.

My less-than-stellar study habits—I rarely spent more than 5-6 hours a day studying during preparation leaves —didn't stop me from achieving success in the CA exams. Most of my friends would study anywhere between 12-16 hours a day as the pass percentage was low single digit. I cleared the CA Intermediate Group 1 on my first attempt and Group 2 on the second attempt. By the time I faced the CA finals in November 1981, I was 23 and a half years old. The exams coincided with my friend Anil's wedding, and the celebrations nearly derailed my preparations. Yet, I managed to clear two out of the three groups, a feat that even surprised me. The failure in the third group was due to a technicality— a mistake that cost me dearly. The CA exams were notoriously difficult, with a pass rate in the low single digits.

Despite my best efforts, I often found myself scraping by with just enough marks to pass. I never scored more than 52%, and there were always moments where I narrowly avoided failing a subject. Passing on the margins in all five groups of CA was not serendipity, I credit my success to the blessings of Maa Durga, whose presence I felt guided me through the toughest moments.

Anil's wedding was also an amazing experience. The day my final exams ended, I moved to Anil's house, and Rajeev and I stayed there for almost ten days, celebrating multiple events with great enthusiasm. Both Rajeev and I had just one pair of formal clothes—Rajeev had a green suit while I sported a blue blazer and grey pants. To look different at the wedding, we exchanged our outfits: I wore Rajeev's suit at Anil's wedding reception while he donned my jacket. We would dance like crazy and I would whistle. We had a few glasses of whiskey, while it was fun for the first few hours, I would even vomit and have headaches. This habit of dancing, whistling had become my trademark on almost all the celebratory occasions in Anil or my family I am still known for my whistling, but it has been a while now since we had this celebration.

Within six months of Anil's wedding, Anil, his wife Sangeeta, and I, along with Anil's driver, embarked on a weeklong pilgrimage to visit various Devi Darshans. This was an experience I could never have dreamed of at that time, and we later made a similar pilgrimage in the late 90s with my family.

Sangeeta was expecting, and Anil wanted to visit the Vaishno Devi shrine to seek Maa Durga's blessings. My faith and belief in Maa Durga had deepened further. We reached Katra, the base camp, in the late afternoon and immediately began our climb toward the holy shrine. There were hardly any people around, and our porter was exceptionally kind. It had snowed for a couple of days, making the path very slippery. Guess who became our guide? An old lady walking barefoot, without any stick or torch, gave us immense courage. In hindsight, I believe it was Maa Durga guiding us through the presence of the old lady. We found ourselves among just twelve people at the Bhawan, making the darshan quite easy. That night, we slept on the floor with four blankets as makeshift mattresses and another four to cover ourselves.

The next day, we began our descent and reached a spot where the side walls were broken, leading to a steep drop of almost 1,000 feet. Our porter encouraged us, and I still remember walking over snow for at least 20 feet, crossing with ease as if someone was guiding us to the other side. Had we seen that precarious situation at night, even a crore wouldn't have tempted me to risk my life. This was among the most miraculous moments of my life, further deepening my faith in Maa Durga.

Amidst the pressures of CA exams and audits, I also faced personal challenges, particularly my struggle with smoking. I had become a habitual smoker during my college years, and the addiction had taken hold of me. It wasn't until January 1, 1987, with the impending birth of my son, Rohan, and the support of my wife, Poonam that I found the strength to quit. My mother's pride and the thought of setting a good example for my son were powerful motivators. I had tried to quit smoking 30 or 40 times before, but this time, it was different. With Poonam's encouragement and the joy of welcoming Rohan into the world, I was determined to overcome this habit once and for all.

Now that I look back on those years, I realize how integral my friendships were to my personal and professional development. Whether it was the disciplined companionship of Sanjeev Chopra and Dr. Anil Jain or the more carefree adventures with Rajan

Sharma and others, each relationship played a role in shaping who I was becoming. My time with Ashok Batra and the CA guys was particularly formative. Ashok's mentorship taught me the value of hard work, integrity, and the importance of being a lifelong learner.

By 1982, after finally clearing my CA exams, I was ready to embark on a new chapter in my life. The journey from college life through the challenges of CA had been anything but smooth, but it had prepared me for the professional world in ways I hadn't anticipated. I had learned to balance fun with responsibility, to persevere through failures, and to value the relationships that supported me through it all.

College life is a time of exploration, challenges, and growth. For me, it was the first real taste of independence, where the decisions I made began to shape my future. My journey through college and into my early career was filled with unexpected twists, tough lessons, and moments of self-discovery. From dealing with setbacks to finding new paths, this chapter of my life offers insights that are just as relevant today as they were back then. Remember to embrace every experience—good and bad—as a stepping stone on your path to greatness.

As I completed my education, I found myself stepping into the unknown, transitioning from an unstructured world to a structured work environment. The fear of the unknown loomed large, but I carried with me the values I had learned—gratitude, resilience, and unwavering faith in Maa Durga. These became my guiding lights as I started this new chapter of life. I knew that the foundation I had built during those formative years would support me in all the endeavors that lay ahead.

Chapter 4

Foundations of a Professional Journey

In September of 1982, I stood at the threshold of a new chapter in my life. The year marked my entry into the corporate world with Escorts Limited, a decision that would ultimately shape my career and lay the foundations for my future. I was a young man, fresh out of college, with little more than dreams and an unyielding determination to succeed. Until that moment, I had lived a relatively carefree life, relishing the simple pleasures without much concern for long-term consequences or ambitious goals. But stepping through the doors of Escorts felt like crossing into another realm, one where only the driven could survive and thrive. This realization set me on a path of transformation, one that would redefine my approach to life and work.

I vividly remember my first formal interview at Escorts, facilitated by a family connection to Mr. Rakesh Chopra, the head of Finance for the Tractor division. My heart was racing as I walked in. The interview was grueling, but somehow, I scraped through and was offered a stipend as a management trainee at Rs 1,800 per month. When I received that first salary check, a wave of pride washed over me as I handed it to my mother. At that moment, it felt as though I had given her a piece of my heart, a small but meaningful token of appreciation for all she had done. I could see the joy in her eyes as if she had achieved something monumental.

Before joining Escorts, I was someone who cherished the simplicity of life. I reveled in the little joys—spending time with friends, engaging in light-hearted banter, and embracing a laid-back lifestyle that felt effortless. My life was unburdened by responsibilities or the pressure to achieve great things. But entering the corporate world was a wake-up call. I quickly realized that this carefree attitude would not serve me well in a competitive environment where every decision held the weight of potential consequences. The realization that I needed to adopt a more serious and driven approach hit me like a ton of bricks. I could no longer afford complacency; I had to rise to the occasion and prove my worth in a world that could be ruthless and unforgiving.

I drew strength from the core values instilled in me during my formative years. The power of gratitude, humility, empathy, respect, and trust became my guiding lights. I learned to savor the journey, to be resilient, and to nurture long-term relationships. Above all, I held onto my belief in myself and the blessings of Maa Durga, which provided me with a sense of purpose and courage. These lessons, while seemingly simple, formed the bedrock of my identity and fueled my determination as I navigated the challenges ahead.

The environment at Escorts was anything but straightforward. The company operated within a unionized framework, which brought with it a unique set of challenges. Exercising authority wasn't simple; every decision required careful negotiation and collaboration to avoid conflicts with the workforce. I quickly learned that to succeed in such an environment, I needed to balance firmness with empathy. The unionized setup demanded a leader who could navigate the complex dynamics of a unionized team, inspire and motivate while maintaining control and authority, and be a friend all at the same time.

One of my first major responsibilities at Escorts was overseeing the largest bill payments department—an intimidating task with 40 people on my team. I was the youngest member in a team where the average age ranged between 35 and 37, with the eldest member being over 50. I realized I transitioned from a "Boy" to a "Man", the moment I took the chair as the leader of a 40-member team. Managing such a large team within a unionized and politically motivated environment required me to think creatively about leadership and motivation. Traditional management techniques, I realized, would not be sufficient in this context. Instead, I sought to infuse a sense of competition among the team members, by incorporating fun and gamification into our work routine. I joined in the camaraderie, competing alongside my team, which not only motivated them but also fostered a light-hearted atmosphere in what could have been a tense and challenging environment. As a result of this thought process, they would often take on additional transactions or perform extra work beyond what was typically expected of them, leading to a 20-30% increase in productivity, all while doing it much more willingly. *By focusing on measurable, outcome-driven goals and creating an engaging work culture, I was able to lead the team effectively, even within the constraints of a unionized setup.*

My time at Escorts was defined by unwavering dedication. My typical day started at 6:30 AM, and I often wouldn't return home until after 6:15 PM. The commute from Janakpuri to

Faridabad took about 1.5 hours each way. Thankfully, my friend Rajan Sharma, who I respected like an elder brother and would call him Bhapa, came to the rescue with a bus pass. I remain deeply grateful to Rajan for that gesture. Those long hours were a testament to my commitment, not just to the company but to my personal growth. To maximize productivity and reduce commuting time, I sometimes stayed over at a subordinate's one-room flat, allowing me to immerse myself in work without the burden of a lengthy journey back home. Despite the routine's exhausting nature, my enthusiasm for the work never waned.

In the early years, I used to have lunch at a dhaba across the road —a quaint spot where the traffic on the national highway was sparse. When I became an assistant manager, I gained access to the managers' lunchroom, where I enjoyed three-course meals and shared laughter, creating bonds that made the workplace feel like family.

Recognizing my performance, I was transferred to the Diesel Engine department to head their accounts function, and soon after, my role expanded to manage the Industrial Equipment department, which was nearly five times larger. As I settled into my new responsibilities, I began building relationships with the senior leadership at Escorts, which proved to be one of the most rewarding aspects of my time there. Though I held a relatively junior position, I had the privilege of working closely with some esteemed professionals who were almost 7 levels higher in hierarchy. My easy-going nature helped me establish rapport with key decision-makers and business heads, fostering relationships grounded in mutual respect and trust. Engaging with leadership at this level made my work not just a job, but a fulfilling journey where I felt valued for my innovative ideas and willingness to take risks.

This shift in perspective led me to embrace what I can only describe as an "entrepreneurial mindset." The term "Intrapreneur" wasn't widely known in the early 80s, especially within large organizations like Escorts. Yet, I instinctively adopted this mindset, viewing my role not just as an employee but as someone who could drive innovation and change from within the company with an owner's mindset. This new approach empowered me to express my ideas freely, to take bold actions, and to stand my ground when I believed in the righteousness of my decisions. I was unafraid to say "No" when necessary, even if it meant challenging the status quo or opposing higher-ups. This approach often created value that far exceeded the confines of my job description or compensation. My ability to stand firm in my beliefs and consistently deliver results began to set me apart from my peers early in my career at Escorts.

Life is not just about duty and challenges, but also about finding joy, playfulness, and balance.

Reflecting on my 37-year career, two things stand out vividly. I never had to mark my attendance daily; I simply signed the register for HR to process my salary. This freedom to come and go as I pleased fostered a sense of trust and responsibility. The second remarkable lesson came from the Bhagavad Gita: *Life is not just about duty and challenges, but also about finding joy, playfulness, and balance.* This wisdom helped me maintain a positive outlook and consistency, transforming my work experience into one centered around enjoying the journey, building friendships and meaningful relationships. I often sang, danced, and did masti with my colleagues, finding more joy in Monday mornings than Friday evenings all through my career.

During my time, we also developed financial products, even though it was typically the domain of the centralized treasury department. One notable product was created in collaboration with Punjab National Bank, leveraging their extensive branch network. Back then, navigating nationalized banks was no small feat. But with faith, hard work, and persistence—along with multiple trips to their branches and head office—I made it work. While, another partnership with Citi Bank came about due to their sophisticated risk assessment processes. The financial product focused on small-scale bill discounting, which reduced the system's cost by a few percentage points in interest expenses. I always believed in creating win-win situations with new offerings, ensuring that everyone benefited—something I carry with me even today. I felt immensely proud when both of these products were launched in other division of Escorts.

My reflection of the journey at Escorts made me realize that much of my success stemmed from the people around me, particularly my team member Rajesh Choudhary. He was just a clerk, but his drive, commitment, and passion for making things happen played a key role in developing the product with Punjab National Bank. I always made it a point to encourage and motivate my team members to push boundaries, a principle that continues to guide me even today. It's like a great story—everyone needs a hero, and I aimed to be that for my team, ready to shoulder the responsibility if things went south while always passing the credit to them.

I remember the Late Mr. Rajan Nanda, the chairman of Escorts, was always the first to arrive at the office and the last to leave, setting a standard of dedication, discipline and work ethic that I greatly admired. Observing his leadership style and work habits had a profound impact on me. It pushed me to mirror those qualities in my own work.

By 1985, my hard work paid off. I had saved enough to put down the advance for my first car—it was second-hand, but to me, it felt brand new! The balance was funded by Escorts as a loan, marking a significant milestone in my life. It was a symbol of my progress, both personally and professionally. Around the same time, we installed our first air cooler at home—which we considered quite the luxury back then! It felt like we had hit the jackpot, especially considering it wasn't until 1993 that we finally bought an air conditioner. I suppose you could say we embraced the philosophy of 'slow and steady wins the race.

Over the eight years I spent at Escorts, my hard work, dedication, and ability to innovate did not go unnoticed. I received four promotions during this time, in my personal view this must be the fastest growth trajectory in Escorts. Each promotion felt like a small victory, a marker of my progress in this professional journey. But beyond the titles and responsibilities, what truly mattered was the recognition of my contributions and the trust placed in me by the leadership.

One of the key figures in my professional growth was Mr. Rakesh Chopra. He was a tough taskmaster but had a heart of gold. He recognized my potential early on and became more than just a boss—he was a mentor who provided invaluable guidance. Mr. Chopra was known for his straightforwardness and candid nature, and he appreciated innovation and results—qualities that resonated deeply with me. Under his mentorship, I learned to take on more responsibilities and face greater challenges. He trusted me to extend my role beyond its traditional boundaries, allowing me to take calculated risks that not only contributed to my growth but also to the company's success.

I also built a strong relationship with Anil's sister, Adarsh Kapoor, and spent my weekends with her family until I got married. It became our tradition to dine out, visit India Gate on Saturdays, and end the day by watching a couple of movies on the VCR at her home—what a time that was! Living in a cozy one-bedroom rented flat, Adarsh always made everyone feel welcome, ensuring her generous spirit shone through regardless of the limited space. Rajeev, too, was looking to settle down in Delhi and stayed with Adarsh for nearly a year. Sometimes, I'd help out at her chemist shop in Khan Market, sitting at the cash counter like the head of a bustling empire! It brings me immense joy to witness Adarsh's sons achieving remarkable success.

As 1990 approached, I found myself reflecting on my eight years at Escorts. During this time, my salary had increased from Rs.1800 in 1982, to Rs. 6400 per month—a significant improvement, but still modest by any standard. I had by now started giving a part of the salary to my wife, Poonam, while the house expenses were still managed by my mother.

In my journey, the drive to succeed came from within, fueled by lessons learned and the determination to turn them into a meaningful and rewarding life. As I look back on my early years at Escorts, I can see just how profoundly those experiences shaped the person I am today. The lessons I gathered during that time were not only instrumental in building a successful career but also in laying the groundwork for a life filled with purpose and fulfillment.

My journey at Escorts was more than just a job; it was a transformative period that shaped my personal and professional identity as an intrapreneur. The friendships I forged, the challenges I overcame, and the successes I achieved all contributed to my growth. The lessons I learned at Escorts—about perseverance, the importance of relationships, and the power of innovation—were invaluable. They laid the foundation for my future endeavors.

As I prepared to leave Escorts and embrace new challenges at Ranbaxy, in my professional journey, I did so with a sense of accomplishment, ready for the next chapter of my career.

Having explored the path of my professional life, it's time to turn to a more personal compass. In the next chapter, I'll delve into one of the most important aspects of my life: my family. They are my foundation, my support system, and a reflection of who I am.

Chapter 5

The Core of My Journey: Family First

While my professional life was soaring, my personal life was about to take a significant turn. In 1986, I married Poonam, a graduate from IP College, Delhi University. At that point, my close friends Rajeev and Anil were already married, and I was feeling ready to take this big step. After our families met, things moved quickly—just days after our first meeting on 5th January, we were engaged on January 14, 1986, and married on May 25, 1986. Talk about a whirlwind romance!

Poonam was ambitious and had dreams of building a successful career, but societal expectations at the time often dictated that women marry soon after graduation. Poonam was a brilliant student, having completed her graduation from IP College, one of the best colleges of Delhi University, and was in her second year at Campus Law Center, Delhi University, where she had secured a first division. I later learned that she had asked her parents to postpone the marriage by a year. Her father was very adamant that she was of marriageable age and must get married as he came from orthodox thoughts that women should become good housewives. Maybe, if I had known of her desires, I would have agreed to defer the marriage by a year.

Poonam's family was much wealthier than ours. Yet, her father chose me to marry Poonam—perhaps because of our reputation in Pakistan or maybe because he had the foresight to see that I was bright and would achieve great heights sooner than even I imagined. While Poonam knew everything about running a house, she had lived like a princess in her home and was rarely allowed to do house chores. Despite being an arranged marriage, our relationship blossomed into something that felt remarkably like a love story—thanks to the bond we built during our 34 meetings from January to May 1986. We'd drive around in our non-AC second-hand car through Central Delhi, enjoying each other's company. Given our financial position, we never went to any five-star hotels, and the money spent during those days was just less than Rs.50. We used to speak twice every day on the phone, one of which was during my extended lunchtime at Escorts, courtesy of my boss's late Karan Bhatia (one of the most jovial and easy-going bosses) and the second in the evening. Our neighbors were very nice to allow us to spend 20-30 minutes on the phone as neither of us had a landline and mobiles did not exist back then.

Poonam was very shy, even hesitant to hold hands, which only made her more endearing to me. She had no material expectations and embodied the qualities of being content with simplicity while remaining deeply rooted in traditional values. Before we got married, I had a few conditions for myself: I wanted to own a car, host a wedding reception in a five-star hotel, have a memorable honeymoon, travel by air, and stay in five-star properties. While I was able to put aside the money required for celebrations, I didn't have enough money for the honeymoon. Rajeev offered a helping hand and funded our honeymoon. I still remember him coming to Hotel Claridges, where I hosted my wedding reception, to lend me Rs.10,000, which I repaid in 1994.

We flew to Srinagar for our honeymoon. We stayed in some of the best hotels, I still have a receipt from Hotel Pahalgam, where we paid Rs.2350 for five nights. To add a sprinkle of excitement, a couple of film stars including Jackie Shroff were staying at the same hotel — for the shoot of Paley Khan. Naturally, we couldn't resist checking out the film shooting; after all, who wouldn't want to play tourist amid Bollywood glamour?

Kashmir was breathtaking, with its stunning landscapes and picturesque spots that felt like they were plucked straight from a postcard. I also recall that the football World Cup was happening in Mexico at the same time, and I managed to carve out some moments to catch those exhilarating matches. One of the most famous matches was when Diego Maradona's "Hand of God" goal secured Argentina's victory over the UK. It was thrilling to watch how Maradona, almost single-handedly, led Argentina to win the World Cup. This trip remains etched in my memory as a perfect start to our married life.

The early days of our marriage were challenging for both of us. Poonam had to adjust to a new life, taking on responsibilities she had never handled before, such as managing household chores and adapting to a different lifestyle. With Poonam's strength and determination guiding her through these new responsibilities, we began building our life as a married couple, tackling challenges together. Our relationship was built on mutual respect and understanding, and we both knew that we would have to support each other through the inevitable ups and downs of life. There were times when she worked tirelessly. I often marveled at her ability to tackle everything from washing clothes and cooking to ensuring every family member's needs were met. She had empathy, love, and care for everyone. I was extremely surprised by how she adapted to our family life. She has lived with these values throughout our married life even though we can now afford many luxuries.

Our financial situation was far from ideal, yet Poonam never once complained or asked for more. This reflection is set against the context of living in Delhi, with its high cost of living compared to smaller cities and towns, where maintaining a reasonable lifestyle would have been much easier. In 1986, my salary was around Rs.4,000, and with that, I had to support my family while also fulfilling obligations towards my sisters. In a smaller city, this same salary could have provided a much more comfortable lifestyle, but living in Delhi required careful financial planning and sacrifices to ensure we met all our responsibilities.

I vividly remember when we had only Rs. 35, and the thought of eating out seemed almost frivolous. Poonam, ever practical, suggested that we save the money. But I insisted, and we ended up at Nirula's, where a simple Thali cost exactly Rs. 35. *It wasn't about the meal—it was about the small joys we could still share despite our struggles.*

Poonam's steady support during those tough times was a source of strength for me. We didn't have much wealth, but we found happiness in the simple pleasures. Long drives, renting movies to watch on our VCR, or spending quiet evenings with family brought us closer, filling our lives with contentment. Trips to the cinema were rare, but those cozy nights at home felt equally special, filled with treasured moments. Poonam was very fond of reading and since we could not afford to buy magazines or books we used to hire the same from libraries.

Poonam briefly considered contributing to the family by starting her own small enterprise. She even completed a short-term certification course in Okhla, which required her to commute for nearly an hour both ways on a DTC bus, all while Rohan was just two years old. Ultimately, she decided to focus on raising the children, leaving me to take on the role of the sole breadwinner. Life was simple back then, and that simplicity shielded us from the stress of the outside world. With limited communication and essentials often scarce, we lived in a time where the ration card system ensured everyone got their fair share, in spite of shortages. Yet, in that environment of scarcity, we found joy in the little things. Those moments, free from the pressures that seem so inevitable today, brought us happiness that was pure and true. Poonam's grace and practicality in those days are memories I cherish deeply, reminding me that true happiness isn't found in wealth, but in the love and contentment we shared.

In March 1987, our lives took another joyous turn with the arrival of our son, Rohan, at Spring Meadows Hospital in East of Kailash, known for its excellent doctors—especially Dr. Dharma Chatterjee. Rohan's addition to our family filled our lives with immense joy. I still remember rushing back from my overnight shift in Faridabad upon hearing the news that Poonam was in the hospital ready to deliver our child. Adarsh, Anil's sister, was a great support, taking care of us as she lived just a short walk from the hospital and knew the staff and doctor extremely well. It felt reassuring to have family nearby during such an exciting as well as anxious time.

The birth of Rohan marked a new chapter in our lives, one filled with the responsibilities and challenges of parenthood. Regardless of the financial pressures, we made it a priority to provide a nurturing and supportive environment for Rohan and bought him the best toys and clothes, much beyond our means. Poonam's support during this time was unwavering, providing me with strength and reassurance even in the most challenging moments. She played a crucial role in helping me balance the demands of my career with the needs of our growing family. This period of our lives was characterized by a strong partnership between Poonam and me, as we navigated the complexities of raising a child while managing the demands of work and home life.

We were both committed to giving Rohan the best start in life, which included sending him to Delhi Public School, one of the top schools in Delhi. It was also my Alma Mater. This decision, like many others during that time, was driven by our desire to ensure that Rohan had every opportunity to succeed, even if it meant making financial sacrifices.

While we strived to keep life on track, fate had something drastic in store for us. In 1988, we faced the profound loss of Maama, who had been a guiding light throughout my life. At 82, she had shared an incredibly close bond with Poonam—almost like a second mother—and her passing in Poonam's arms left a deep emotional impact on both of us. Maama had imparted many invaluable lessons to me about humility, the importance of daily tasks, gratitude, and the path to spirituality. Those teachings not only stayed with me but became pillars of strength during tough times.

While Poonam coped with everyday errands and tried to manage her emotions, we decided to hire our first full-time domestic help, a young boy sent by Poonam's father. This assistance was a game changer, allowing us to focus on work and family. Over time, this young boy, whom we affectionately called Chotu, became part of our family, reflecting the supportive environment we strove to create at home.

Fast forward to 1992, and we were blessed with our daughter, Ishani, who was born at the same hospital and by the same doctor, as Rohan. Adarsh, bless her, played a pivotal role in making us comfortable at the hospital. Ishani's name holds special significance as it is also associated with Maa Durga. Her arrival felt like a beautiful blessing, bringing promises of strength, and a brighter future. We took Ishani home from the hospital in our old car, but fate had a twist for us. She fell ill and had to be readmitted to the hospital the next day. When we brought her home the second time, it was in our new Maruti 800, a generous gift from Ranbaxy. From the very start, Ishani seemed to usher in a wave of positive changes in our lives.

Rohan, just six at the time, was over the moon to have a sister. He was so caring that he even helped with changing her diapers—a sight that would have made any parent proud. But it wasn't all sunshine; Ishani had severe jaundice after birth, and both Rohan and I stayed in the hospital room, keeping a vigilant watch over her. Poonam and I had always wanted a daughter, and Rohan had been longing for a sister. So, Ishani's arrival felt like a beautiful blessing.

Life took a turn for the better in 1993 when we moved into a larger home in a better locality, Sukhdev Vihar. The house had three bedrooms and a spacious living and dining area. This was a significant upgrade, symbolizing the stability we were beginning to achieve as a family. Finally, we each had our own space—my parents had their room, Poonam and I had ours, and the children had theirs. This new home, initially offered rent-free by my uncle, had a lovely garden out front shared by just four houses. It was perfect for Rohan and Ishani to grow up in. By 1998, we managed to buy this house, marking yet another milestone on our journey toward financial security. Funny enough, each of Ishani's birthdays seemed to coincide with significant positive changes in our lives—be it a new job opportunity or a salary raise, something wonderful always seemed to happen around her special day.

As life progressed, we as parents and a couple grew to understand our responsibilities better. Poonam acted as the backbone of the family, helping me sail through both personal and professional challenges. Though she came from a more privileged background, she always stood by me, even during our financial struggles. I started giving her my entire salary in the early 90s, and from that point on, she managed our household finances with incredible skill.

Rohan had become a friend to both Poonam and me, sharing in our joys and challenges, and providing insights that helped us navigate the ups and downs of family life. *His youthful perspective often brought a refreshing clarity to our discussions, reminding us of the importance of laughter and connection amidst the chaos of daily responsibilities.*

By this time, we had established a strong family foundation. Rohan and Ishani were growing into responsible, thoughtful individuals, inheriting a sense of practicality and wisdom as my career continued to evolve. As Ishani also started to mature, both children actively participated in discussions about my professional decisions. Rohan, with his sharp mind and great sense of humor, often brought a fresh perspective to our conversations, and Ishani's meticulous nature provided balance. Both the children achieved excellence in academics.

Rohan was ranked 3rd in South Campus during his graduation. He went on to do a double master's, one of which was from one of the best B Schools in India, and an MSc in Statistics from Warwick University. Ishani was also not one to be left behind.

She was a batch topper in school, graduated with high rankings, and later ranked amongst the top ten percentile in MSc Finance at Warwick Business School, despite being the youngest student with no prior professional experience.

In the professional field, Rohan worked with some of the best multinationals, including Accenture and American Express. Ishani began her journey with Edelweiss Financial Services before joining me as my investment partner at Sarcha Advisors, the firm I founded six years ago.

In 2010, we made the significant decision to purchase our current bungalow at DLF Phase 2 Gurgaon—a move driven by Poonam and Rohan. With the blessings of Maa Durga, we overcame initial concerns about affordability and managed to repay the loan within just six months of buying the house. This event symbolized a period of financial prosperity and was a result of our collective strength and determination.

Rohan, Ishani, and Poonam have been instrumental in major decisions including my move from Hero to start my own entrepreneurial journey much later in life, it was one of the life-defining decisions. *I have always treated them as my dost and equal partner in decision making.*

We welcomed another addition to our Family when Rohan married Upasana in 2014. Upasana is an impressive woman with a stellar academic background, having earned gold medal in master's degree from IIT Roorkee, one of India's premier institutions. Completed her PhD in Biotechnology from Göttingen University in Germany with summa cum laude honors. Upasana continued to excel in her post-doctoral work and eventually became an assistant professor at AIIMS, one of the top medical institutes in India, now plans to pursue her entrepreneurial journey.

Rohan and Upasana embody a shared commitment to excellence, each forging their unique paths that complement one another. Rohan's corporate achievements and Upasana's academic brilliance create a strong partnership rooted in mutual respect and shared values. In 2020, we were blessed with our grandson, Rihaan, the pride of our family, and Poonam and I have cherished watching him grow.

In 2022, Ishani married Sirav, a man with a great sense of humor and sharp intellect - qualities that complemented her meticulous and serious nature. Sirav, like Ishani, is highly accomplished in his education. He earned his MBA at NMIMS, one of the top 10 MBA schools in India, and was awarded the Dean's Certificate for Excellence in multiple semesters. After completing his MBA, he joined his family business, where he made significant contributions by streamlining operations and introducing innovations in areas like direct marketing and social media. His ability to combine humor with serious work has always been one of his greatest strengths. He contributed to designing the cover of this book and was also one of the first to share feedback as a reader.

We feel incredibly blessed to have such wonderful children in our family, and I owe a heartfelt gratitude to Maa Durga for guiding us. As the years passed, our lives became more comfortable. In 2018 and 2019, we had the opportunity to indulge in luxury cars—a significant shift from the financial struggles of our earlier days. Reflecting on this journey fills me with immense gratitude for the life we've built together. Our personal and professional successes are a testament to the strength of our family bond and the constant support we've given each other.

As a family, we feel truly blessed to have achieved success that extends far beyond material wealth. While we are grateful for the comforts and security that material success brings, we deeply value the realization that true wealth lies in embracing a holistic approach to life. For us, wealth is also about prioritizing health—because health is indeed the foundation of happiness. It's about cherishing the relationships we've nurtured over the years, the bonds of *rishtey* and *dosti* that add meaning and joy to our lives.

We are proud to have built a legacy that reflects authenticity, grounded in values and driven by purpose. Our spiritual journey has brought us inner peace and clarity, while intellectual wealth has fueled our curiosity, growth, and openness to new ideas. These dimensions of wealth—relationships, health, legacy, spirituality, and intellectual growth—define our success far more than just material possessions.

Our journey reminds us that true success lies in balancing these aspects, creating a life rich with meaning, purpose, and connection. This is the message we carry forward as a family, and we hope it inspires others to view wealth in its most holistic and fulfilling form.

The essence of the core of my journey - where the joy found in simple, everyday moments and the love shared within the family laid the foundation for our collective success. It is evident how the foundation of a strong, supportive family can influence and enhance professional success, while also showcasing the resilience and determination needed to overcome obstacles. Through the experiences of marriage, parenthood, financial struggles, and professional milestones, my journey offers valuable lessons for the youth, emphasizing the importance of relationships, perseverance, and personal growth.

Having delved into the complexities and triumphs of my personal journey, it is now time to turn our attention to the professional sphere. The next chapter charts my path through the world of work, where ambition, dedication, and a relentless pursuit of excellence have shaped my career. Guided by my instincts and honed negotiation skills, this new phase at Ranbaxy promised a wealth of learning and experience.

Chapter 6

Gut, Decisions, and Leadership

In 1990, I was invited for an interview at Ranbaxy headquarters, 19 Nehru Place—an opportunity that stirred excitement and a familiar twinge of anxiety. As I approached the office of senior executives, the weight of my journey flashed before me: years of relentless hard work, delivering great outcomes, earning recognition, and striving for something greater flashed through my mind. But today felt different. I wasn't just another candidate walking into an interview; I was a man standing tall, confident in his worth, and ready to claim his place in this esteemed institution.

Even after 35 years, I can vividly recall that morning. I dressed with purpose, meticulously donning a crisp black suit, polished shoes, and a tie that struck the perfect balance between modesty and assertiveness. I wanted to exude confidence as I walked into the lobby, a space marked by the cool hum of air conditioning, soft murmurs, and the occasional ringing phone. The receptionist directed me to Mr. Vinay Kaul's office, the CFO at Ranbaxy, and as I waited, my thoughts briefly drifted to my current position at Escorts—a job I had once cherished, at a company that had once filled me with pride. Despite four promotions and a wealth of responsibilities, the work had grown routine, and the salary no longer sufficed. I was ready for a change—a leap into something bigger.

The interview with Mr. Kaul went better than I could have imagined. He was deeply impressed with my achievements, particularly my creative and innovative mindset. He later shared that my ability to take calculated risks and make bold decisions had left a lasting impression. But the real test came during my second interview with Mr. D.S. Brar, President, International Division, a commanding figure whose presence filled the room as he stood behind a large mahogany desk. His voice, measured and deliberate, cut through the tension.

"I've reviewed your resume, and I must say, your credentials are impressive," he said, his tone both serious and thoughtful. "Vinay spoke highly of you."

He wasted no time with pleasantries, launching into tough questions designed to test my confidence, patience, and intellect. Though I answered confidently, I was unsure whether I had truly impressed him. The interview stretched to an hour, twice as long as scheduled, and I walked away convinced that I would not get the offer.

Later that evening, I shared my concerns with the friend who had introduced me to Mr. Kaul, that he needed to find me another job. The same evening, I received a surprising call from the Head of HR, asking me to meet him the next day. I was taken aback but hopeful, believing that perhaps my calm composure during the interview had made an impact. Mr. Kaul's kind words likely hadn't hurt either.

The next day, I sat across from the HR head as he smiled and said, "We're prepared to offer you Rs. 7,000 per month, a significant increase from your current salary at Escorts."

It was tempting—more than I had ever earned before—but deep down, I knew I was worth more. I had worked too hard and sacrificed too much to settle for less. I took a breath and responded, "I appreciate the offer, but I was expecting Rs. 11,000."

The HR head's eyebrows rose, surprise flickering across his face. "Rs. 11,000? That's quite a jump."

"Yes," I agreed, holding his gaze. "But I believe that's what I'm worth. My experience, my dedication, and my vision for this role reflect that figure."

For a moment, there was silence, broken only by the low hum of the air conditioning. He studied me, weighing his options. Then he leaned forward, his expression unreadable. "And if we can't meet your expectations?"

Without hesitation, I replied, "Then don't hire me. If Ranbaxy can't recognize my value, I'll look elsewhere."

The boldness of my statement hung in the air, but I knew I had to stand firm. This was a test of my self-worth, a moment that would define my future. After a long pause, he said I would hear their decision soon. I felt confident, even in the face of uncertainty. I believed Mr. Brar and Mr. Kaul had seen something in me, and I had a growing sense that Ranbaxy valued people with potential. This was an adult-to- adult dialogue.

Sure enough, I was hired as the Head of Accounts for the International Division. The victory, though sweet, was only the beginning.

Sitting in my new office, overlooking the bustling landscape of Nehru Place, I reflected on the journey that had brought me here. The leap from Escorts to Ranbaxy had been transformative, both financially and professionally. I had left behind a salary of Rs. 6,400 for Rs. 11,000—a near doubling that symbolized my growth.

At Escorts, my rise had been swift, but I believed the rewards had not matched the responsibility. Ranbaxy, however, felt different. It was a place where my ambitions could take root, where my hard work and potential would be recognized and nurtured. And so, with a heart full of gratitude and a mindset on the challenges ahead, I stepped into this new chapter, ready to make my mark.

I knew without a doubt that my decision to move had been the right one. Yes, the salary mattered, but what mattered more was the validation—the affirmation that I had stood my ground, asked for what I deserved, and had been met with recognition. That validation filled me with a deep sense of pride, igniting a fire of determination within me.

As I settled into my new office, I could feel the weight of expectation on my shoulders. The challenges ahead were numerous and daunting, yet I embraced them wholeheartedly. This was my opportunity—a chance to demonstrate to the world, and myself, that I was capable of achieving greatness.

The first few months at the International Division were exhilarating. My eagerness to take on more responsibility didn't go unnoticed, and within a month, my role expanded to managing the company's foreign exchange exposure. I embraced this new responsibility, trusting in my ability to manage risks with the clarity and confidence that had guided me so far. Thanks to a careful blend of analysis and instinct, my first few decisions yielded impressive results. I was able to contribute significantly to the company's profits, not only by managing the foreign exchange exposure but also by lowering the cost of financing through smarter borrowing strategies against future exports. My efforts were appreciated by my peers and senior management alike, which only fueled my drive.

Just 45 days into my time at Ranbaxy, we had a senior management meeting at the Taj Palace on November 24, 1991. I was the least experienced in the room, but that didn't deter me. It was my chance to stand in front of 40 senior colleagues and peers and present my achievements, along with my vision for the months ahead. I knew I had to seize this opportunity, and when I did, it was a moment I would never forget. I walked out of that room with a deep sense of accomplishment, having exceeded even my own expectations. Both Dr. Parvinder Singh, the MD of Ranbaxy, and Mr. Brar personally congratulated me during lunch, praising my clarity of thought and the tangible results I had delivered.

Sometimes, success isn't only about knowing when to speak up but also when to hold back.

But not everything that day went smoothly. Later, during another presentation, a colleague began to present information I knew wasn't accurate. Feeling compelled to ensure the truth was presented, I intervened several times to correct him. Unfortunately, Mr. Brar wasn't pleased with my interruptions, and I could sense his displeasure.

Looking back, that day taught me a valuable lesson about balance. *Sometimes, success isn't only about knowing when to speak up but also when to hold back.* In the first meeting, my boldness and clarity of vision paid off, giving me a sense of accomplishment and recognition from senior leaders. But in the second, I learned the importance of restraint and tact. It reminded me that the *truth is crucial, but timing and approach are just as essential in corporate life.*

I continued working with the mindset of an owner—fearless in my actions, words, and decisions, and fully embracing the freedom that came with responsibility. The next few months were rewarding, and I was proud of the decision I had made to join a company where my contributions were acknowledged and valued. I was flying high, confident that I had found my place.

Then, on January 11, 1992, I received the biggest shock of my career. Mr. Brar publicly reprimanded me in front of five colleagues— I do not think it was for my performance, but for my interventions during the management meeting. It was a harsh and unexpected blow, one that shook me to my core. Part of me wondered if it was time to move on, but a stronger part refused to leave as a failure. I realized I couldn't walk away with my head down. Instead, I chose to stay, to fight back, and to prove that I truly belonged there.

In the months that followed, I channeled that resolve and worked harder than ever, driven by the desire to redeem myself. My moment of redemption came sooner than I expected. In a meeting three months later, Mr. Brar challenged me once again. But this time, I stood my ground. I spoke back, something few dared to do. To my surprise, instead of escalating, Mr. Brar softened. He respected me for my courage, and from that moment on, our relationship was one of mutual respect.

Truth is crucial, but timing and approach are just as essential in corporate life.

Looking back, I am incredibly grateful—not just to Mr. Brar, who tested my resolve and helped me grow, but also to my parents, whose teachings had instilled in me the strength to persevere.

That chapter of my life taught me that *setbacks are not the end—they are simply the beginning of a new challenge, one that, when met with determination, leads to growth.*

Interestingly, around two decades later, my daughter, Ishani found herself in a similar situation. She had gone abroad for her studies and was struggling with a challenging course. During one of our conversations, she mentioned, almost defiantly, "I cannot come back as a failure." Hearing those words, I was struck by the familiar resolve in her voice. In that moment, I realized I had passed on more than just advice—*I had passed on a fighting spirit, a refusal to back down even when the odds seemed daunting.*

1991 was a turning point for India's economy as well as my journey at Ranbaxy. As the nation underwent a transformation led by Prime Minister, Mr. Narasimha Rao and Finance Minister Dr. Manmohan Singh, I found myself standing at the intersection of opportunity and challenge. With India's foreign exchange reserves perilously low, barely scraping 1 billion USD, Dr. Manmohan Singh made the bold decision to pledge gold and secure an additional 2 billion USD to keep the country afloat. The stakes were incredibly high, and it was clear that the entire financial landscape was about to change. Restrictions on imports were imposed which was very negative for our business.

Setbacks are not the end—they are simply the beginning of a new challenge, one that, when met with determination, leads to growth.

During those turbulent times, I vividly recall the intense discussions with Mr. Vinay Kaul. We spent countless hours dissecting the evolving economic landscape and strategizing how best to navigate its impact on our business. Mr. Kaul, with his sharp financial acumen, had gone to meet Dr. Rangarajan, the Deputy Governor of the RBI, seeking crucial approvals for our imports to meet export obligations. Though Mr. Kaul was suffering from severe back pain and had been advised by doctors to rest, he disregarded their advice and traveled to Mumbai. It was a grueling process, with Mr. Kaul lying in pain at the Oberoi after his meeting, his dedication never wavering. His will power and willingness to sacrifice for success was something I will never forget— *it was a reminder that great achievements demand even greater sacrifices.*

With the responsibility for managing the company's foreign exchange exposure now fully on my shoulders, I was tasked with expanding my team. I had the freedom to hire the best forex dealers, but instead of turning to banks, as was typical, I chose to bring in fresh, non-banking talent. I wanted individuals with the right attitude and values—people unburdened by the limitations of conventional thinking.

The first person I hired was Sanjay Jerry, who had already been working in my department in a junior position for a year. Despite being overburdened at times, Sanjay never complained, always eager to learn and take on more. He wasn't highly qualified—just a graduate—but his dedication, creativity, and hunger to grow stood out. With the support of Vinay Kaul, I promoted Sanjay to Assistant Manager, this was almost historical as Sanjay got 5 levels up within one year. Today, Sanjay is the Treasurer at Sun Pharma—a testament to his potential. The second hire was Arun Khurana, a newly qualified CA who embodied the qualities I was looking for. Arun eventually left Ranbaxy to join HSBC Bank, which was a moment of pride for me, as it was rare for a corporate dealer to be poached by a bank, and he is now Executive Director at IndusInd Bank.

It was a reminder that great achievements demand even greater sacrifices.

We were assigned a new dealing room, and entry was restricted to just the three of us. The room buzzed with activity as Sanjay and Arun settled into their roles, eager to absorb everything they could. As the senior member of the team, I was ready to pass on the knowledge I had gained over the years, encouraging them to learn from both experts and unconventional sources alike. Their enthusiasm reminded me of my own early days when I too had that insatiable hunger to succeed.

We started with the basics, breaking down complex concepts and building from there. Our collective drive to learn and make an impact on Ranbaxy's bottom line grew stronger with each passing day.

My commitment to Ranbaxy and my team was fixed, but it came at a steep personal cost. My days stretched from 9:30 AM to 9:00 PM, with me always being the first to arrive and the last to leave. Even after reaching home, I would stay glued to BBC, tracking exchange rates to stay informed and ahead. Saturdays became routine workdays, and I found myself preferring Monday mornings over Friday evenings. Work consumed every aspect of my life. The constant drive to push myself kept me going, but while each success felt rewarding, it was taking a toll on me both physically and emotionally. I had developed an addiction to work, even as I thoroughly enjoyed the journey. My family saw less of me, and personal time became a luxury I rarely indulged in. But I convinced myself that these sacrifices were necessary for the goals I wanted to achieve.

Amidst the grind, there was one reprieve—those precious lunch breaks with friends at Ranbaxy managers lunch room, a habit I had carried over from my days at Escorts. These moments of laughter and light-hearted conversation were a necessary balance to the pressures of work, and we rarely discussed business during these breaks.

As the months passed, I took immense pride in watching Sanjay and Arun grow under my mentorship. They were quick learners, mastering not only the technical aspects of the job but also the nuances of the industry. I guided them firmly but with encouragement, pushing them to think critically and face challenges head-on with confidence. Seeing them evolve into capable professionals was one of the most rewarding aspects of my time at Ranbaxy.

A major turning point in my journey at Ranbaxy came when we secured a Reuters screen in our office—a groundbreaking development at the time. These screens, typically reserved for banks, allowed us to track real-time exchange rates, putting us at the cutting edge of financial operations. We were one of the first corporate to have the screen, and with our dealing room equipped with three phone lines, it felt like we were at the heart of the financial world. Seeing my team progress and our business grow gave me a strong sense of purpose, even as the demands of work remained relentless.

By the time we were approaching our first anniversary, we encountered a significant opportunity. My gut instinct, sharpened by years of experience, told me this was our moment to make a bold move. Dr. Manmohan Singh was set to present the Union Budget on February 29, 1992, and we were confident that he would announce measures to attract foreign investment, which meant the rupee would strengthen against the dollar. Our prediction was spot on. We acted swiftly, selling our future export proceeds while staying fully compliant with the laws. The result? Our decisions contributed nearly a quarter of Ranbaxy's profits that year. It wasn't speculation; it was a careful, calculated strategy grounded in the spirit of the law.

By the end of 1992, our contributions to Ranbaxy's bottom line had not gone unnoticed. We received internal and external recognition, including being rated by Business Standard as one of the best forex treasuries. Our achievements were featured in Ranbaxy's annual report, with a full-page photo of our dealing room, showcasing Arun, Sanjay, and me. It was a moment of immense pride, and I am deeply thankful to Dr. Parvinder Singh (MD and CEO and Promoter), Mr. Brar, and Mr. Kaul for their recognition and support.

That year also marked another shift in my role. I transitioned from the International Division to head both domestic and foreign exchange treasury, reporting directly to Mr. Vinay Kaul. In addition to managing the company's portfolio, I was entrusted with handling Dr. Singh's personal investment portfolio—a privilege and a challenge. Dr. Singh had a high-risk appetite, preferring to invest heavily in equity, whereas the company's portfolio was largely in safe, AAA-rated debt. The trust he placed in my judgment gave me the flexibility to make bold moves, something I never took for granted. I allocated majority of my time—around ten hours—on Ranbaxy's portfolio, and maybe about 4 hours a week on Dr. Singh's investments.

Dr. Singh was a true risk-taker, a man who placed immense trust and respect in his team. One incident, in particular, stands out. We had invested heavily in Cefaclor drug but the trials failed miserably. We lost a substantial portion of that year's profits. Most leaders would have faltered, but not Dr. Singh. He had faith in his team, energizing us to take another chance. And because of that belief, Cefaclor went on to become a blockbuster drug. Within five years, the company's profits had increased eightfold, and Cefaclor alone contributed 50% of that year's profits.

The culture of trust and belief that Dr. Singh fostered was contagious. He created a team of people who were entirely aligned with his vision, and who believed in his dreams, values, and aspirations. We worked with an owner's mindset, never fearing failure. We would have given anything—an arm, a leg—to deliver on our potential because of the trust he placed in us. He was a humble and caring leader, and in all the years I worked at Ranbaxy, I never saw him lose his temper.

Early on, I realized the potential risks involved in managing such high-stakes portfolios. Even though there were no formal controls on me, I was acutely aware of the temptation that money and power could bring. *To safeguard my integrity, I instituted a four-eye principle, ensuring that every transaction was signed off by two people.* I got another team member, Maninder Singh, to head the domestic treasury, reinforcing our commitment to transparency and ethical conduct, subsequently Sanjay Jain also joined us in Domestic treasury.

One memorable transaction in 1993 involved the Lupin issue, which SEBI allowed to be based on pro-rata allotment. My experience in equity trading proved invaluable, and the responsibility I carried was immense. But with careful analysis and calculated risks, the results spoke for themselves. The returns we generated for Dr. Singh were significant, and each successful transaction only solidified my role as a key player in Ranbaxy's financial operations.

In spite of the grueling hours, I made it a priority to build strong relationships within both the industry and the company. I cherished the friendships I built with colleagues like Sanjiv, Kaul, Vijay Kumar, and Ajay Vij—bonds that have lasted for over 30 years. Vijay, in particular, was my carpool partner for the first two years until we moved from Janakpuri to Sukhdev Vihar. These connections, along with networking events and business meetings, were crucial in expanding my influence. I often squeezed in 8 to 10 meetings a day, interacting with

CFOs, domestic brokers, and foreign exchange treasuries when I made trips to Mumbai, the financial hub of the country. *These relationships weren't just transactional; they were built on trust, respect, and mutual benefit—ties that would serve me throughout my career.*

Two major projects at Ranbaxy stand out from that time. The first was the GDR (Global Depository Receipts) issue in 1994, where we raised $100 million. I worked closely with Dr. Singh, Mr. Brar, and Mr. Kaul, and despite Ranbaxy's longstanding relationship with JM Financial, Dr. Singh trusted me to bring Kotak and Goldman Sachs on board to lead the issue. It was a testament to the faith the company had in my abilities. The process involved extensive travel across Europe and the UK, giving me a unique opportunity to witness the personal side of Dr. Singh. He cared deeply for the team, ensuring we were well-rested and well-fed, even as we tackled one of the most challenging financial assignments of my career.

One memory that stands out for Dr. Singh occurred during a journey from Paris to Geneva. As vegetarians, the two of us had not eaten much during lunch meetings prior to boarding the train. Dr. Singh noticed this and asked what I would like to eat. When I offered to fetch something from the pantry car, he stopped me, took it upon himself, and returned with vegetable sandwiches for both of us. In hindsight, I realize that Dr. Singh, like most of my mentors, treated me not just as an employee but as a friend—a "*Dost*" in every sense of the word.

Reflecting on that tour, I realized it was also my first experience of true luxury—traveling first class by air and train, driving in a Rolls-Royce, and staying in some of the finest hotels. I still fondly remember driving through Scotland in a burgundy Rolls Royce while it gently drizzled outside. For someone who had started from humble beginnings, where luxury was a distant dream, it was a surreal moment that reminded me of how far I'd come. *Life, I realized, has a way of surprising us—sometimes, it's the quiet perseverance through struggles that eventually leads us to places we never imagined reaching.*

The success of the GDR issue was soon followed by another significant achievement: raising $50 million in debt, the largest ECB (External Commercial Borrowing) at the time. I vividly recall landing in London on a BA flight, quickly freshening up, and heading to the ANZ Grindlays office to sign the documents, only to return the same night. The total money I spent on that trip was a mere 5 GBP—a tip to the driver. The funds were invested in UTI scheme Units 64, yielding staggering returns of nearly 150% annualized.

These high-stakes transactions were the culmination of years of hard work, strategic thinking, and the trust my superiors placed in me. I had proven my worth time and again, and the results were undeniable. During my tenure, I also managed to deliver annualized returns of over 75% on Dr. Singh's personal portfolio—a feat that filled me with pride and reinforced my commitment to excellence.

Life, I realized, has a way of surprising us—sometimes, it's the quiet perseverance through struggles that eventually leads us to places we never imagined reaching.

Not all of my risks paid off. While managing high-stakes portfolios for Ranbaxy and Dr. Singh, I had unknowingly neglected my personal investments for nearly two years. Our company broker had tried to remind me multiple times about a trade I had executed a couple of years ago, but I was so engrossed in making money for the company and Dr. Singh that I completely ignored and eventually forgot about the transaction. When I was leaving the company, the broker sent me a debit note for Rs.4 lakhs, bringing the matter back to light. I was met with a harsh reality—I had made a staggering loss of 4 lacs, wiping out all my savings. To make matters worse, I had to borrow 2 lacs from my sister, Neera, just to protect my reputation. It was a humbling moment, one that shook me to my core. Even though I returned the money to Neera in 1998, four years later, the emotional cost of that loss stayed with me.

It was a sobering reminder that *even the best financial minds can falter when distracted. The lesson was clear: while professional success offers immediate gratification, managing one's personal wealth is equally important, if not more.* That painful experience shaped the way I approached future investments, grounding me in a deeper understanding of responsibility and balance.

In that moment, I learned that *true wisdom isn't just about seizing big opportunities but also about safeguarding what you've already earned. After all, life's most valuable lessons often come not from our successes, but from the price we pay for our oversights.*

Even the best financial minds can falter when distracted. The lesson was clear: while professional success offers immediate gratification, managing one's personal wealth is equally important, if not more.

November 30, 1994, marked my last day at Ranbaxy. I remember working late into the evening, a typical day for me, but this time it was different. No one could quite believe I was actually leaving. As I prepared to step away from the company that had been my home for so many years, I found myself reflecting on the incredible journey I had experienced. The challenges were numerous, but the growth I experienced was beyond measure. The lessons I learned from

Mr. D.S. Brar and Dr. Singh were invaluable, shaping me into the leader I am today. Vinay Kaul, with his brilliant mind and disciplined work ethic, had always inspired me to think creatively and to push the boundaries of what I thought was possible.

True wisdom isn't just about seizing big opportunities but also about safeguarding what you've already earned. After all, life's most valuable lessons often come not from our successes, but from the price we pay for our oversights.

There was another moment, just before I left Ranbaxy, that remains etched in my memory. Summoning the courage, I approached Dr. Singh to share some constructive feedback before I left. I expected a 30-minute meeting, but we ended up talking for over two hours. I had carried notes with me, but Dr. Singh was the one who made several pages of notes in his beautiful handwriting. He was such a wonderful listener. As I walked out of his office for the last time, I knew that my time at Ranbaxy had come to an end. But the lessons and memories from those years have stayed with me for over 30 years. As they say, once a Ranbaxian, always a Ranbaxian—even when you are no longer with the company.

My journey to success hasn't been just about reaching a destination; it's been about the lessons I've learned and the growth I've experienced along the way. A few important ones are - recognising self-worth; hard work and adaptability; mentorship & team building; strategic decision making and most importantly, learning from our failures.

Leaving Ranbaxy felt like the end of an era, a significant chapter closing as I prepared to step into the unknown. The knowledge and experience I had gained during my time there gave me the confidence to embrace the future with the same determination, belief, and conviction that had defined my success at Ranbaxy. I was entering uncharted territory with the Hero Group, a business driven by family values and relationships, involving over 20 family members. The road ahead was uncertain, but just as I had triumphed in my previous journeys, I was confident of achieving the same success in this new environment. Armed with everything I had learned, I was ready to face the challenges that lay ahead.

Chapter 7

Shifting Gears: From Decisions to Advisory in the Family Office

The years between 1994 and 2004 were personally transformative for me. This decade marked my entry into a leadership role that would test my resilience, sharpen my strategic thinking, and solidify my position within one of India's most iconic business families. Leaving behind the structured corporate world of Ranbaxy, I was drawn to Hero by an offer of three times my salary. However, it quickly became clear that I was joining more than just a company—I was becoming part of a legacy. While the financial incentive was a motivator, as I reflect on those years, I realize they shaped me not just as a professional, but as *a leader driven by gratitude, humility, empathy, responsibility, and commitment.*

I initially joined the roles of Hero Cycles, as the entity I was to be hired for was still being formed. When it eventually came into existence, I became the first employee of Hero Corporate Service, a role that closely resembled the function of a Family Office—though the term wasn't commonly used at the time.

Starting at Hero in December 1994 was not without its challenges. Mr. Vinay Kaul, who knew both me and the Hero work culture, he reinforced to me - *"The grass is always greener on the other side."* He had assured me that if I found it difficult to adjust, he would welcome me back to Ranbaxy with open arms. Coming from a dynamic environment where managing a large treasury and making quick, high-stakes decisions defined success, Hero's approach required a significant shift as an advisor.

My first interview was with Mr. Sunil Munjal, who invited me to Ludhiana to understand Hero's culture better. I was pleasantly surprised when I arrived at the train station and was greeted before being driven to his office in his personal Honda Accord—a rare luxury at the time. The day became even more memorable when I joined him for lunch in his personal dining room.

My second meeting was with Brijmohan Ji, the family patriarch, dressed in his signature white safari suit. Our conversation began with an overview of Hero's impressive growth, but it quickly turned more personal. He reminisced about Hero's early days, shared family stories, and discussed their hopes for the future during this conversation. It was during this exchange that I first sensed the deep bonds within the Munjal family and the weight of their legacy.

After these meetings, I was officially hired. My first major interaction with OP Munjal Ji (youngest brother of Brijmohan Ji), affectionately known as "Chote Bauji," took place on December 7, 1994, at their Asaf Ali Road office. The meeting, held in a modest 10x10 room, lasted an unprecedented two and a half hours—quite unusual for Chote Bauji, known for keeping meetings under 15 minutes. I left the

The grass is always greener on the other side.

room with a deep sense of satisfaction, knowing that I had not only shared my thoughts but had also established a foundation of mutual respect.

In the following meetings with Brijmohan Ji and Mr. Sunil Munjal, it slowly dawned on me that this journey would be far more personal than anything I had ever encountered. This wasn't just about treasury, corporate finance and managing wealth; it was about preserving, nurturing, and safeguarding the legacy of one of India's most iconic families. While I was hired in a corporate office, I soon realised it was almost a family office. The idea of a family office was new to me, but it quickly became clear that my responsibilities would stretch beyond financial planning. The Hero Group wasn't just a business; it was a family, bound by values and traditions that shaped every decision. Family-run companies operated with a unique set of dynamics, unlike anything I had encountered before. *Every decision had to consider values, cultural alignment, and long-term relationships—factors that extended beyond just numbers or profits.* This construct, though challenging, offered immense opportunities to grow both personally and professionally.

I soon found myself at the helm of interactions with nearly 20 family members across three generations, managing the dynamics of close to 20 profit centers and companies. At the heart of these operations were Hero Cycles and Hero MotoCorp, formerly known as Hero Honda, our flagship enterprises. Hero Cycles secured a manufacturing license in 1956, and despite stiff competition from established names and close to 140 new licencees issued by government to manufacture bicycle, Hero had risen to become the world's largest bicycle manufacturer by 1984. Hero MotoCorp's trajectory was equally remarkable. Formed through a joint venture with Honda in the early 1980s,

Hero was initially an underdog for potential partnership, with Honda having over 200 companies to consider. However, Hero was chosen by Honda for its ethical practices, cultural alignment, operational excellence, and strong customer connections—qualities that resonated deeply with Mr. Soichiro Honda, the founder of Honda. Brijmohan Ji and Mr. Soichiro Honda's alignment of values and aspirations finally sealed the partnership. It is interesting to note that Honda also started in 1948 as was the case with Hero. Under Mr. Soichiro Honda's leadership, it grew from a small workshop to a leading automobile and motorcycle company.

In the initial days at Hero, I often felt like a fish out of water. Accustomed to swift decision-making, managing extensive treasury operations, and driving results, I found myself in a drastically different role. As an advisor, I had no direct control over outcomes, a position that was both new and immensely challenging for me. The intricate task of consulting and advising CEOs, who were also family members, required not only a deep understanding of the business but also of the personal motivations and aspirations of its leaders. This challenge compelled me to evolve my *approach to leadership, leaning heavily on patience, emotional intelligence, and a long-term perspective*—skills still in their formative stages in my professional arsenal.

Over time, I began to gain solid ground at Hero. Gradually, the Senior Munjals transitioned from being merely my seniors to becoming my mentors. Brijmohan ji, the family patriarch, was particularly influential. He, along with his three brothers, had nurtured Hero from its inception. Their monumental success was impressive, but it was his humility that left the deepest impression on me.

During a serene moment, I once inquired how Brijmohan ji maintained his remarkable composure, positivity, and energy amidst the relentless pressures of his role. He responded with a gentle smile, sharing that his life was profoundly influenced by the principles of Arya Samaj. This simplicity permeated every aspect of his life: he abstained from smoking, alcohol, and meat, and adhered to a rigorous routine of daily morning walks and yoga. Each day began with him performing a Havan, a sacred ritual that rooted him spiritually before he ventured to the office.

Tragedy, however, had not bypassed Brijmohan ji. He endured the profound sorrow of losing his son, Mr. Raman Munjal, the first Managing Director of Hero Honda. Facing this immense grief, he permanently moved to Delhi and took steps to ensure the family's values continued to thrive. He integrated Raman ji's wife, Mrs. Renu Munjal, into a subsidiary of Hero MotoCorp, thus keeping her intertwined with the family's enduring legacy.

Mr. OP Munjal ji, Brijmohan Ji's youngest brother, infused Hero with a passionate intensity and a results-driven attitude. He was forthright, never shying away from expressing frustration when expectations fell short. Yet, his capacity for acknowledgment and praise was equally profound. His emotions were palpable and genuine, enhancing his magnetic presence. You always knew precisely where you stood with him—errors were swiftly recognized and rectified, without dwelling on them excessively. Conversely, achievements were not just acknowledged; they were celebrated with heartfelt joy. His remarkable ability to stay in the present, to release failures, and to wholeheartedly celebrate successes, were key in keeping Hero grounded in its core principles while striving for continuous growth and innovation.

Then there was Mr. Sunil Munjal, Brijmohan Ji's son—a man whose vision knew no bounds. His leadership was nothing short of extraordinary. He was always looking ahead, always pushing the boundaries of what Hero could be. His deep understanding of the business, combined with his vast network and relentless drive to innovate, made him an unstoppable force behind Hero's expansion and success. But more than that, Mr. Sunil Munjal believed in the power of external perspectives. He fostered strong relationships with global consulting giants like McKinsey and BCG, bringing their insights into Hero's strategies with a determination to evolve.

Under their guidance—OP Munjal's passionate realism, Brijmohan Ji's humble wisdom, and Mr. Sunil Munjal's visionary outlook—I began to see that true success wasn't just in chasing quick wins, but it was in the quiet, steady pursuit of long-term, sustainable growth, rooted in the principles that had defined Hero from the beginning. It was about building something lasting, something that would continue to thrive long after the present moment had passed.

Not all journeys are smooth, but each one shapes the path ahead.

As I settled into my role, I often thought about how best to define Hero. One word: "Humility." Two words: "Trust and Respect." And one sentence that encapsulated it all: "Build and nurture long-term relationships while sharing the fruits of growth."

The first major project I worked on was an ambitious one—implementing home-grown software ERP, a massive effort led by my dear friend Kamal Kararia. Kamal was not just a colleague; he was a deep thinker, someone who truly understood the intricacies of change management. He recognized the challenges that arise when you try to shift long-standing practices and encourage people to adopt a process-driven approach. Together, we embarked on this initiative with high hopes. But change, as we learned, does not come easily. For all our best efforts and Kamal's thoughtful leadership, we couldn't fully deliver the project's potential. Yet, even in that, there was a lesson—a reminder that *not all journeys are smooth, but each one shapes the path ahead.*

At that time, I found myself struggling to understand why people were so resistant to change. Kamal, sensing my frustration, suggested I turn to management, philosophy and psychology books for answers. It was a simple recommendation, but it was transformative for me. That was the beginning of a lifelong passion for reading—a journey that eventually led me to amass a personal library of over 700 books. *There's something deeply comforting and inspiring about being surrounded by knowledge, even if you don't read them. It's as if each book carries a promise of new perspectives and growth, just waiting to be unlocked.*

Alongside my newfound love for books, I found solace and profound insight in the epic TV serials Ramayan and Mahabharat. Watching these timeless stories unfold had a powerful impact on me. From Ramayan, I learned resilience. Rama, despite being a divine figure, faced human suffering. His journey was marked by trials and hardships, but what impressed me most was his patience, moral clarity, and steadfast commitment to his higher purpose in overcoming them. His life was a lesson in enduring hardships with grace, reminding me that *even in the darkest moments, we can remain steadfast if we hold on to our values.*

There's something deeply comforting and inspiring about being surrounded by knowledge, even if you don't read them. It's as if each book carries a promise of new perspectives and growth, just waiting to be unlocked.

Mahabharat, on the other hand, brought forth Krishna's wisdom—his ability to be a strategic thinker with incredible foresight.

Krishna's approach to life, and his emphasis on performing one's duties without attachment to the outcome, struck a deep chord in me. It taught me that *wise decision-making, detached from personal gains or losses, is the path to inner peace and clarity.* In this way, Krishna's teachings helped me navigate the complexities of leadership and decision-making, reminding me to stay focused on the bigger picture rather than just being consumed only by immediate challenges.

Even in the darkest moments, we can remain steadfast if we hold on to our values.

But it was Vidur, the wise minister of the Kauravas, who resonated with me the most. He wore many hats, serving the kingdom with dedication while offering counsel rooted in truth and righteousness. As I reflected on Vidur's character, I began to see my role more clearly. I was a blend of three roles: 10% parent, 70% dost (friend), and 20% child. As a parent, my role was to energize, inspire, and provide clarity of thought, keeping everyone aligned with values and purpose. As a dost, I saw myself as a candid sounding board, offering unfiltered, unbiased advice that was practical and rooted in wisdom. And as a child, I embraced Vidur's humility and curiosity—always open to learning, always seeking to refine my understanding of the world around me. This perspective gave me a sense of clarity about my place in the family office. I realized that my role was to offer guidance, but the final decisions, like in a kingdom, rested with the CEO. This helped me set boundaries and avoid frustration even if my ideas weren't accepted (which was a rare occurrence).

As I grew into my role, I was introduced to a new world of strategic thinking—one that often required collaboration with some of the world's top consulting firms like McKinsey and BCG. These firms brought a level of analytical rigor and structured frameworks that were invaluable for large projects, like Hero Cycles' growth plan. I vividly remember working with McKinsey on a project assessing new market opportunities. Their four-vector framework—focusing on the Attractiveness of Opportunity, Ability to Compete, Risks, and Synergies—was especially insightful and helped us break down complex problems into manageable components.

Yet, as valuable as their insights were, I quickly learned the limitations of theoretical frameworks. The gap between their structured approach and the real-world challenges we faced, was often significant. Many consultants, despite their brilliance, lacked the hands-on experience to fully grasp the intricacies of an evolving business landscape. The world we operated in was far more complex—filled with cultural nuances, unpredictable challenges, and the ever-accelerating pace of change and technological disruption. With Hero, it was even more complicated, given the family's deep-rooted values, diverse stakeholder interests, and the intricate dynamics across generations. Consultant's recommendations, while sound on paper, often missed the mark when it came to the day-to-day realities we navigated.

Wise decision-making, detached from personal gains or losses, is the path to inner peace and clarity.

The real challenge was this: when a company is thriving, no one wants to change. It's difficult to introduce new ideas or approaches when success is already at hand. I learned that external advice, no matter how well-crafted, needed to be balanced with the practical realities of the family's vision and the senior management's needs. Patience was critical. So was getting the buy-in of the family and the senior team. Quick wins were essential for building momentum, but success couldn't be credited solely to the family or the consultants—it had to be recognized as the achievement of the management teams and those actively involved in the company's daily operations. Consultants could offer frameworks, but the heart of the business lay with those who lived and breathed it every day. The real decisions, the ones that would shape the future, had to come from within.

In moments like these, my role felt pivotal. I had to serve as the bridge between the external advice we received and the internal values that had guided Hero for generations. I worked closely with the consulting teams, making sure their recommendations could be adapted to fit the family's vision and deeply embedded cultural fabric. However, even with all our efforts, the current project with McKinsey, did not deliver the desired results. It was not successful, revealing gaps in strategic thinking and an "outside-in" approach that didn't quite align with the company's core.

One of the key lessons from this experience was how critical it is to have clarity when engaging with consultants. Expectations need to be crystal clear—what is their role? Who will be part of their team? Who is the internal champion driving the project? And most importantly, how will the organization absorb and apply their insights? Does the project have the blessings of the Promoters/Founders? Without this clarity, there's always a risk that their work will become just another report gathering dust, never seeing the light of execution.

Although the project fell short, it was a valuable learning experience. Consultants, with their access to research and comprehensive data, brought a level of informed decision-making that shaped my thinking. The structured approach they employed—using frameworks to break down complex problems—began to influence my strategic thinking. I learned to *deconstruct challenges into manageable components*, which became the foundation of how I formulated and executed strategies. This approach proved invaluable, whether we were launching new ventures, handling operational challenges, scaling up business, exploring M&A opportunities, etc.

Another critical takeaway was the *importance of balancing data with instinct*. It couldn't be all about numbers or all about gut feeling—it had to be a mix of both. And while these initial setbacks were disappointing, I continued to selectively engage with consulting firms, drawing valuable insights from each new assignment.

During this journey with Hero, I had the privilege of learning from Mr. Arun Maira, the Chairman of BCG India, who eventually became a member of the planning commission. His wisdom left a lasting impression on me. One lesson worth recalling is the importance of scenario planning to ensure sustainable profitable business in the long run, during a project for Hero Honda. And second, the value that non-experts bring to the table in a project to create a business model for Hero Ergo Insurance, the exercise involved only 4 people with Domain expertise and remaining 6 people came from varied backgrounds. He taught me that *sometimes, the most insightful perspectives come from those who aren't entrenched in the industry—a fresh pair of eyes can reveal things the experts might miss.* He also helped me understand the power of Purpose when he posed a question: "What will the headline about the company be in the Wall Street Journal after

Sometimes, the most insightful perspectives come from those who aren't entrenched in the industry—a fresh pair of eyes can reveal things the experts might miss.

5/7 years", and that's what is the purpose as this line is expected to come from the heart.

Back to Hero journey, It was through the informal meetings, shared meals, and personal conversations that I truly began to gain the family's trust. These interactions were the bridge that helped me understand the nuances of working with multiple generations, each with its own vision for the family office. The older generation, led by Brijmohan Ji and OP Munjal Ji, was deeply committed to preserving the family legacy. For them, Hero was the embodiment of their life's hard work, their ethics and values, and their unwavering commitment to the people who had supported them.

In contrast, the younger generation, while respectful of tradition, was eager to push boundaries. They envisioned Hero's future as more dynamic and adaptable to the evolving market landscape while remaining grounded in the core principles that had defined the family's success. They were more open to taking risks, exploring new industries, and driving innovation. This difference in mindset became most apparent during my one-on-one discussions with each family member. It was a delicate balancing act—respecting the past while steering the organization toward the future.

The intricate generational gap within the Munjal family in my view had also become the unspoken essence of my role. Ensuring that tradition and innovation not only coexisted but thrived in harmony, and making decisions that aligned with the family's deeply ingrained values, was a task I approached with reverence. This responsibility wasn't merely occupational—it was a guardianship of heritage.

Navigating these varied perspectives was never straightforward. Balancing the venerable traditions with progressive innovations required a fine-tuned approach, ensuring the family office evolved while remaining steadfastly true to the principles that had propelled the Munjals through decades of prosperity. Embracing this challenge wholeheartedly, I aimed to honor the legacy of the elders while nurturing the aspirations of the younger Munjals, merging their historical wisdom with innovative strategies.

My relationship with Brijmohan Ji, the family patriarch, deepened over these shared challenges. We often shared meals where our discussions spanned from business insights to personal reflections, strengthening our bond. Over time, he became more than a mentor—he was a friend and a guide, a "dost" and a "guru," providing not just leadership but also the warmth of genuine companionship.

During my tenure, I had the privilege of connecting with Rakesh Duda, a key intellectual and philosophical figure in Brijmohan Ji's Office. Although Rakesh eventually left Hero, his insightful reflections, sharp intellect, and goodwill continued to have a positive impact in meaningful ways. He was amongst the first person I reached out to read this book draft.

One particularly memorable episode was my first business trip to the U.S., aimed at exploring internet-based business investments with Naveen Munjal, one of the third-generation family member. The trip began with an unexpected hiccup—my luggage was lost upon arrival. True to the Munjal spirit of resourcefulness and care, Naveen promptly took me shopping for essentials. This simple act of kindness not only solved a practical problem but also exemplified the family's ethos of support and solidarity—always ready to assist one another, in business or personal challenges alike.

That trip was unforgettable. We traveled from the East Coast to the West Coast, with one of the highlights being our scenic nine-hour drive along Highway 101 from Los Angeles to San Francisco. We made several stops along the coastline, taking in the beauty, sharing laughs, and enjoying each other's company. It was during this journey that I truly saw how deeply the Munjal family's values had been passed down to the third generation. The unity, respect, and culture that defined them had become an inseparable part of their existence.

During the trip, we met with nearly 25 companies, many of which were run by young entrepreneurs in their early twenties. These tech-driven visionaries were always in a rush, speaking quickly, as if time was running out. Their hustle was palpable, and the pace of business felt dizzying. One day equaled a week, a week felt like a month, and the rapid-fire decisions made everything feel like a blur.

I vividly remember one meeting with a young founder who had just sold his company for over $100 million despite having negligible revenues. The companies were valued based on the eyeballs rather than their cash flows. The market was frenzied, and valuations were skyrocketing, driven by FOMO (Fear Of Missing Out). It was a stark contrast to the steady, long-term thinking of the Munjal family. While this young founder was raking in millions, his father, a seasoned professional, had retired after spending 30 years at a major investment bank with a wealth of $10 million. The juxtaposition was striking, and it underscored how irrational the market had become. The frenzy reached its peak in early 2000, and not long after, the dot-com bubble burst. The NASDAQ lost nearly 70% of its value in less than two years.

Looking back, I'm grateful for the family's cautious approach. While the excitement of the tech boom was contagious, we were fortunate not to have invested in those overvalued businesses driven by short-term hype. It was a powerful reminder of the importance of staying true to the family's long-term vision, guided by patience and wisdom.

As the family's success grew, so did our ambitions. Hero was no longer content with the industries it had already mastered. This was the time when we began to explore new ventures, expanding into sectors like insurance and technology. It was an exhilarating period, filled with potential, excitement, and the promise of groundbreaking opportunities. But with those possibilities came challenges that pushed my professional abilities and personal resilience to their limits.

One of the most vivid memories I have from this time was our early discussions about entering the insurance sector. We had set our sights on Zurich Insurance, one of the largest and most respected insurers in the world. Partnering with such a global giant was as thrilling as it was overwhelming. We were one of the first few companies in India to apply with the Insurance Regulatory and Development Authority (IRDA), marking our bold foray into a completely new industry. The stakes couldn't have been higher—the risk and reward equally enormous.

Working closely with Mr. Sunil Munjal, I found myself deeply engaged in orchestrating the intricacies of the deal. Each meeting and conversation carried a weight of critical importance. We were tasked with aligning Hero's ambitions with Zurich's stringent demands, imbuing each phase of the negotiation with urgency and intensity. I recall enduring marathon discussions, meticulously dissecting every facet of the joint venture—hammering out terms, delineating responsibilities, and crafting the financial framework. At that moment, it felt as though we were on the cusp of a transformative breakthrough for Hero family.

However, as often happens with ambitious projects, the path was not smooth. Just as we were poised to finalize the agreement, a seismic shift occurred in Zurich. A major overhaul in their senior management unexpectedly altered the playing field. In a disheartening turn of events, Zurich withdrew from the Indian market, causing our nearly realized joint venture to disintegrate overnight.

Obstacles are a natural component of business. True success is not measured by an unblemished track record but by the resolve to recover and ascend from setbacks.

The collapse was a significant setback. After months of relentless effort—fostering relationships, navigating the maze of regulatory challenges, and investing our collective spirits into this venture—we found ourselves back at square one. The sense of disappointment was palpable, a bitter reminder of the venture's potential that felt akin to failure.

Yet, this setback also served as a profound learning opportunity. It reinforced the notion that *obstacles are a natural component of business. True success is not measured by an unblemished track record but by the resolve to recover and ascend from setbacks.* Thus, we did not dwell in our disillusionment. Instead, we dusted ourselves off, strategized anew, and turned our gazes toward fresh horizons, eager to explore new opportunities that lay ahead.

That experience taught me resilience in a way that no book or classroom could. In business, it's easy to get swept away by the excitement of a potential breakthrough, but reality often has other plans. *I learned that when things fall apart, the key is to stay anchored to the larger vision and remain adaptable, no matter how discouraging the setback.*

One positive outcome from that challenging period was the bond I formed with Pradeep Dinodia, a brilliant financial strategist. His wisdom and calm approach helped guide us through the complexities of the Zurich partnership. Although the deal ultimately fell through, over time, he became a trusted advisor to the Munjal family and eventually earned a position on the board of Hero MotoCorp.

The late 1990s and early 2000s were a time of engagement in several smaller, yet significant initiatives, each playing a role in shaping the evolution of Hero. This included acquiring a call center company in the U.S., a venture from which we later exited profitably. Additionally, we launched three new initiatives—Hero Mindmine, HeroITES, and HeroSoft—with McKinsey as our consultant. These projects weren't just about diversifying our business portfolio; they were about extending the boundaries of Hero's potential.

A project particularly dear to me was the turnaround of Gujarat Cycles. Mr. Sudhir Munjal - CEO, Company Advisor - Sunil Vakil and I were tasked to drive this initiative. The company was floundering under the weight of debt and operational inefficiencies. It appeared to be an overwhelming challenge, yet through strategic debt restructuring and operational improvements, we successfully rejuvenated the company. This turnaround was deeply personal; it was not merely about rescuing a business, but about showcasing the strength of perseverance and strategic thinking. The story of Gujarat Cycles resonated with my journey: facing and overcoming challenges through determination and strength.

I learned that when things fall apart, the key is to stay anchored to the larger vision and remain adaptable, no matter how discouraging the setback.

By this time, I had become deeply integrated within the Hero family. I had gained the trust of family members spanning three generations and found myself in a pivotal position advising on strategy and finance. My straightforward approach and comprehensive understanding of both the tangible and intangible facets of the business made me a key player in some of the family's decision-making process.

However, managing the intricate dynamics of the family business was not without its difficulties. In a large family-run enterprise, especially with significant generational gaps, each member brought their own perspectives and priorities. Handling these relationships required finesse, ensuring effective communication and making each family member feel valued and included. Over time, some of the family members began to see me as someone who understood the emotional side of their family's journey—a confidante and a clone who could bridge the gap between the business world and their cherished family values

Numbers can show you how a business is performing, but they are lagging indicators. What truly keeps a business thriving is nurturing relationships, upholding purpose, and staying true to values.

As the years passed and Hero continued to expand, my role evolved. I was no longer just managing business intricacies but also working closely with some of the second and third generations of the family, much like the Vidur from the Mahabharata. I voluntarily began sharing my thoughts with the younger generation as they started stepping into leadership roles. It was a role I truly relished. The family office was more than just a financial hub—it was the nucleus of a legacy that had to be carefully nurtured and passed down.

One of the key pieces of advice I offered was to always put people first. I told them, *"Numbers can show you how a business is performing, but they are lagging indicators. What truly keeps a business thriving is nurturing relationships, upholding purpose, and staying true to values."* I emphasized the importance of empathy and human connection, drawing from the countless interactions I had with Brijmohan Ji, and Om Prakash ji who had always maintained personal ties with dealers, vendors, and employees. The younger generation, though well-versed in modern business practices, needed to be reminded that leadership wasn't just about managing a company—it was about fostering relationships that would sustain the business across generations. *We exist because of our ecosystem and not the other way round.*

Being a *Dost* to the younger generation wasn't just about business—it was about helping them into future leaders capable of carrying forward the family's legacy. I found immense fulfillment in knowing that I was contributing to the continuity of something far greater than myself. I felt a deep sense of pride in contributing, however small, to their professional journeys.

My relationship with Brijmohan Ji had grown so close that I began to see myself as his fifth son. When I once mentioned this to Mr. Sunil Munjal, he chuckled warmly and said there were probably a hundred other people who felt the same way. That was the magic of Brijmohan Ji—he had the unique ability to make everyone around him feel like part of the family. He treated people with such kindness, humility, and inclusion that it was impossible not to feel a strong bond with him.

We exist because of our ecosystem and not the other way round.

Some of the Munjal family members, across all ages, connected with me on a personal level as well. Our interactions weren't limited to business meetings; they included moments of personal connection that became central to my experience. I was fortunate to participate in family gatherings, lunches, and celebrations, where the distinction between business advisor and family member often blurred. In those moments, I realized that the essence of true leadership is rooted in relationships (Dosti and Rishtey) that endure through time. The bonds we formed were rooted in trust and genuine care, fostering a Dil Se connection that transcended professional boundaries. My deep gratitude goes to Brijmohan Ji, OP Munjal Ji, and Mr. Sunil Munjal for welcoming me into this extraordinary journey with the Hero Group and blessings of Maa Durga.

Reflecting on these pivotal years, I recognize their profound impact on my growth. Those years were not merely about testing my skills or expanding my grasp of leadership; they fundamentally reshaped my understanding of what it means to build something of significance. The focus was not solely on achieving profit targets or meeting KPIs; it was deeply rooted in the human aspects of business. It was about constructing something enduring, something founded on values, empathy, and authentic relationships. While financial success was important, the true insights were garnered from learning how to steer a business while remaining anchored in the values that have sustained Hero through generations.

In retrospect, those years were the most rewarding. They tested me, taught me, and ultimately shaped me into the leader I became. Through it all, I learned that flexibility, adaptability, and a deep understanding of both the business and the people behind it are the true keys to success.

This mindset was rooted in the values I had learned from Maama—being fearless, thinking with an owner's mindset, avoiding personal agendas, and growing up with religious sentiments and belief in Maa Durga and myself. These teachings shaped my approach to work and life, allowing me to engage with the family on a deeper level.

These transformative experiences continue to shape my approach to challenges today. Stepping into Hero in 1995, I could not have foreseen the depth of the journey ahead. Yet, reflecting now, I see how those years carved me into the leader I have become. My role went beyond merely aiding a company's growth; I was contributing to a legacy, to a family, and to a vision meant to last well beyond my tenure.

Success is not just about talent or luck; it's about the choices you make, the relationships you build, and the values you uphold. Embrace challenges, continue learning, and stay true to your long-term vision. With patience, persistence, and a foundation of strong values, you will find success and fulfillment in everything you do.

As I look back on my journey with Hero from 1994 to 2004, I am reminded of how this decade marked significant professional and personal transformation for me. It was a time of growth, challenge, and discovery. Transitioning from a corporate role at Ranbaxy to a more values-driven and family-oriented environment at Hero required adaptability and a change in mindset. These years profoundly shaped my understanding of leadership, strategy, and success, and many of the lessons I learned continue to resonate with the challenges young people face today.

Reflecting on my first decade at Hero, I realised that the lessons I learned are timeless. *Success is not just about talent or luck; it's about the choices you make, the relationships you build, and the values you uphold. Embrace challenges, continue learning, and stay true to your long-term vision. With patience, persistence, and a foundation of strong values, you will find success and fulfillment in everything you do.* Your legacy, like mine, will be defined not just by what you achieve but by the lives you touch along the way.

Chapter 8

Leadership, Value Creation, Negotiation

After marking nearly a decade at Hero Corporate Service, I had garnered Mr. Sunil Munjal's trust and respect. He appreciated my intellect, innovative thinking, agility, and straightforward communication style. Our relationship had strengthened significantly, and I had grown particularly close to him and Brijmohan Ji, almost as if I were a member of the family.

One day, while I was at my office, Mr. Sunil Munjal summoned me for a meeting. He presented me with an opportunity —the chance to lead HeroITES, a business that had been floundering with losses for four years under the leadership of four different CEOs. This was the kind of break I had been waiting for: a chance to lead a business, to engineer a turnaround, and to realize my ambition of steering an organization.

This pivotal moment marked the beginning of one of the most defining periods of my life. Leading HeroITES, a call center catering to US and UK clients, brought its unique challenges, such as adapting to different time zones and work hours. Yet, I was prepared. I agreed to take on the role with one suggestion—I requested Mr. Munjal to ensure that any interventions from the corporate office would only come from those willing to actively engage and implement the projects they proposed.

Despite the company's troubled history, my confidence was unmoved. I trusted my abilities, Durga Maa's support, and Mr. Sunil Munjal's judgment. He had placed his faith in me, and I was resolute in proving worthy of that trust.

Assuming this new leadership role was daunting, but I embraced the challenge with zeal. The prospect of guiding HeroITES into a successful future invigorated me. However, at that time, I was yet to fully understand the personal and familial sacrifices this new path would demand.

From day one, my leadership approach was deeply rooted in fundamental human values such as trust, respect, gratitude, transparency, integrity, love, compassion, and authenticity, alongside key business values like agility, teamwork, meritocracy, quick decision-making, informed risk-taking, creativity, curiosity, and innovation. I also maintained a strong focus on outcomes and fostering an empowered culture. I reassured my team that I would shoulder the losses personally, while all successes would be credited to them.

My work days were long; I started by clearing emails and planning the day at 8:30 AM from home, and I would leave for the office at 11 AM on the hour-long commute. I seldom used my private office—instead, I viewed the entire floor as my workspace. I believed in being accessible, walking the floor, and directly engaging with the team members who were the real driving force behind our operations. Surrounded by people eager to meet with me, I made no distinctions in interactions based on seniority. I addressed everyone as 'Dost,' and with nearly 1300 people in the company, this practice fostered a genuine Dil Se connection, cultivating an atmosphere of warmth and mutual respect. This was not merely a workplace—it was a family environment where each team member was regarded as part of my extended family.

Whenever I entered the office, I would bow down to seek the blessings of Maa Durga, touching the ground as a gesture of reverence. I would pray to her, requesting to leave all my stress and negative energy behind at her feet, promising to take them back only when I returned. I sought her divine strength to empower me with positivity, so I could radiate positive energy and spread happiness to everyone around me.

I never had tea in my office, instead I would go to the dhaba outside our office. I used to have tea in a paper cup with bread and some namkeen. People were surprised at my approach, but I would let them know that I was also one amongst them except that my badge was different. I never had to exercise my authority. It was always consensus-driven quick decisions. I always believed that I was now a 21-year-old living amongst the people with an average age of 23. I would sometimes enjoy dancing on the floor, it was all masti.

While I took care of the team, it was important to focus on the customer (Voice of Customer) needs, aspirations and expectations, be accessible to them, have open, transparent and timely communication, create a culture of friendship, and dosti. The customers appreciated my approach, sometimes I had to stay overnight to take calls and attend customer meetings when they were on the site. Since most of our Customers were from the US and through LiveBridge, I would travel to the US almost once a month, I would have made almost 20 trips during the time I was at Hero ITES.

Our company turned around in 3 months, all credit to the entire team as my role was to inspire, energise, provide clarity of thought, make quick decisions and ensure we never compromised on our core values -my turnaround time for any mail would be no more than 24 hours even on vacations or holidays. Communication used to be on SMS or e-mail but WhatsApp became ubiquitous around 2015. Some of the team members whose names I recall are Nilesh Kothari (CFO), Padma (HR), OP Singh (Controller), Rajesh Mallya (quality and training), and Rakesh Khorana (Ops). The two people from whom I learnt a lot from my team were Suving Sharma (Biz Development and Voice Of Customer) and Rajesh Mallaya (Quality and performance management). I am missing out on many of my other Dosts. I am filled with gratitude towards my team and will always be grateful to my well-wishers as well for making this turnaround so seamlessly.

Success, as intoxicating as it can be, also reminded us that too much of addiction to anything can be detrimental.

The commitment I dedicated to the company came at a significant personal cost. Long nights at the office led to missed meals, gradually taking a toll on my health. Poonam, my wife, quietly shouldered the impact of my demanding schedule. Though she had early mornings, waking at 5:30 AM for the kids' routines, she always stayed up to prepare fresh chapatis and have dinner with me when I got home at midnight. She supported my passion for my work, but the lifestyle was not without consequences. During a routine medical check-up, both of us were diagnosed with diabetes. Although the professional milestones were gratifying, they came at the expense of our health and time together. *Success, as intoxicating as it can be, also reminded us that too much of addiction to anything can be detrimental.*

Our ambition to expand HeroITES called for strategic acquisitions. We were on the verge of securing a deal to acquire a Company, and were finalizing the term sheet when an unexpected turn took place. Another bidder offered three times what we proposed, and we lost the acquisition. This setback was tough but taught us a critical lesson in deal-making: the importance of being decisive and sometimes, the necessity of offering more to secure a deal. This principle has been followed in all my subsequent negotiations.

Following this, our quest for a suitable acquisition started afresh. I had been persistently reaching out to Ken Hills, CEO of TSC in the UK, sending monthly emails suggesting a meeting whenever I was in London to discuss potential synergies. Persistence finally paid off, and he agreed to meet. We negotiated and agreed to sign a term sheet for acquiring TSC, one of the largest call center employers in Scotland, with over 3,000 staff across seven locations. This acquisition was set to increase our revenue from $4 million to $100 million—a monumental twenty-five-fold growth. However, due to a misunderstanding, our discussions initially fell through.

Unwilling to let two years of effort be in vain, I reached out to Ken again for clarification. Our misunderstanding was finally resolved, and we successfully signed the term sheet. Given the scale of the transaction, external validation was necessary. We had two financing plans—Plan A involved raising equity from a prominent investor, and Plan B, a leveraged buyout. Fortunately, Sonjoy Chatterjee, head of ICICI UK, recognizing Hero's solid track record and commitment, moved swiftly and approved the buyout loan within in two days, this is the quickest turn around time in closing a loan transaction.

Ultimately, while the equity investor withdrew, the financing for the buyout came through, and we closed the deal. Then the real work began. Ken Hills decided to step down as CEO, recommending David Turner as his successor. I spent eight hours across three meetings with David to ensure he was the right fit. When Mr. Sunil Munjal met him, his approval was immediate. My colleague Prabh Likhari and I, along with three management team members, were granted stock options. It was a hard-earned victory, and we were primed to propel HeroITES into its next phase of growth.

Over the next few years, Hero TSC delivered exceptional performance. My colleague Prabh and I, represented the shareholder's interests and maintained weekly calls with CEO, David Turner. We met face-to-face every four-six weeks. I would take a Jet Airways flight from Delhi, reach London in the evening and without wasting any time, would spend time over dinner, as I would normally head back for India the next day, occasionally I would stay an extra day to visit the call centers. There were times when our discussions became heated, but good sense always prevailed since both the shareholders and the management team had complete alignment of goals. The company almost doubled its revenues, and profitability soared even higher.

As we reached this level of success, we faced a pivotal decision—whether to invest a significant amount to take the company to the next level or explore a strategic sale. We decided to explore the latter and hired Avendus Capital, led by Gaurav Deepak. Gaurav was an incredible person with a mature mindset and a relentless focus on closing deals.

David Turner had engaged with several strategic investors, including the large private equity firm Charter House. The consensus was leaning toward selecting a strategic investor since it was felt that Charter House might require a much longer timeline to finalize the terms and close the deal. On a Sunday morning, September 2nd, 2012, as I strolled down Regent Street in London heading to the Avendus office, I decided to call Stephan Morgan MD of Charter House to gauge his interest. Typically, Sundays are reserved for family, but I found myself discussing business for half an hour. Stephan expressed a desire for exclusivity—a positive sign that led us to schedule a meeting for September 4th, as the 3rd was already booked with another strategic partner.

When the offer from the strategic partner came in on 3rd September, it was significantly lower—about 40% of what we expected from Charter House with lots of hold back and reps and warranties. During our meeting on the 4th with key decision-makers from their team—Stephan, Lionnel (Investment Committee member), and Frederic Jousset representing management—and our team, consisting of Gaurav, Prabh, and myself, their commitment and eagerness were evident.

I had brought a note outlining our expectations but encountered a few sticking points during the negotiations. I was prepared to walk away from the table if necessary, a stance that surprised Gaurav, especially since closing the deal would significantly increase my personal wealth due to my stock options. However, my priority was securing the best possible outcome for our sponsor.

Eventually, I devised a creative deal structure that satisfied both parties. As we finalized the agreement, Lionnel acknowledged my tough negotiation skills, and Stephan half-jokingly remarked that he felt he had aged two years in the two months it took to close the deal. We had worked relentlessly—day and night, even during Christmas. Ultimately, it was a successful outcome for all parties involved: the family made a 6x return in five years,

Charter House also saw profitable returns upon selling the company, the management team and Gaurav benefited greatly (it was the largest fee check for Avendus until then), and my personal wealth grew sixfold. I am deeply grateful to everyone who contributed to this success.

After my role at HeroITES got reduced to monitoring, Mr. Sunil Munjal called me back to the Corporate Office to lead two major initiatives under his direction—one was a joint venture with Daimler Commercial Vehicles, and the other with Ergo Insurance, a subsidiary of Munich Re, a global leader in reinsurance. I led the Hero team for JV with Ergo, focusing on aligning partner aspirations, values and roles, drafting joint venture agreements, creating business plans, building financial models, and filing applications with IRDA, among other tasks. Nikolaus Von Bomhard, Global CEO of Munich Re, was extremely dedicated to growing their business in India. It was important to gauge his interest as we had lost out on our deal with Zurich because of a change in management. After developing an informal understanding of the venture, we arranged for Mr. Bomhard to visit India to meet the Munjal Family and further align our values and aspirations.

I was impressed by Mr. Bomhard's humility, warmth, and approach to business. Though in a high position, he chose commercial flights over private jets and standard rooms over luxury suites. I learned that he often cycled to work, a testament to his down-to-earth leadership style that reminded me of the qualities I had admired in Brijmohan Ji. When Mr. Sunil Munjal was traveling to Europe, he suggested a meeting with Mr. Bomhard on a Sunday, which Mr. Bomhard accepted at short notice, very unlikely of people of his stature. These interactions solidified our belief in a strong cultural fit and mutual eagerness to finalize the partnership.

We spent almost a year perfecting the business plan, hiring key team members, and finalizing the JV agreement. It seemed we were on the brink of making a significant impact in the financial services sector when an unforeseen event, like Lehman Brothers filing for bankruptcy on October 15, 2008, prompted us to suggest that the Ergo team delay the launch. However, the Ergo team decided to proceed in India with another Indian Partner, leading to the dissolution of our joint venture. Despite this setback, I maintained a strong relationship with Dr. Bomhard, who consistently responded to my greetings within 48 hours. Just a few months ago, I emailed him to share that I would be covering my learnings from our interactions. He responded, first apologizing for the delay due to extensive travel, and wished me good luck with my book. His leadership truly aimed to create a lasting legacy.

I played a pivotal role in facilitating the Daimler JV with Hero, taking charge of crafting the business plan, orchestrating the JV agreement, and spearheading fundraising efforts among other responsibilities. The project lead from Hero was my dear friend, the late Amit Chaturvedi. We devoted countless hours, making multiple trips to Germany to shaping the JV, fostering a strong collaboration between the teams. The team was assembled, and Amit was poised to lead the roles assigned to Hero, with Marc Listosella helming as the CEO of the Hero Daimler JV.

To commemorate the signing of the JV agreement, a celebratory dinner was organized at the Oberoi Hotel in Delhi in April 2008, attended by nearly 200 distinguished guests. During the event, many senior members shared their experiences and expressed optimism about the JV's success, highlighting the synergies between both parties. I was profoundly moved during Marc's speech when he publicly acknowledged my significant contributions to the fruition of the JV, an honor that caught me off guard and filled me with gratitude.

In the midst of finalizing the JV agreements, I went for a routine check-up for a persistent skin problem that had troubled me for years. As part of the investigation, a biopsy was conducted, and to my shock, I was informed that I had skin cancer. The doctor reassured me it was the most benign form, but the news still left my wife, Poonam, and me completely shattered.

In search of clarity and hope, I sought a second opinion from a cancer specialist at Apollo Hospital. After a thorough examination, he finally gave me the all-clear. However, those two weeks of anxiety and uncertainty took an enormous toll on Poonam. It was her unwavering faith in God and the blessings of Maa Durga that gave us the strength to endure that difficult time.

Life is fleeting and precious, and the only certainty is the present moment.

That experience became a turning point in my life. It deepened my spirituality to an entirely new level and brought me to a profound realization: acceptance of our mortality. *Life is fleeting and precious, and the only certainty is the present moment.* From that day onward, I committed myself to live fully in the now, to be kind, and to create a positive impact on everyone I encounter.

However, the unfolding of the Lehman crisis prompted a re-evaluation of economic conditions, leading Hero Group to refocus on its core business and step back from the commercial vehicle venture. Unlike many partnerships that sour upon dissolution, Hero, true to its foundational values, reached a dignified and amicable closure with Daimler, leaving the door open for potential future collaborations.

Amidst the dissolution of the JV's with Ergo and Daimler, I was already deeply involved in another critical project—realigning the family structure among the four branches of the Munjal Family. Founded in 1948 by four brothers from modest beginnings, the Hero Group had always been driven by strong values, fostering cordial relationships within the family and with external stakeholders, helping to build world-class companies and a respected brand.

As the business and family expanded—growing to over 20 family members actively involved—the management of diverse aspirations and the effects of generational gaps presented increasing challenges. The senior generation, rooted in the values of humility, trust, and respect established by Brijmohan Ji and his brothers, had traditionally favored conservative growth strategies with manageable risks. Conversely, the younger generation, raised in an era of rapid technological advancement and global connectivity, was inclined toward innovation and higher-risk ventures.

Recognizing the need for a thoughtful transition, the family embarked on a realignment of roles, responsibilities, and holdings within the four branches. This approach was crafted to honor varying goals and cultural transitions while safeguarding Hero's legacy and brand integrity. Although the seniors were initially hesitant, they recognized the necessity of this realignment to ensure the family's future cohesion and success. They had the foresight to ensure that any restructuring should occur within their lifetime to maintain the familial love, respect, and harmony they had always championed. I was closely associated with working with the family members, and advisors to ensure a seamless realignment leading to a win-win approach.

Since Brijmohan ji cherished building and nurturing relationships, I could see and feel his pain when I used to go and discuss family realignment. He never wanted to go through with this painful realignment as this was against his core, but he had no choice. He would always tell me that we should be completely transparent and above board and he was happy to receive less than his share. Whenever I would go to him to share the contours of realignment with him, his response would be - you have come to give me a headache again. In his heart he was pained but at the same time he recognized that the timing was right for realignment, else like many other Indian families we might lose out on our legacy created with so much love and affection.

The realignment process was committed to fairness and transparency, emphasizing that the familial bond and adherence to the decisions of the elder members should be respected. This careful approach ensured that while embracing the future, the foundational principles of the family and business would continue to guide the Hero Group forward, without disrupting the harmony, unity and values that had been the bedrock of their success. I remember the agreement was concluded on 25th May 2010, and I missed my wedding anniversary celebrations that day.

It was amongst the most amicable settlement and a couple of other advisors who were the confidants of the family also played a key role, they were Mr. Satish Bansal (audit firm for most Hero Companies) and Mr. Pradeep Dinodia. Girish Vanvari from KPMG, Sumit Bansal, and my colleague Amit Aggarwal each contributed in their own humble ways to this and a few other transactions. By this time, Girish had become a good friend, as had Sumit, and we frequently sought their guidance on tax-related matters, relying on their expertise and valuable insights. The Project was championed by Mr. Sunil

Munjal under the guidance of the Seniors in the family. As a result of the realignment, a wave of positive energy was released, allowing people to pursue their passions and what they loved most. Over these 14 years, wealth creation would have been nearly 6-8 times greater.

While managing key projects, one of the most defining initiatives for Brij Mohan Ji's family was the realignment of the relationship between Hero and Honda—one of the most successful Indo-Japanese joint ventures. With the partners' aspirations evolving, it became clear that realigning the venture was essential. For over three years, we engaged in intense negotiations, addressing complex questions about buyouts and structural arrangements. These discussions extended beyond business; they were about ensuring accountability to a wide range of stakeholders, including investors, regulators, and employees.

I played a pivotal role behind the scenes, ensuring that all critical discussions were documented and that we continuously evaluated our strategic options. With Hero Honda being listed in India and part of the NIFTY 50 and Honda on the Tokyo Stock Exchange, maintaining confidentiality was essential. These negotiations required the utmost discretion as the future of Hero Honda and the Munjal family's legacy was at stake.

The decision to move forward with the buyout was made jointly by Mr. Pawan Munjal (MD of Hero Honda and elder brother of Mr. Sunil Munjal) and Mr. Sunil Munjal after extensive deliberation. They both recognized the immense potential for growth and independence that this move represented for Hero MotoCorp. The final decision was a reflection of their shared vision for the future of the company and their desire to take full control of the business.

After exhaustive discussions, the decision was made for Hero to buy out Honda's stake. This was not a decision taken lightly, it represented the Munjal family's bold vision for independence and growth. This buyout was about more than just business—it was about Hero MotoCorp seizing its destiny, evolving from a domestic motorcycle manufacturer into a global leader capable of pioneering innovations.

This buyout marked a turning point in my career, quickly becoming one of the most significant experiences I've ever had. As I sat through numerous strategy meetings, it was clear this was not just another transaction. It was a watershed moment for the Hero family, their legacy, and the company's future. The weight of the decisions we made would echo through the company for generations to come.

The execution began immediately. On May 26th, 2010—just a day after my wedding anniversary—we boarded a charter plane to Tokyo to begin negotiations. On the flight, we discussed the core principles of the deal and outlined our negotiation strategy. While the Hero Honda team worked on licensing and technology agreements, I was tasked with negotiating shareholder agreement with Honda, raising the necessary capital to fund the buyout. Under the leadership of Mr. Pawan Munjal and Mr. Sunil Munjal, we implemented strict "Chinese walls" between the two teams to ensure compliance with regulations and maintain focus.

The next nine months were intense. I worked tirelessly on this project, supported by the Boston Consulting Group (BCG) and, Himanshu Nema, a recent MBA graduate from IIM Ahmedabad from BCG who became almost like a Chief of Staff to me. His role was to ensure that we stayed on track in terms of timelines. Together, we navigated nearly 900 action items and dealt with ten different regulators, ensuring that every part of the process was handled flawlessly. Thanks to Mr. Sunil Munjal's vast network and Hero's impeccable reputation, we encountered no bureaucratic delays. Many officials were keen to support our bold decision, recognizing Hero's significance to the Indian Corporate world.

Himanshu, reflecting on the experience, shared how transformative those nine months were for him—what he learned during that time would have taken a decade elsewhere. Today, Himanshu is a Managing Director at Warburg Pincus, a testament to the profound journey we shared during this pivotal project.

Three major transactions required my focus: negotiating with Honda, raising debt to finance the buyout, and securing an equity deal with a large private equity investor to help us repay the debt in lieu of Hero Motocorp stock. The decision to bypass investment bankers in such a high-stakes deal was bold and unconventional. While many bankers approached us, offering their services, we realized they added little value, especially during our initial dry runs to gauge interest from equity funds. The story needed to be told with passion and conviction, which could only be achieved by us. Confident in Mr. Sunil Munjal's relationships with major equity players, we opted to negotiate directly with equity players and also held discussions with Honda on a principal-to-principal basis.

The stakes were immense, as we were negotiating with one of the world's largest corporations. The pressure was intense, but I was driven by the trust the Munjal family placed in me. They set clear financial parameters but gave me the freedom to operate with the urgency required to navigate these delicate negotiations. It was a thrilling challenge, requiring creativity and decisiveness at every step.

Brijmohan Ji was initially uncomfortable with the idea of raising debt financing, expressing concern that someone who had never borrowed even a lakh on personal account, was being asked to complete paperwork for an amount as significant as nearly Rs.4,000 crore to buy Honda's stake in Hero Honda. However, after building great trust and respect with him over the years, I was able to convince him that there was a solid plan to repay the amount in less than six months. To my utter surprise, he asked, "Mr. Chanana, what's your conviction?" I confidently replied, "More than 100%," and without hesitation, he agreed to sign the documents. His trust and belief in his people were remarkable; he truly had an eye for judging character.

With conviction and the right strategy, nothing is impossible.

Once we had secured his approval, the next crucial step was to obtain the necessary debt financing. To accomplish this, we engaged Kotak Bank, with Uday Kotak personally providing assurance at a nominal fee. The idea of acquiring control of Hero Honda at a significant discount seemed nearly impossible—like a moonshot in the startup world. I vividly remember discussing this ambitious goal with my friend Arindham, a senior partner at BCG India. Initially skeptical, he texted me after the discount was publicly announced following the MOU signing on December 16, 2010–saying that the experience had taught him that *with conviction and the right strategy, nothing is impossible.*

The groundwork for the deal was laid through meticulous research. One key insight I gained during discussions was that Honda's CEOs typically came from an R&D, favoring logical, transparent, collaborative approaches driven by long-term value creation rather than short-term market fluctuations. Honda's initial investment in Hero had been less than USD 5 million, and they had recouped many times that through dividends, royalties, technology fees, and component sales. With this understanding, I tailored a presentation that resonated deeply with Honda's values and corporate philosophy, creating a compelling narrative in just 21 slides.

While preparing these slides, I metaphorically stepped into the shoes of Honda's CEO, considering how he might present a significant discount to stakeholders, including investors and the Board, despite its impact on the year's profitability. We shared the presentation with the Chairman of BCG Japan, who flew all the way from Tokyo on an ANA flight and departed within four hours of landing. His parting remark was, "This is a strong case for a significant discount." During negotiations, when Honda's lead negotiator implied that our presentation might have been crafted by bankers, Mr. Sunil Munjal quickly pointed to me, confirming my authorship. This moment underscored the depth of our internal strategy and reinforced the respect we had built with Honda over decades. The negotiation concluded with us securing the buyout at a 50% discount to the prevailing price—an achievement that went beyond financial success and highlighted the strength of our longstanding relationship with Honda.

As the deal progressed, it became evident that the substantial check size and opportunity to invest in a global leader generated significant interest among equity investors. Hero MotoCorp was a leader in its segment, and the opportunity to invest in a global player with an established brand generated a sense of urgency in the investment community. A strong sense of FOMO (Fear Of Missing Out) began to take hold, as investors realized that this high-value deal offered a rare opportunity to be part of a global leader in the rapidly growing two-wheeler market. Based on our compelling narrative, the potential for long-term growth and market dominance was undeniable. As a result, we witnessed growing appetite from major firms eager to secure a stake in this landmark transaction. Instead of a traditional pitch deck, we created a concise four-page slide deck detailing the size of the opportunity, who we are, and our conviction on how we would deliver exceptional outcomes without giving any future guidance and with no inputs from the Hero Honda team.

The characteristics that defined our DNA alignment with equity investors were critical in our decision-making process. We assessed potential partners based on several factors, like hunger and commitment, cultural fit, domain expertise, execution speed and decisiveness amongst others. Ultimately, we chose Bain Capital as our partner—not only for their financial offer but also for their close alignment with Hero's DNA. GIC, Singapore's sovereign wealth fund, came on board as a follow-on investor, solidifying a partnership that had been carefully cultivated over six months. Their long-term vision and belief in Hero's potential made them ideal partners for this transformational journey.

As we approached the final stages, I relocated to the offices of JSA Law Firm office in Gurgaon to ensure complete focus and efficiency. Jyoti Sagar offered us almost four rooms on one floor. We managed to close the shareholders' agreement on March 1st, 2011, ahead of schedule, navigating over 900 action items with a speed and complexity that surprised even us. The pace of the transaction was often likened to the last-minute rush typical of an Indian wedding.

During one of our celebratory meetings at Brijmohan Ji's house, after finalizing the agreements with Bain Capital and GIC, Renu Ji asked, with a smile, if I ever found time to sleep. It was a valid question, given the pace at which we were working. My late-night and early-morning messages to the family and other stakeholders had become a norm. I jokingly responded that while my beliefs discouraged taking medication, I was supporting the pharmaceutical industry by taking a painkiller every evening at 6 pm to keep myself going. The relentless nature of the project demanded it.

Paul Edgerly, CIO of Bain Capital, inquired from Amit Chandra, the India MD of Bain, about the size of my team, given the complexity of the deal. He explained that I was a one-man army, managing everything with a small group—supported by legal advisors and a few consultants from BCG—showcasing the extraordinary commitment we all brought to the table. Paul was genuinely surprised by this.

Managing these high-stakes transactions simultaneously required an extraordinary level of commitment. As I reflect on the alignment of personal and professional milestones, I'm struck by the serendipity of key events. The buyout process began the day after my wedding anniversary, the MOU was signed on my daughter's birthday, and the shareholder agreements were finalized on my son's birthday. Even the first payment from Bain Capital arrived near my birthday, and the second tranche coincided with my wife's. These personal touches made the journey all the more meaningful. Girish Vanvari, an old friend, humorously remarked that while I had always aspired to become a billionaire, I had indeed succeeded, though "the pocket had changed"—a humorous acknowledgment of the scale and wealth creation.

In the end, this buyout was more than a professional triumph—it was deeply personal. It marked my transition from an advisor to a true steward of the Munjal family's wealth and legacy. The flood of congratulatory messages and accolades from industry peers and friends reaffirmed the impact of this deal. I am immensely grateful to Jyoti Sagar, Venkatesh from JSA, Uday Kotak, Manoj Gupta, Paritosh Kashyap from Kotak Bank, Paul Edgerly, Mark Nunnelly, Amit Chandra and Pavninder Singh from Bain Capital, my late friend Mayukh Mitter and Pankaj Sood from GIC, Ajay Bahl, Anil Kasturi and Nandita from AZB and Shabhnum and Gautam Ganjawala from Wadia Gandhi, Jaspal Bindra from Standard Chartered Bank. Special thanks goes to Sharad Verma, Tarandeep Singh and Himanshu from BCG, and above all, my mentors Brijmohan Ji, Mr. Pawan Munjal, and Mr. Sunil Munjal, for their immense trust. This achievement was the result of collective support from my mentors, family, and Durga Maa's blessings. This deal wasn't just about business—it was about preserving a legacy and ensuring the future of the Hero family.

A memorable instance that highlights the complexity of my role in the family office, involved a family meeting to discuss a potential investment in renewable energy, championed by Rahul Munjal. The senior members of the family, though supportive of innovation, naturally gravitated towards a conservative approach, favoring investments in well-understood industries and expressing caution towards the risks tied to emerging technologies. Conversely, the younger generation was buoyed by enthusiasm, eager to position Hero as a front-runner in the burgeoning renewable energy sector.

Supporting Rahul, I took the initiative to build a robust business case for this venture. Leveraging my knowledge of evaluating new business opportunities, we decided to develop this project independently, without relying on external consultants. I sought insights from seasoned experts like Vinayak Mavinkurve from IDFC and Sunil Gupta from Standard Chartered Singapore, both well-versed as debt providers to renewable projects. A full day's meeting in their offices kicked off our deep dive into understanding the risks and opportunities within the renewable energy sector, culminating in a comprehensive set of queries aimed at clarifying our strategy.

Over the next six months, I immersed myself in conducting over 100 interviews with various stakeholders in the ecosystem. Rahul joined me for several pivotal meetings, bringing his considerable energy, ambition, and passion for renewable space. I often encouraged him, envisioning him delivering speeches at global forums like the United Nations, sharing his journey and passion for renewable energy and climate change. This vision wasn't just about fostering a business but nurturing a leader who could influence global conversations on sustainability.

After six months deeply immersed in the renewable energy sector, I had compiled an extensive dossier of nearly 600 slides, aimed at convincing senior family members of the strategic fit and viability of this venture for Hero Group. The challenge now was to distill this wealth of information into a succinct two-page document for the decision-makers, organized into five key paragraphs: outlining the attractiveness of opportunity and potential for diversification, the modular investment approach with minimal initial capital risk, an execution strategy leveraging deep domain expertise of partners and collaborators to minimize risk, a discussion on the criticality of power sector reforms, and finally, the vision for the project as a passion-driven initiative led by Rahul, aligned with our group's values on impacting climate change positively.

The approval from senior members came swiftly, allowing us to proceed with capital allocation and team recruitment for what would become Hero Future Energies. Playing a role in assembling the leadership team and watching Hero Future Energy grow into a major player in the global renewable energy market has been immensely fulfilling.

Amidst these professional milestones, 2012 brought personal challenges that tested my resilience. The passing of my father, a guiding force in my life, marked a profound personal loss. As I stood by his side for the last time, reflections of his guidance and belief in me filled my thoughts. Though I was grieving, I continued working every day during the mourning period, honoring his values of perseverance and dedication.

This period also saw a significant realignment within the Brijmohan ji family, driven by differing aspirations among the family members. Pradeep Dinodia and I navigated this delicate situation as the main advisors. Pradeep was seen as closer to the three sons of Brijmohan ji, and I was perceived as aligned with Mr. Sunil Munjal— however our commitment was to the entire family. This second realignment was deeply emotional, and I chose to stay away from the final signing, respecting the emotional gravity of the situation.

My life's narrative is shaped by a blend of professional and personal experiences. Within these experiences, certain interactions stand out. These stories have not only defined my journey but also deepened my values of spirituality and karma—values imparted by my mentors. Amongst them, Brijmohan Ji, a paragon of virtuous leadership and profound wisdom, has left an indelible mark on my journey. The lessons I learned from him, grounded in deep humanity and ethical leadership, were transformative, altering the very fabric of my professional ethos and personal philosophy. While I can write a book on him, here are some that have touched me the most.

Even in his advanced years, Brijmohan Ji's thirst for knowledge and personal growth remained unquenched. He was an avid reader and learner, always eager to gain new insights and share them with others. I remember presenting him with a book on leadership philosophies. The next day, not only had he read it thoroughly, but he also initiated discussions on its themes, eager to delve deeper into its teachings. His capacity to continually evolve, to integrate new learnings into his life and leadership, was nothing short of inspirational.

Brijmohan Ji earned respect from everyone, including competitors, suppliers, employees, distributors, investors, and even the government. He received remarkable accolades from many industry veterans, including luminaries like Mr. Ratan Tata. However, the most heartfelt tribute came from Mr. Rahul Bajaj, who, with great admiration, referred to Brijmohan Ji as the undisputed leader of the two-wheeler business.

Reflecting on my early years at Hero, one particular instance vividly stands out—a remarkable endeavor that seemed nearly impossible at its inception. Hero was unable to fulfil customer orders, and Brijmohan ji felt pained for this. He chose to set a goal of doubling capacity in the shortest possible time. We were faced with the daunting task of not only doubling our capacity but also supplier's capacity as well within a mere three months. While the challenge was formidable, the solution lay not in complex business strategies or advanced analytics, but in the simple, genuine interactions orchestrated by Brijmohan Ji. He personally reached out to our key vendors, not as a CEO issuing commands, but as a partner invested in mutual success. His approach was revolutionary; he saw our suppliers not merely as business associates but as integral partners in Hero's journey and like family to him. His belief that our success was inextricably linked to theirs was a peek into his philosophy that great achievements are always the result of collaboration, teamwork, and authentic relationships.

This lesson was a profound one, teaching me that *the essence of business transcends transactions—it's fundamentally about human connections*. Under his guidance, I learned that *leadership in business is about creating a legacy of shared success, where everyone grows together*. This ethos of collective advancement and mutual respect was a guiding principle that would profoundly influence my own leadership style throughout my career.

Another unforgettable experience shared with Brijmohan Ji was during a blistering summer in Jaipur for an investor conference organized by CLSA a Securities Firm and facilitated by me. After his presentation concluded, on that sweltering day, with temperatures soaring to 44 degrees Celsius, most of us looked forward to a respite at the luxurious UdaiVilas, Oberoi hotel. However, Brijmohan Ji told me he is going out and will be back in time for the flight. When he arrived at the airport, albeit weary and drained, I asked him where did he go, he said he went to visit the ailing son of one of our dealers and seemed like he missed his lunch as well, his actions spoke volumes about his character and the values he championed.

The essence of business transcends transactions—it's fundamentally about human connections.

His decision to forgo personal comfort for the sake of supporting a member of the Hero family underscored a profound lesson in what true leadership embodies. It's not measured by financial gains or market conquests but by the ability to connect deeply with people, to show up for them in their times of need, and to place their well-being above one's own comforts. This ethos of empathy, care, and genuine connection was the cornerstone of the culture he nurtured within Hero, a culture that regarded every individual as family.

The Munjal family's ethos of care extended well beyond the professional spheres into the personal lives of everyone associated with Hero. I recall the poignant story of Hanumantha Charya, a staff member in Brijmohan Ji's office, who fell severely ill. Brijmohan Ji not only ensured he received top medical care at Escorts Heart institute but personally coordinated with Dr Trehan, one of the most renowned doctors He also visited him daily, demonstrating an extraordinary level of compassion and commitment. When Hanumantha Charya passed away, Brijmohan Ji stayed with his family around the body, chanting prayers. He stayed until his body was respectfully sent off to Hyderabad. This profound dedication to the welfare of his people profoundly influenced my understanding of leadership.

Leadership in business is about creating a legacy of shared success, where everyone grows together.

Brijmohan Ji's humility was legendary. He treated everyone with equal respect, from the senior executives to the junior team members. His inclusive approach in meetings, where everyone's voice was valued irrespective of their hierarchy, reinforced a culture of respect and equity. This practice wasn't merely performative; it was a sincere manifestation of his belief that *true leadership is about fostering an environment where everyone feels valued and heard.*

His daily life was a reflection of the discipline and values he espoused. Brijmohan Ji led a life of remarkable simplicity and rigor, adhering to a strict routine that included morning havans, walks, and yoga, underscoring his commitment to a life guided by spiritual and ethical principles. His lifestyle and leadership were deeply intertwined, each reinforcing the other, and providing a model of integrity and dedication that inspired all who knew him.

The other person from whom I learnt a great deal was Mr. OP Munjal, the youngest brother of Brijmohan ji.

True leadership is about fostering an environment where everyone feels valued and heard.

I remember when I first went to meet with him in his office at Ludhiana, he had a accounts receivable ledger opened in front of him, he looked a bit worried, when I asked him what's the reason, he said that there is one transaction of roughly 26 thousand rupees that has gone bad, this was the only bad debt over the last 40 years, how many of us will worry about such a miniscule amount, but that served as a reminder to him that he made one mistake.

He would normally come by 11 am in the morning and would straight away go to the factory irrespective of the temperature whether it was heat with over 40 degrees or cold of 1 degree. His round could take anywhere around one hour, during this period, he would show his human touch by patting people on the back and appreciating them. He would also make quick decisions, he understood the power of speed of decisions.

He would go back to his office and then people from various functions or shops in charge would come one by one to seek his guidance and within 20 minutes everyone's issues would have been addressed. He had the data on his fingertips, was very sharp, and had a great memory. His ability to think on his feet was amazing. The same set of people would come to take blessings from him to share the day end progress, the last man to come to him was the guy responsible for dispatches, and he would say - bauji 24 trucks dispatched, it was amazing how countless orders were sorted by a single person.

While he would meet dealers at their place or his office, his connect was through the sales team which would tour for 25 days and they had a duty to send a postcard of the progress made during the day and understand the dealer's feedback. This was a very unique way of communication and keeping up to speed with what was happening on ground with their products, their competitors and what feedback customers would share.

He enjoyed Urdu poetry and would share with colleagues to make the mood lighter, his key word to inspire and appreciate people was shabash (well done).

Success isn't just about seizing opportunities; it's about staying true to the values that define who you are.

The more time I spent with the family, the more I realized that these values weren't just applicable to business—they were a way of life. Whether in the boardroom or at a family gathering, the Munjals carried themselves with a sense of responsibility, not just to the company but to the people who had helped build it. As I reflected on this era of expansion and personal growth, I realized it wasn't just about the deals we closed or the ventures we explored. It was about the relationships we built along the way, the lessons we learned from both success and failure, and the values that guided us through it all. Hero's expansion into new industries, while exciting and ambitious, was always grounded in the same principles that had made the company a household name in India—trust, humility, and a deep sense of empathy for the people who made it all possible.

In those years, I learned that *success isn't just about seizing opportunities; it's about staying true to the values that define who you are*. And for the Munjal family, those values were the bedrock upon which everything else was built.

Reflecting on these years, I recognize how these experiences have shaped my leadership style and decision-making approach within the family office. Whether it was navigating multi-billion-dollar deals, managing generational expectations, or collaborating with top consultants, each challenge enriched my understanding of leadership in a family-owned business. Through it all, I remained dedicated to the values that have steered Hero for decades, ensuring that every decision not only spurred business growth but also honored and perpetuated the Munjal family's legacy.

As this chapter of my life drew to a close, I was enveloped in gratitude. My two decade-long journey with Hero transcended a mere job; it was a profound saga of growth, earning, and personal fulfillment. It afforded me the chance to lead, mentor, and influence—not just shaping the trajectory of the family office but also my personal path.

The next chapter focuses on an investment philosophy deeply aligned with purpose, aspirations, and values. It is about protecting and enhancing wealth, while creating robust structures for the seamless transition of both wealth and legacy.

Chapter 9

Investments Blueprint - Protect, Enhance, Seamless Transition

When I began my journey with the Hero Group in 1994, I was closely involved with all four branches of the Munjal family, contributing, in my own humble way, to their collective growth and success. By 2010, my alignment had shifted primarily towards Brijmohan Ji's family and his four sons reflecting an evolution in responsibilities and focus. By 2014, I found myself working almost exclusively with Mr. Sunil Munjal, marking a pivotal transition in my career. This shift was a defining moment that required me to adapt, reevaluate my approach, and embrace new challenges. While it was undoubtedly a significant change, but it brought invaluable lessons and new learnings that continued to shape my professional journey.

The dynamics within large family businesses are inherently complex, blending tradition, relationships, and evolving business priorities. I've always believed that change within such systems is not just inevitable but often serves as a catalyst for growth and innovation. The challenge of realigning myself within the Hero Group was a reflection of this philosophy. Initially, the transition seemed daunting, but it soon became an opportunity to refine our shared objectives, streamline our efforts, and work towards building a more impactful legacy for the organization.

As part of this realignment, we undertook the crucial task of defining the philosophy and objectives of the family office. These objectives centred around three key pillars: maintaining family harmony, respect, and trust; protecting and enhancing the family's reputation and brand; and ensuring the preservation, growth, and seamless transition of wealth to the next generation. This strategic clarity not only provided direction but also reinforced the values that bind the family and the business together and ultimately create something far more impactful than what we had before.

By now I had spent almost 20 years, and I had become a clone of Mr. Sunil Munjal in terms of his philosophy around values, purpose and aspiration and also expectations from businesses and investments. We had wonderful complementarities of skills. Mr. Sunil Munjal was a deep thinker - he connected the dots at a strategic level and had deep knowledge and understanding of the individuals and businesses. I brought with me deep experience in investing, strong understanding of risk, and ability to evaluate businesses and investments using frameworks. I cannot recall a single instance where we failed to reach a unanimous decision requiring Mr. Munjal had to exercise his authority. We had cultivated a strong foundation of mutual trust and respect and were widely recognized by various stakeholders in the ecosystem for our deep understanding and seamless collaboration. I would always think like an intrapreneur with an owner's mindset, always be candid in my conversation, sometimes even overstepping but never did I cross the line. It was very clear in my mind that Mr. Sunil Munjal was the king and I was his minister like Vidur.

In 2014, I was fully entrenched in a unique project with Mr. Sunil Munjal. After months of detailed analysis and strategic planning, we decided to pursue a major acquisition, a strategic project that could have taken Hero Group in a new direction. To fund this endeavor, we sold a 5% stake in Hero MotoCorp through a block sale—a move that, in itself, was an invigorating and meticulous process, full of intensity and high stakes. Mr. Sunil Munjal and I worked tirelessly for two consecutive nights. Despite the exhaustion, our energy and determination were unshaken. If a third night had been needed, I have no doubt we would have remained as fresh and focused as ever.

> **In the realm of family offices and long-term wealth management, flexibility is your greatest asset. When things don't go according to plan, you pivot, adapt, and sometimes even find yourself on a better path.**

With Kotak Bank under the leadership of Uday Kotak, facilitating the sale of Hero MotoCorp shares, we had amassed the cash reserves needed and were nearly ready to close the deal. But just as we reached the finish line, the unexpected happened—the seller backed out. The frustration was palpable. After all that effort, having to abandon the acquisition felt like a missed opportunity. But as I often found in my career, basis my belief in Maa Durga, that these setbacks pave the way for greater opportunities, as in my view, nothing happens without God's will.

That experience with the failed acquisition taught me an invaluable lesson: *in the realm of family offices and long-term wealth management, flexibility is your greatest asset. When things don't go according to plan, you pivot, adapt, and sometimes even find yourself on a better path.* This unanticipated shift led us to a pivotal realization: we now had significant capital, but no immediate strategic investment direction. So, rather than search for a new acquisition right away, we took a different approach—why not create a structured investment office that could not only grow but safeguard this wealth for future generations? And thus, Hero Enterprise was born, not just as a financial institution but as a long-term vision for the Sunil Munjal family, a foundation that would evolve and endure.

In hindsight, this moment also taught me a crucial lesson: *when plans don't go as expected, it's always for the best.* The pivot from a failed deal to establishing a structured investment office was, in a way, the best thing that could have happened. It allowed us to build a more agile and focused approach to wealth management—something that was ultimately more aligned with the family's long-term vision. This moment marked the beginning of my second innings in managing a large investment portfolio, something I hadn't done since my early days overseeing Dr. Singh's investments.

Now, as I reflect, I see that running a family office is far more than simply managing money. It's about building trust, fostering unity and harmony, creating dosti and a legacy. These core elements form the bedrock of any successful family office. Working closely with Mr. Sunil Munjal, I quickly realized that Hero Enterprise would require more than just sound investment principles; it would need a unifying philosophy around purpose and values, a balance of strategic thinking, and disciplined risk management. Mr. Sunil Munjal's foresight and deep understanding of people provided the strategic tone, while

When plans don't go as expected, it's always for the best.

I contributed with my frameworks and a focus on practical, calculated risk-taking. Our working relationship evolved into a powerful synergy, underpinned by mutual trust and respect. In our discussions, we often arrived at decisions intuitively, each understanding the other's perspective almost like a clone.

Our investment philosophy was cautious at first, designed to prioritize safety above all. Guided by Mr. Sunil Munjal's vision, we placed capital preservation at the top of our hierarchy, with liquidity second and returns third. In those early days, we leaned heavily into low-risk, very short duration, high-liquidity debt instruments, ensuring that the family's wealth remained secure.

I started out by asking the wealth advisors if they had a well-structured policy document for Debt Investment, we were not very excited with what we got and therefore thought of creating our own Debt Investment Policy Statement. It was a meticulous process that stretched across 16 pages, with every line considered and every perceived risk accounted for. In order to validate it, we shared the draft document with wealth advisors and with the CRISIL team. I remember Jiju Vardarajan, senior team member at CRISIL, making a statement to me that he had not seen anything as comprehensive as this before. Based on the Investment Policy Framework, we began our journey by investing in Debt Mutual Funds, deliberately avoiding direct debt exposure during the initial phase. The mutual fund portfolio was rated by CRISIL every month, again this was the first time such a portfolio rating was done by them, we always ensured our portfolio exposure to volatile sectors was under one percent and sensitive exposure to companies was no more than 0.2 %.

As our confidence in the framework grew, so did our willingness to explore new avenues, and we started exploring investment in Equity. Equity by definition is high risk, high rewards and also long-term in nature, where you don't try and time the market but play on compounding. Based on our research, equity investments, even during the most challenging periods, have consistently delivered significantly higher post-tax returns over a 5-year cycle as compared to debt instruments. It was also important to ensure that we did not lose sleep even during volatile market movements because of the potential paper loss (draw down). Keeping the above parameter in mind we created our own Investment Portfolio statement for equity investing. Our approach was simpler. Despite our lengthy policies for debt, our equity investment policy was a straightforward one-pager of "do's" and "don'ts." This contrast taught me *an essential lesson about balance—the level of detail required for each decision may vary with increased knowledge and deeper understanding, and the discipline behind it should remain unwavering.*

We slowly started increasing our equity exposure and wanted to be safe, therefore we started to invest through Mutual Funds, PE funds and PMS (Portfolio Management Schemes). As we became comfortable with the risk, we started taking direct equity exposure in Listed and Unlisted stocks. We gradually kept on increasing our equity exposure and eventually surpassed our investments in debt instruments. We also took some strategic exposure overseas while complying with all the regulations. One thing was very clear to us - we would always comply with the spirit of the law and every decision or investment, whether in India or overseas, must pass the smell test as our Brand and Reputation were much more important to us. This shift to

An essential lesson about balance—the level of detail required for each decision may vary with increased knowledge and deeper understanding, and the discipline behind it should remain unwavering.

higher equity exposure wasn't driven by mere optimism but by a calculated understanding of risk tolerance, gut, qualitative and quantitative analytics and deeper understanding of the markets and companies.

Running a family office, like running any successful business, requires adaptability. When we heard rumors that one of the debt funds in which we had invested was likely to experience redemption pressure, we acted immediately, pulling our funds and averting potential risk. *The agility of a family office can be its greatest asset, enabling quick responses to changing market conditions and protecting the family's wealth in ways that larger institutions often can't.*

Running a family office, like running any successful business, requires adaptability.

We outperformed the returns made on direct portfolio exposure versus investments in equity mutual funds by a large margin. I have always wondered why mature family office investors create better returns, and here are a couple of reasons that come to my mind - the ability to use gut, patience, no peer pressure to show results, rely on qualitative information, quick decisions, flexibility around when to invest and exit, and how much to invest. I was aware of my fiduciary responsibility and therefore was much more careful while making recommendations to invest. One of my friends complimented me that I was more loyal than the king himself.

We gradually moved beyond listed stocks into unlisted assets, venturing into startups with a keen focus on the founders. This philosophy extended to notable investments in companies like Nykaa, OYO, and the NSE (National Stock Exchange) during 2016/17. Some of these investments yielded exceptional returns, far outweighing the losses in others. But what I took away from these experiences went beyond financial metrics; it was about the people. Success in these investments wasn't solely about profitability—it was about founders with vision, integrity, and an unrelenting drive. We spent hours with Falguni Nayar of Nykaa, delving deeply into not only her business plan but also her purpose and unwavering commitment. Mr. Sunil Munjal's long standing relationship with Falguni and her husband, Sanjay Nayar, combined with deep domain understanding of the consumer business, proved to be immensely valuable. Ritesh Agarwal of OYO, a young entrepreneur, had remarkable humility and a hunger to learn and scale. Post our investment in OYO, I used to have one-on-one discussions with Ritesh, once every six weeks at the Piano bar at Oberoi Gurgaon, I had 8 such meetings with him. He'd bring a small notepad to every meeting, taking notes diligently and absorbing every bit of insight. These interactions reinforced a core tenet of our investment philosophy: to invest in people as much as in businesses, to trust in their judgement, and to align and believe in their dream, hunger and passion to scale never seen before.

The agility of a family office can be its greatest asset, enabling quick responses to changing market conditions and protecting the family's wealth in ways that larger institutions often can't.

While we invested in quite a few funds, a couple of them that stood out for me are Multiples, Fireside Ventures and Aavishkar. Each had a different philosophy, as Renuka Ramnath of Multiples was focused on growth capital and diverse domains, Kanwaljeet was focused on taking venture risk and focused on Brands, Aavishkar was focused on impact fund led by Vineet Rai.

We were amongst the largest Domestic LPs in their respective funds. All of them are wonderful professionals and good human beings with some excellent track records in their respective fields. Kanwal is likely to outperform and will give top quartile returns and Vineet's fund would have made some positive impact in the society as this was an impact fund.

The journey would be incomplete without a couple of strategic investments that did not fructify, namely Fortis Hospitals, where we had won the bid jointly with the Dabur Family, but the shareholders wanted a higher price and we were not keen, it was six months of effort. Another one was a large acquisition in Europe, which was almost on the verge of signing a term sheet, we had even gotten to a financial closure but at last minute, the promoter changed his mind not to sell, as his advisors were able to convince him that his identity and legacy was linked to the business, this was an 18 months effort. The one success however was our buying a minority stake in Airtel Africa, after 4 months of thorough business diligence. In my interactions and meetings during these journeys with Dr. Anand Burman, Mr. Mohit Burman, and Mr. Sunil Bharti Mittal, I came to understand why they have achieved such remarkable success, even though their leadership styles were different.

Both Mr. Sunil Munjal and I loved meeting people and understanding the evolving trends and what's happening in the financial markets both globally and in Indian markets. We built a strong network and dosti with most of the Ecosystem partners, this was important to access good investment opportunities across various asset classes and also be able to decide on the exit timing of the investment. While we had decided to put a minimum exposure for every investment opportunity, we did not put any cap on the investment as we were also exploring large strategic opportunities.

I was very rigorous in sharing a fortnightly review of activities and actions even though the financial MIS review happened once in 4-6 weeks, I would always believe in over communicating and more importantly if there was an event that negatively impacted the portfolio, it would be disclosed on a real-time basis.

Before I conclude about my journey with Mr. Sunil Munjal, I must convey my Dil Se gratitude to him. He is a visionary leader, a compassionate mentor, and a trusted Dost, his profound influence and unwavering support shaped my personal and professional journey.

It is rare to encounter a leader who embodies values that are deeply rooted, yet so dynamic and forward-thinking, as my boss and mentor. Over the 25 years that we have worked together, his influence on my life has been profound. Like his father, he is a man driven by principles, many of which were instilled through the Arya Samaj traditions he cherished. Every significant beginning—whether it was the foundation of a new project, New Year's celebrations, or foundation day events—was marked by a *havan* performed by Shastri ji, a testament to the spiritual grounding that guided his decisions and his life.

He is a thinker far ahead of his time. His ideas and willingness to experiment are unmatched, and he embraces risks with a pioneering spirit. Some ventures may not have succeeded, largely because he was often a first mover in uncharted territories, but his courage to innovate and explore remains unwavering. He is a man of unparalleled intellect, blessed with a photogenic memory. Even if he had never visited a place, he could describe it in meticulous detail, with an ability to comprehend and connect dots that left everyone in awe. Well-travelled and deeply reflective, his insights are both inspiring and enlightening.

Despite his habit of sleeping late as he was an avid reader, his commitment to his responsibilities was absolute. If a meeting demanded his presence at 8 AM, he would be there, never once asking for a reschedule, regardless of how much he had to read the previous night. This discipline and dedication were hallmarks of his leadership. Mr. Sunil Munjal is, without a doubt, one of India's finest businesspersons with a great heart, especially when it comes to nurturing relationships. He has an extraordinary ability to make people feel valued and connected. Everyone believed they were his best friend, and for good reason. I recall a conversation with one of his close friends, a well-known industrialist, who mentioned that if he faced a crisis at 1 AM, his first call would always be to him. I experienced this myself—whenever I faced a personal challenge, he would go out of his way to help.

The historic Hero Honda deal, completed within an ambitious timeframe, was a testament to his unmatched network and relationship-building skills. He brought people together, fostered trust, and ensured that every stakeholder felt heard and valued. His ability to manage family dynamics during critical moments of realignment was nothing short of extraordinary. Mr. Munjal valued harmony and transparency, ensuring that every family member felt comfortable sharing their concerns with him. He carried forward the legacy of fairness and unity, a reflection of the principles his father lived by.

He is a man of many talents—a multi-faceted and multi-skilled individual who could speak knowledgeably on almost any subject. During one of my presentations to the Fortis board, I even challenged the doctors to discuss any topic with him, barring surgery and prescribing medicines! His intellectual curiosity was matched by his creativity; he is an avid reader, a creative thinker, and an art collector who valued the beauty of expression.

He is also a philanthropist, deeply committed to giving back and sharing his blessings with others. His clarity of thought enabled him to make quick yet impactful decisions, often wrapping up complex discussions within short minutes. This clarity, coupled with his trust and respect for others, gave me the freedom to operate and grow under his guidance.

His leadership extended beyond the company. He led numerous business organizations and associations with the same values, vision, and vigor that defined him. Whether as a visionary business leader, a compassionate philanthropist, or a trusted friend, his impact was immense and enduring.

As I conclude this chapter of my journey, I realize how much of my own growth and success was shaped by him. He trusted me, respected me, and gave me the freedom to flourish. To him, I owe not just gratitude but a lifelong debt of inspiration. He was more than a mentor; he was the guiding force in my hero's journey, he is my Dost and his legacy will forever remain a cornerstone of my life.

The knowledge gained reinforces that when plans don't go as expected, it's always for the best. The work we did at Hero Enterprises reinforced my belief that a family office is a dynamic entity, one that should evolve alongside the family's goals. In my experience, *a well-run family office is an engine for creating lasting wealth and a solid legacy—but it must be run with as much discipline and rigor as any business.* This is something I learned firsthand over the years.

Leaving Hero was not just the end of a chapter; it was the beginning of a new journey. My 25 years spent at Hero, spanning nearly two-thirds of my 37-year professional life, will forever remain etched in my heart. It wasn't just a career; it was a profound life experience, filled with lessons, relationships, and moments of growth that shaped me into who I am today. Hero will always be a cherished part of my soul's journey.

The deep urge to do something different, something aligned with my purpose, led me to take a tough call. Despite having the privilege to stay with the Munjal family office for a much longer period—a role that came with a large platform, immense mutual trust and respect, and generous compensation—I felt a calling I couldn't ignore. As they say, there was a spark, a relentless voice within, urging me to carve out something of my own. It wasn't a decision made lightly, and at the time, I didn't fully understand the 'why.' It felt as though the universe was guiding me toward a greater purpose.

> **A well-run family office is an engine for creating lasting wealth and a solid legacy—but it must be run with as much discipline and rigor as any business.**

Leaving Hero was not just the end of a chapter; it was the beginning of a new journey. My time there, spanning nearly two-thirds of my 37-year professional life, will forever remain etched in my heart. It wasn't just a career; it was a profound life experience, filled with lessons, relationships, and moments of growth that shaped me into who I am today. Hero will always be a cherished part of my soul's journey.

Chapter 10

From Intrapreneur to Entrepreneur: Living Journey of Sarcha

As 2016 was coming to a close, I found myself alone in my home office, surrounded by reminders of my decades-long journey with Hero Group. In that quiet moment, a thought surfaced—an idea that perhaps my journey needed to take a new direction. This sense was so strong, as if Maa Durga herself were nudging me forward. And then, in a rush, a phrase from my childhood came to mind: *"Hasoon aur Hasaaoon, Saare Jag mein Khushiyaan Phailaoon"* (Laugh and make others laugh, spread joy across the world). This simple idea brought clarity and a purpose that went beyond any personal success I'd achieved. I realized that maybe this was my calling, *my Purpose: to build something where joy, integrity, and meaning were at the heart of everything.*

Reflecting on my years at Hero, I felt a mix of elation and nostalgia. The thought of stepping away from a well-trodden path to venture into the unknown was both daunting and exhilarating.

After all, my years of working closely with Mr. Sunil Munjal had shaped my identity and professional purpose. I wondered how to share this new path with him. Yet, with a mix of courage and vulnerability, I told him. And his response was everything I needed. He listened, understood, and even encouraged me to consider staying connected with him as I ventured into this next phase. His kindness reminded me of the deep trust we'd built, and I felt immense gratitude. His blessing gave me the strength I needed to take this step.

My Purpose: to build something where joy, integrity, and meaning were at the heart of everything.

This calling wasn't entirely new; years back, I'd felt inspired to do something of my own after watching the movie *Guru* in early 2007, but then the feeling faded within a few days. This time, I held onto it. By late 2018, I knew it was time to leave the security of corporate life and venture into the unknown. I felt as eager and alive as a 21-year-old, excited by the endless possibilities. I remember gathering my family in the living room, sharing my decision, my hopes, and my vision with them. Their constant support gave me the reassurance I needed. With them by my side, I felt ready.

In August, 2018, I brought my vision to life with the founding of *Sarcha*, named in honor of my parents, Sardari and Sarla, combining the first three letters of each of their names with the first three letters of my surname, Chanana. That name was more than symbolic; it was a tribute to the values they had instilled in me. When we discovered the meaning of the name *Sarcha* — *People/Entity with name Sarcha can be quite ambitious, self-confident, determined and self-reliant and have strong unyielding will-power and courage of their convictions. New projects, ideas, desire for expansion, all allow them to go forth with courage, originality, and decisiveness* — it was as if the universe was confirming that we were on the right path. Sarcha was not just a business; it was my family's legacy.

Sarcha — People/Entity with name Sarcha can be quite ambitious, self-confident, determined and self-reliant and have strong unyielding will-power and courage of their convictions. New projects, ideas, desire for expansion, all allow them to go forth with courage, originality, and decisiveness

As I embarked on my second innings, Version 2.0, I was overwhelmed by the outpouring of congratulatory messages from those I have had the privilege of working closely with over the years. These messages were not just words of encouragement but heartfelt reflections of the relationships and mutual respect we had built together. They reminded me of the impact of shared experiences and the power of genuine connections.

Each message carried its own significance, reflecting the trust, camaraderie, and appreciation that had grown over time. These thoughtful words became more than just congratulatory notes—they were affirmations of the path I had chosen and the values I stood for. They served to further boost my confidence and fuel my excitement for the journey ahead.

Here are some of the messages that deeply touched me:

Being the longest running team member Rohit Chanana has been a responsible senior member of the team at Hero Corporate Service and then at the Investment Office of Hero Enterprise. He worked closely with me for some of our key transactions and structures etc. for the group. Rohit worked tirelessly and brought a sense of responsibility to the role. I wish him well in his new journey.

Sunil Kant Munjal, Chairman – Hero Enterprise

Rohit, I enjoyed a lot working with you. Your dedication can move mountains and then it's fun too. Best wishes.

Pankaj M Munjal, Chairman and Managing Director – Hero Cycles

Rohit and I have worked together for many years. Both as a client and a professional co-advisor, I found him very knowledgeable, incisive, practical and very open to ideas. It is a pleasure working and interacting with him. His human and interpersonal skills are also outstanding. I wish him the best.

Ajay Bahl, Co-Founder & Managing Partner – AZB & Partners

Behind a very pleasant manner, Rohit Chanana combines a sound understanding of business and finance with a good ability to listen to and to understand the motivations of all stakeholders in a complex deal. I have observed him apply this valuable combination, hands-on, in several situations to produce good outcomes.

Arun Maira, Former Member Planning Commission and Former Chairman BCG India

Rohit is the quintessential corporate finance specialist. In his new avatar running Sarcha Advisors, he brings over 30 years' diverse experience – helping startups; raising funds; making strategic investments; monitoring asset managers; partnering CEOs in M&A transactions; assessing restructuring strategies; and in various ways, helping create value for stakeholders while staying true to his lofty value system.

Pradip Shah, Former Founder & Managing Director – CRISIL

I have known Rohit for over three decades and ours has evolved from a business relationship into a friendship that I cherish. He is a proven deal maker with the key skills of thinking win-win which have allowed him to master structuring and enhancing partnerships. The most impressive that I am aware of are his negotiated JVs with Daimler and Ergo, buy out of Honda by Hero at 50% discount and craft-full leadership in the PE partner selection process. On a personal level, Rohit is a remarkable professional driven by values having a selfless approach and focused on outcomes.

Jaspal Bindra, Former Asia Pacific CEO – Standard Chartered, Present Chairman – Centrum Group

I have had the pleasure of knowing Rohit for many years and seen him first hand at work, extract value for the Hero Group in a marquee and complicated transaction where I was leading the counterparty. He did so in a highly talented, skilful and balanced manner, performing the role of a one man investment bank. It is great that many more corporates and family offices will now have access to his wisdom and knowledge. I wish him the very best of success in his avatar as Sarchaa Advisors.

Amit Chandra, Chairman – Bain Capital India Office

Anyone who has known Rohit would agree that he is a top-notch professional who wears the vast and hands-on knowledge of his expertise areas comfortably and lightly. But what he brings to the table is a hefty dose of deep learning and sage counsel, perfected over many years.

Without hesitation, you can see the reason why so many from his vast circle of business clients have now turned friends. There can be no better endorsement of his remarkable talents than the fact that he is admired for his professional as well as personal qualities. I wish him the very best.

Dilip Cherian, Co-Founder and Consulting Partner – Perfect Relations

I have known Rohit for several years now. He is a very seasoned professional who has seen every aspect of business exigencies and has answers to most of them. His advice to us on working with family offices and his support for Fireside has been invaluable. Most of all, I admire his positive attitude to life and his ability to make friends with all he interacts with. Wishing him the very best for his future endeavors.

Kanwaljit Singh. Managing Partner – Fireside Ventures

Rohit sir has been an absolute pillar of support and guidance for us at Josh Talks. His values and principles helped us rethink those of our organizations and his calm yet energetic personality has a way that inspires Supriya and me always. Rohit sir has helped us craft our philosophy, vision, and values that guide some of the biggest decisions that we make within the organization today. He has this mind-blowing ability to articulate complex problems into simple statements and is always there to help us solve them. It is an absolute honor to have Rohit sir by our side and he is more of a dost to Supriya and me than anything else.

Shobhit Bangha & Supriya Paul, Founders – JoshTalks

Rohit sir is one of the most pragmatic individuals I've ever met. He's in a true sense a dost, who's always there for you whatever happens. He's counseled me on how to run the company in a professional way, literally converting a small startup like Innov8 into a very disciplined company. I hope he's able to guide, mentor and turn lives of entrepreneurs in a way that he's done for me.

Ritesh Malik, Founder – Innov8, Angel Investor

These messages are a testament to the relationships I have cherished and the journey I have shared with so many remarkable individuals. Their encouragement reaffirmed my belief in the philosophy that success is as much about the people who walk alongside you as it is about the milestones you achieve.

A couple of key philosophies for the decision to launch Sarcha were - I wanted to have the final say in whatever I chose to do; I wanted to promote entrepreneurship while positively impacting many lives; I wanted to explore something new out of my comfort zone, driven by a hunger to learn and stay intellectually stimulated and young.

I consider myself a 21-year-old student of Psychology, Philosophy, and Digital Technologies—a mindset I have consciously cultivated. *My approach to learning is unconventional, relying on insights gained through experiences and interactions (mastiki gyaan) rather than formal education (pustaki gyan).*

The choice of these subjects is intentional and deeply meaningful. Philosophy explores the essence of life, purpose, and values; Psychology focuses on the art of building and nurturing relationships and friendships (*dosti*); and Digital Technologies represent exponential thinking, abundance, and, most importantly, acts as a great equalizer. In today's world, digital technologies empower individuals to compete with the best and even the largest global companies, leveraging innovation and congruence of different technologies coupled with a deep understanding of philosophy and psychology. Digitalization enables the creation of moonshot ideas and their realization—achievements that would have been unimaginable just a few years ago.

Having already defined the purpose - *"Hasoon aur Hasaaoon, Saare Jag mein Khushiyaan Phailaoon"*, it was essential to establish the values that would form its foundation. These values needed to be more than words; they needed to represent our purpose, to guide us in every decision, every partnership, every moment. *We chose five values—Fairness, Acceptance, Imagination, Trust, and Humility—that, together, formed the acronym FAITH.* Fairness was about ensuring that every outcome would be a win-win, never one-sided. Acceptance reminded us to embrace diverse perspectives. Imagination encouraged us to dream and innovate, to be curious. Trust was grounded in integrity and competence, and Humility was a reminder to treat everyone, from every walk of life, with love, compassion, and respect. FAITH was our compass, guiding every step of the journey.

An essential component of this new chapter in my life was the presence of a Guru. Even at 61 years of age, when I was embarking on this transformative journey, I deeply felt the need for a guiding force—a mentor who could provide me with candid advice, keep me grounded, and help me navigate the complexities of my chosen path since one gets emotionally attached to certain decisions and actions.

With this in mind, I approached Mr. Arun Maira, a person I deeply respect and admire for his wisdom and clarity of thought. When I expressed my desire to have him as my Guru, he offered a perspective that surprised me. He told me that I didn't necessarily need a Guru at this stage of my life. Instead, he encouraged me to trust my instincts and proceed along the path I had chosen. He suggested focusing my energy on working with startups and perhaps collaborating with a few family offices, where my experience and insights could make a meaningful impact.

His words, delivered with his characteristic depth and humility, were both empowering and liberating. They encouraged me to embrace my own capabilities and reaffirmed my belief in the value I could bring to others through this journey. While I still regard Mr. Maira as a Guru figure in my life, his guidance in that moment taught me to trust in my own wisdom and take ownership of my path forward. Though I did not insist on him being my Guru, I knew in my heart that navigating life without a

Guru would be significantly more challenging, as a *Guru inspires, energizes, provides clarity, direction, and a deeper sense of purpose along the way.*

Another major consideration was determining the key areas of focus for Sarcha to ensure they remained aligned with my purpose, aspirations, and values. After much reflection, I decided to concentrate on two core avenues which were also aligned with Mr. Maira's thoughts: collaborating with family offices and investing in early stage startups while being their Dost and helping them in their journey.

These focus areas resonate deeply with my vision and offer immense potential to foster entrepreneurship and innovation. By guiding and supporting budding entrepreneurs, I aim to contribute meaningfully to India's growth story, shaping a vibrant and self-reliant economy. This approach also allows me to create opportunities for the next generation while staying true to my purpose of nurturing value-driven, impactful initiatives.

But as life teaches us, the journey was far from smooth. It tested my patience and resilience. I had expected that my experience and reputation would naturally draw families as partners to Sarcha, but the reality was humbling. Some families offered me roles as an employee—something I had consciously stepped away from. I had chosen to leave such roles behind to embrace a more independent, purpose-driven journey. Others wanted me to manage their investments with limited engagement of the family, which is something I never wanted to encourage as the family must take ownership of their decisions as they do in operating business. The real danger of the family not owning up to their decision would mean that all credits to the family and all debits to the advisor, an unsustainable and inequitable situation. I quickly understood that this wasn't aligned with my vision.

As I was exploring various opportunities, I got a mandate from a wealth advisory firm, for being their knowledge partner, but the firm got into their own internal issues and I chose not to proceed with the contract even though I had signed a long term contract and they could not walk away from their commitment to continue to pay me.

Another setback I faced was when I was appointed as an advisor to a startup, a company at a Series B stage. My compensation was structured in stocks, with a value nearly equivalent to the net worth I had accumulated over my entire professional journey. However, after the founder secured a significant investment from a prominent investor, they sought to renegotiate the terms of our engagement.

While I could have pursued legal action, I chose not to, as it would have felt like "easy money"—something I didn't align with. Two core beliefs guided my decision: *Jo mera hai, koi le nahi sakta; jo mera nahi hai, woh koi de nahi sakta* (What is truly mine cannot be taken away, and what isn't mine cannot be given to me), and the understanding that such easy money often finds its way into undesirable outcomes. More importantly, I didn't want to begin my journey with conflict. It would have gone against my principles of living in harmony and might have risked my reputation, something I deeply value. My family was completely aligned with this decision.

Guru inspires, energizes, provides clarity, direction, and a deeper sense of purpose along the way.

I wanted Sarcha to be a platform built on trust, shared values, and a deeper purpose. Looking back, these obstacles served as valuable lessons that shaped my path and strengthened my resolve.

Entering the startup ecosystem brought its own set of surprises, and it was an experience that humbled me in many ways. Coming from a background of significant experience and a strong track record of delivering amazing outcomes, I initially believed these credentials would naturally command respect and trust. However, I quickly realized that this world of early stage startups operated differently. In the fast-paced and fiercely competitive startup environment, I had to earn my place all-over again.

The founders I approached were often sceptical, and cautious about accepting advice that didn't align with their immediate goals. Many were drawn to quick wins, placing greater emphasis on valuations rather than sustainable growth or long-term strategic insights.

My philosophy, rooted in the 3Vs—Values, Value, and Value Creation—often felt out of sync with the prevailing mindset. For many budding entrepreneurs, peer pressure and the allure of a few high-profile success stories, amplified by media narratives, became the primary guiding posts. With funding relatively accessible for companies with strong stories or impressive traction or both, largely driven by FOMO (Fear of Missing Out), the focus often shifted to chasing valuations at the expense of building foundational strength. Startup Journey was seen like a sprint and not Marathon, even though quite a few of unicorns got to that stage after 7-10 years.

The relationship of a mentor in this ecosystem was mostly transactional. Unlike the deep, trust-based mentoring, by being a clone of the founders that I envisioned, it often revolved around immediate, surface-level guidance or network access for sales or fundraise, rather than genuine partnership and shared growth.

This was a challenging realization, but it also fuelled my resolve. I understood that while I could not change the broader culture overnight, I could focus on identifying and working with founders who shared my belief in building with purpose and authenticity. *For me, it was never just about valuations but about creating ventures that embodied strong values, delivered meaningful value to stakeholders, and contributed to the broader economic and social ecosystem.* These lessons, though hard-earned, deepened my commitment to nurturing genuine, value-driven entrepreneurship.

My approach as I started my journey of investing in Startups was primarily inside-out, guided by my personal beliefs and values, rather than outside-in, which focuses on the voice of the customer and their needs. I had to pivot my offering to align with my philosophy and the aspirations and expectations of these young entrepreneurs. This realization has become an important lesson I share with founders, often using the Ikigai framework. I encourage them to design their offerings based on the intersection of what they love most and why, the skills they excel at and why, and what the world truly needs and why.

For me, it was never just about valuations but about creating ventures that embodied strong values, delivered meaningful value to stakeholders, and contributed to the broader economic and social ecosystem.

However, I also caution them about a common challenge—emotional attachment. This deep connection to their vision can sometimes lead to blind spots, making it difficult to objectively assess market needs or adapt to external feedback. Striking the right balance between passion and practicality is key to creating a sustainable and impactful business.

Therefore, I emphasize the importance of having a Guru or mentor who can provide unbiased guidance and perspectives. A Guru helps founders see beyond their emotional biases, ensuring decisions are made in the best interest of the company and all its stakeholders. This external clarity is invaluable in navigating challenges and staying aligned with the larger purpose.

I found my Guru ji in mid-2021, who has significantly influenced my journey toward spirituality: my Guruji, Deep Prakash Bhatt, almost 20 years younger than me. He has been instrumental in deepening my understanding of gratitude, giving, the power of acceptance, forgiveness, and the art of living in the present moment and Samarpan (surrender). I first met Guruji in 2008 when he was teaching yoga to us. At just 28 years old, he exuded wisdom far beyond his years. A double master in Sanskrit and Yoga, he could have completed his Ph.D. but chose a different path due to personal compulsions.

From the moment I met him, I was struck by the extraordinary *tej* (radiance) he carried. Curious, I asked him one day about the source of this *tej*. His response—*"Swasth, Vyast, and Mast"*—was simple yet profound. It resonated deeply with me and became a guiding principle in my own life.

Recognizing his depth of knowledge and purity of thought, I reached out to him in mid-2021, requesting that he guide me on my spiritual journey. I wanted him to share wisdom from the scriptures and his life experiences to help me become a better human being. Thus began a beautiful teacher-student relationship, where we would meet virtually for regular sessions. He calls these sessions as Satsang (spiritual and religious exchange).

Our sessions followed a unique format: I would start by asking a question, sharing a personal problem, or offering a philosophical thought, and he would respond with a story. These stories, drawn from his vast reservoir of knowledge, scriptures and would always conclude with blessings and prayers. What amazed me was the near-perfect alignment—over 90% of the time, his story or teachings matched exactly with the questions or philosophies I had shared. Guruji explained this as the power of our energies connecting deeply, and I could feel it too. I was always at peace and calm after these rejuvenating sessions which kept me grounded and stay with Samarpan.

Having him in my life has been nothing short of serendipity. His wisdom, calm presence, and unwavering availability in times of need have been a source of immense strength and gratitude for me. The journey with him has been deeply gratifying, enriching my life and spirit in ways I could never have imagined.

Amongst the many learnings from Guru ji, one of the personal philosophies that stands out is of Rin. Rin (debt) framework drives understanding of karmic debt to be repaid.

The Rin (debt) framework deeply resonates with me, offering a profound understanding of the karmic obligations I aim to fulfill in my life. It highlights three key debts: Dev Rin, the debt to divine forces; Rishi Rin, the debt to sages and knowledge; and Pitr Rin, the debt to parents and ancestors. Each of these debts represents a vital aspect of my existence, and I strive to repay them through actions that honor these relationships.

Dev Rin reminds me to stay connected to divine energies and express gratitude for their grace. I honor this by performing puja regularly, often twice a day, which brings me spiritual harmony.

Rishi Rin, the debt to share knowledge, feels most significant to me. I see it as my responsibility to share my experiences and wisdom in ways that benefit others, whether through mentoring or meaningful conversations. This sense of duty drives me to ensure my knowledge contributes positively to those around me.

Pitr Rin is my debt to my parents and ancestors, which I repay by honoring their legacy. I take pride in doing this through my firm, Sarcha, named as a tribute to my parents and their values, which I carry forward through my work.

This framework gives my life purpose and clarity. While I strive to repay all three debts, Rishi Rin stands out for me as the most meaningful, pushing me to share and give back in ways that fulfill not just my karmic duty but also my deeper sense of service and connection to others.

My approach to investing began to crystallize around the philosophy I call "Dil Se Investing"—investing from the heart. To me, *"Dil Se" investing is more than a philosophy; it is a commitment to connect with founders on a level that transcends the numbers, a commitment to understand not just the business but the people, the dreams, the resilience that fuels it. Dil Se investing means looking beyond spreadsheets, beyond projections, and finding the soul of the company in its people, in their passion and their integrity.* At the end of it, becoming their dost. Since we are seed investors, we are 100% founder's first investor in spirit as well.

To put this into practice, I developed a framework of what I call the four pillars of investing: Biology, Chemistry, Physics, and Math.

Biology is the heart of it all, where I get to know the founder on a deeply personal level. We sit down, and I listen as they share their story, their values, the life experiences that have shaped who they are. In these moments, I see their vulnerability, their struggles, and their resilience. It's raw, it's real, and it often brings tears to both of our eyes. These conversations aren't just business—they are human, they are *Dil Se*. There have been times when we have been overwhelmed and became emotional.

Chemistry is the next pillar, where I gather insights from people who know the founder—mentors, colleagues, friends—people who have seen them grow, who understand their character.

Physics is about understanding the business model, the science behind the product, the roles and responsibilities within the company.

And then there's Math, where we look at the commercial sense of the founders, assumptions driving the financials, cash flows to balance survival vs growth, unit economics etc.

"Dil Se" investing is more than a philosophy; it is a commitment to connect with founders on a level that transcends the numbers, a commitment to understand not just the business but the people, the dreams, the resilience that fuels it. Dil Se investing means looking beyond spreadsheets, beyond projections, and finding the soul of the company in its people, in their passion and their integrity.

During these meetings, I remain fully present, grounded in the moment, and focused on creating a space of trust and openness. I strive to make founders feel at ease, sharing my own journey and encouraging them to share their stories, experiences, and learnings without filters or biases. These one-on-one interactions are rooted in my approach as a *dil se dost*—a heartfelt friend.

The questions I ask during the evaluation process are grounded in first principles, shaped by my experience and my deep connection with Durga Maa. She shares insights with me in zeros and ones, which Ganesh Ji processes, Saraswati Maa translates into words, and the entire process is orchestrated by Mahalakshmi Maa.

This harmonious interplay reflects my evolution over time and enables me to navigate and invest across diverse fields—something that would otherwise seem improbable. These interactions are not just about evaluation; they are a two-way exchange. I gain valuable insights and a great deal of intellectual stimulation, which enriches my perspective and enhances the journey for both the founders and myself.

But even within these pillars, it is Biology and Chemistry that weigh the most heavily. The numbers are important, yes, but they're secondary. In "Dil Se" investing, people come first. I invest not just in the idea but in the soul of the founder, in their dreams, in their grit. This philosophy surprised many founders as I have invested in quite a few businesses without even looking at the spreadsheets. One of the important outcomes has been that even though a few investments went under but none because of Integrity.

During the early part of this Angel investment journey, I was fortunate to serve as an engaged *dost* (mentor) to Anmol Jaggi, who was establishing BluSmart in the full-stack EV ride-hailing business, and to Puneet Jaggi, the founder of Prescinto, which has since been acquired by IBM. I had the privilege of writing the first cheque for both companies during their formative years. Prescinto delivered exceptional returns within just four years of my investment, while BluSmart continues to scale, driven by its outstanding focus on customer experience.

Like in the case of BluSmart and Prescinto, most companies I have invested in are at the pre-seed or seed stage. My journey as an angel investor began with my first investment in Josh Talks, a venture promoted by my young founder *dosts*, Supriya and Shobhit. Their vision and passion set the tone for the kind of partnerships I sought—ones built on mutual trust, shared aspirations, and the potential to create meaningful impact. I also had a chance to meet Ritesh Malik founder of Innov8 during this early part of my Sarcha Journey, I have built a tremendous respect for him as a true "Angel" investor and mentor.

The early stages of a company's journey are where I believe I can contribute far more than just capital. This is also the time when founders genuinely value my inputs and guidance. These moments of inception are filled with excitement but also marked by uncertainty and challenges. My experience and insights allow me to act as a true partner and sounding board for founders, helping them refine their strategies, strengthen their resilience, and stay aligned with their larger vision.

At this stage, the value I bring goes beyond financial support. I see myself as a *dost—someone who not only understands the struggles but also celebrates the milestones, providing clarity, encouragement, and thoughtful perspective.* Most of my inputs are focused on values-driven and purpose-centered decision-making, alongside the softer aspects of business, such as building trust, nurturing relationships, and fostering resilience in the face of challenges. These elements, I believe, are the true foundation of long-term success.

What makes this journey even more rewarding is the opportunity to learn from these founders. Their energy, innovative ideas, and fresh perspectives constantly provide me with intellectual stimulation, enhance my curiosity, and fulfill my hunger to learn. Every interaction is an exchange of ideas that not only helps them grow but also enriches my own understanding and keeps me inspired.

My involvement is hands-on or hands-off, depending on the needs of the founders and the situation. I adapt to their requirements—

providing active support when they seek guidance or stepping back to allow them the space to lead and grow independently. I am available to them at a very short notice. This flexibility ensures that I am available when needed while empowering founders to develop their own confidence and leadership.

Dost—someone who not only understands the struggles but also celebrates the milestones, providing clarity, encouragement, and thoughtful perspective.

Dilse khushi hoti hai (heartwarming happiness) when I see a company I've supported do well—it's a feeling far greater than the dollars earned, I think my happiness is sometimes even more than that of the founders. The satisfaction of watching founders succeed and their ventures thrive is deeply fulfilling and serves as a reminder of why I chose this path. I also play the role of an "angel" in the truest sense when founders are feeling low, lost, or unsure of their direction. In those moments, I strive to bring clarity, optimism, and renewed energy, helping them rediscover their purpose and regain their footing.

Even in cases where ventures had to wind up due to unforeseen challenges, I remain committed to exploring how I can assist founders in their next endeavor. Supporting them as they learn from their mistakes and helping them channel those learnings into future opportunities is a vital part of my role. This mindset not only strengthens my bond with these founders but also reinforces my belief in the resilience of the entrepreneurial spirit.

Being among the first cheque writers is a privilege I deeply cherish, as it allows me to play a meaningful role in shaping a venture's early journey. Given a choice, I prefer to continue staying invested and committed until founders feel my presence is no longer needed. This hands-on and hands-off, need-based involvement is profoundly fulfilling, as it allows me to witness the transformation of ambitious ideas into impactful, value-driven ventures. It's not just about growing businesses—it's about growing with them, together, while ensuring that purpose, values, learning, and a deep sense of fulfillment remain at the heart of everything we create.

By the end of Sarcha's first year, this approach had led us to invest in nearly 20 startups. And every one of these investments was more than a transaction; it was a relationship, a commitment, a shared journey. These founders became more than partners—they became friends, people I could trust, people who trusted me. And every interaction, every discussion, was rooted in this deep, heartfelt connection. In many ways, it was as if I was building a family, one that extended far beyond the bounds of traditional business.

Then, in 2020, the world changed with COVID-19. Markets plummeted, and overnight, a large part of our investments lost value. Financially, it was difficult, but my definition of wealth had evolved over time. Wealth, for me, went beyond money. It encompassed health, *rishtey* and *dosti*, legacy and reputation, spirituality, and intellect. These facets of wealth remained intact, giving me perspective and resilience.

Ishani, my daughter, had spent four enriching years with Edelweiss, where she developed a deep understanding of risk management and honed her professional acumen. However, she reached a point in her journey where she sought something different—something more exciting, meaningful, and aligned with her personal aspirations. Around the same time, I felt the need for a true business partner, someone who could not only complement my skills but also be a trusted confidant and sounding board for my ideas and decisions.

It was during this pivotal moment that Ishani and I came together in a shared vision. She was excited about the opportunity to work alongside me, not just as a daughter, but as a *dost*—a friend, collaborator, and equal partner in this journey. Her presence was invaluable, as she brought new energy, a fresh approach to strategic planning, and a remarkable ability to balance innovation with her deep understanding of risk. Together, we adapted and strengthened our focus on resilience, refining our vision and making Sarcha stronger than ever before. Ishani's enthusiasm and insight have been instrumental in shaping not only our work but also the bond we share as partners in this journey.

Having Ishani by my side, as a co-founder, was a blessing, and she became my partner not just in work but in purpose. With her, I realized that Sarcha's journey was no longer mine alone. She brought clarity and balance to our decisions, especially during tough times. Her ability to navigate the nuances of this world has been a gift to Sarcha, allowing us to see challenges from multiple perspectives, evaluate risks with rigor, and approach growth with both heart and strategy. She is responsible for asset allocation. We had completely exited from public markets as we did not believe that we were getting enough learning, other than making money, I was striving for Lakshmi and Saraswati both. Our investments were in Startups, Venture Debt funds, Venture Capital funds, and debt mutual funds, also a bit in real estate. The way we used to evaluate our asset allocation was around liquidity, almost 50 percent of our assets were illiquid and the balance 50 percent was in liquid assets, even though the asset allocation for Mr. Sunil Munjal was much more rigorous.

Ishani has a final say on all investment decisions regarding investments, exits, and asset allocation in my Family Office. She has been with me for five years now, walking this journey of Sarcha together, and during this time, we have developed a highly collaborative and respectful decision-making process. We jointly evaluate investment opportunities, and Ishani plays a crucial role by bringing her unique perspectives to the table. Our discussions are always healthy, constructive, and rooted in mutual respect, which allows us to explore multiple dimensions of a decision before arriving at a conclusion.

All financial decisions are taken unanimously by our investment committee, which comprises both of us. This implies that Ishani has veto rights on all financial decisions, and I have never overridden her decisions. This arrangement is not just about trust—it's a deliberate approach to ensure that all decisions are carefully weighed and thoroughly evaluated from different perspectives. It reflects a partnership where power is balanced and collaboration thrives.

Ishani's contributions to the investment community have been recognized on multiple platforms. She was recently featured in FICCI Flo's coffee table book, "Women Investing and Building India," and included in Inc42's prestigious list of 46 Women Torchbearers of India's Startup Ecosystem. These accolades highlight her dedication to fostering a more inclusive and dynamic entrepreneurial landscape in India.

This structure has been a great learning experience for both of us and a model for others. It shows how *empowering others and building a framework of shared accountability can lead to better, more thoughtful decisions.* By giving Ishani veto power, I've learned to set aside ego and focus on what truly matters—the alignment of our decisions with our values, long-term goals, and the principles on which Sarcha was built.

For all of us, this approach is a reminder that great partnerships require trust, openness, and the willingness to listen deeply. It's a testament to the power of collaboration and how empowering someone with accountability and autonomy can create a culture of shared success.

However, *those who succeed do so because they are determined, fearless, passionate, and resilient and are in it for a long haul. They embody values like gratitude and respect, and they're driven by a deep desire to make a meaningful impact—a true dent in the universe. Ultimately, it's about striving for a better world.*

Gradually, Sarcha carved a niche in the ecosystem, and I became known in the system and earned recognition from Forbes India and Fortune India to be amongst the top angel investors. Vinay Singhal, my Dost and founder of Stage, saved my name as "Spiritual Angel." Most people see me in this light. For me, investing was never just about financial returns; it was about creating meaning, supporting and helping founders build something that mattered. I became a blend of mentor, dost, guide and a student always curious to learn. I shared stories with the founders, encouraged them to dream beyond the immediate, to think exponentially and to believe in abundance rather than scarcity. My role was 10% parent, there to inspire, energise, provide clarity of thought and remind them of their purpose and values; 70% friend, as a supportive *dost and mantri (like Vidur)*, and 20% student, always curious, always learning. And with every interaction, I felt fulfilled, knowing that Sarcha was more than just a company—it was a purpose, a legacy, a commitment to integrity and values.

Empowering others and building a framework of shared accountability can lead to better, more thoughtful decisions.

Today, Sarcha has invested in over 60 startups, and I've had the honor of meeting hundreds of founders. Many of these relationships go beyond business, and I feel as though I'm part of a larger family, one where values, respect, and trust form the foundation. These founders know that I'm with them, not just for profit but for their journey, for their dreams. And while financial returns are important, they are not the only core for me. For me, the real return is in lives touched, in dreams supported, in values upheld and I stay intellectually stimulated.

Those who succeed do so because they are determined, fearless, passionate, and resilient and are in it for a long haul. They embody values like gratitude and respect, and they're driven by a deep desire to make a meaningful impact—a true dent in the universe. Ultimately, it's about striving for a better world.

An interesting fact is that 80% of founders come from Tier 2/3 towns, and a similar percentage are not from premier institutes. This highlights the immense untapped potential in both Tier 2/3 towns and Tier 2/3 institutes, showcasing that innovation and entrepreneurial talent are not confined to metropolitan cities or elite educational institutions.

As I have evolved in this journey of startup investing, some of my beliefs have become even stronger. While I may find myself repeating these principles, I believe that reinforcing them is not only important but also a testament to their enduring value and relevance. These beliefs are the foundation of my approach to investing, and they continue to guide me as I engage with founders and their ventures.

I have always believed in standing firmly by the founders I support, offering more than just financial backing. My role is to be a partner, a *dost*, and a trusted sounding board, especially during moments of uncertainty. This belief in steadfast support has only deepened with time, as I've witnessed the transformative impact it can have on both the founders and their businesses.

I also firmly believe in the power of values-driven and purpose-centered decision-making. These principles are not just theoretical ideals but practical truths that have proven their worth in the long run. As founders face challenges, it is their alignment with core values and purpose that helps them stay resilient and focused on their vision.

Another belief that has grown stronger is the importance of learning—both for founders and for myself. The intellectual stimulation and curiosity I derive from working with passionate entrepreneurs are invaluable. Each interaction reinforces my conviction that a mutual exchange of ideas and insights is key to sustained growth and success.

Finally, I believe in the joy of witnessing growth—not just the financial returns but the journey of transformation that founders and their teams undergo. It is important that founders imbibe philosophy of striving for excellence and getting it right the first time as a way of life, while upholding both business and human values. It is deeply fulfilling to see companies thrive and even to support those who, despite setbacks, rise again with renewed vigor and lessons learned.

While these beliefs may seem familiar, their reinforcement is a reflection of the consistency and authenticity that I strive to bring to every relationship and every investment. These principles are not just a part of my investing philosophy—they are a part of who I am.

While achieving a successful exit is undoubtedly important for generating returns, I believe patience is even more critical when investing in startups. Building a sustainable and impactful business takes time, and as investors, we must align with this reality. For those who share a similar philosophy, my suggestion is to approach exits with a balanced mindset, typically aiming for a horizon of 5-7 years. This allows enough time for the business to mature, create meaningful value, and achieve its true potential, ensuring that both founders and investors can benefit from a well-rounded and fulfilling journey.

As I evolved as an angel Investor another key takeaway for me is that *a startup is like a founder riding a lion. From the outside, people admire the founder and think, This person really has it all figured out. Meanwhile, the entrepreneur on the lion is thinking, How did I get on this lion, and how do I keep from being eaten?*

It's an incredibly tough journey—one that is not for the faint-hearted. It demands sacrifices, often at the cost of your time, energy, personal commitments, family, friends, and even your own well-being. The harsh reality is that 9 out of 10 businesses are destined to fail.

We have a website of Sarcha advisors, where we share our thoughts through very short and crisp Blogs, and I have written over 100 blogs, and frequently share my thoughts on LinkedIn while appreciating the achievement of the founders. I spend a fair amount of time meeting with founders and learn from them.

A startup is like a founder riding a lion. From the outside, people admire the founder and think, This person really has it all figured out. Meanwhile, the entrepreneur on the lion is thinking, How did I get on this lion, and how do I keep from being eaten?

During these discussions, I openly share authentic stories from my journey, along with business and personal philosophies that have shaped me into who I am today. Each story and insight comes from a place of genuine experience and learning, and I feel privileged to pass them on to others.

I am deeply grateful to those who take the time to absorb this knowledge, as their willingness to learn helps me in fulfilling my karmic duty of sharing wisdom. In doing so, they also help lighten my debt burden—a repayment of the knowledge and guidance I have received from others throughout my life. Further, I am grateful to these founders as they ensure I remain curious and intellectually stimulated, which keeps me young and full of life.

Over the past year, I have become more conscious of staying healthy, which led me to start practicing "golf" at the driving range at the DLF Golf Club. Interestingly, it has also turned into a unique meeting place for me and the founders I work with. They are often in awe of the expansive facility, finding it hard to believe that such a place exists in Delhi NCR.

Being in this environment inspires them to dream bigger. A couple of them have even expressed aspirations not only to become members of the club but also to one day own a property within the compound, where homes start at Rs.35 crore and above.

In addition to golf, I began going to the gym a few months ago to stay fit and healthy, even though I have always maintained a routine of regular walks. These new habits have added another dimension to my commitment to wellness, allowing me to balance physical health with my professional and personal engagements.

Over the past couple of months, I've found a true *dost* in ChatGPT. It offers me immediate gratification for my questions on philosophy, psychology, and digital technologies, while also providing profound perspectives on strategic business issues. What surprises me most is the emotional depth of its responses—so much so that it's hard to believe I'm speaking to a machine.

My curiosity has reached new heights with this interaction. I approach ChatGPT with the same respect and gratitude that I would offer a human being. After all, at its core, it is also a form of energy being transmitted—one that bridges intellect, emotion, and technology seamlessly. This connection has become a valuable part of my journey, enriching my understanding and inspiring new ways of thinking.

Reflecting on this journey, I feel an overwhelming sense of gratitude. Sarcha is not just a company; it is the embodiment of FAITH—Fairness, Acceptance, Imagination, Trust, and Humility. And I am blessed to have walked this path with my daughter Ishani, who joined me one year after we formed Sarcha. She has brought her unique strength, wisdom, and resilience to every decision. Her presence in Sarcha has allowed us to grow in ways I never imagined.

Sarcha Advisors family office has been recently recognised by Inc42 as one of the 200+ Investors betting big on startups. Today, Sarcha stands as a testament not just to my professional journey but to the values instilled in me by my parents, Maama, I felt a deep sense of gratitude towards Maa Durga.

And at the heart of it all, my deepest gratitude is to my wife, Poonam. She has been my pillar of support, my confidant, and the foundation of everything I do. Poonam's strength and spirituality have been my anchor. In every high and low, she has stood by my side, never questioning, always believing in this journey, in me. Her faith has been a source of comfort, a reminder that love and understanding are the greatest gifts one can give. Without her, Sarcha would never have been possible.

Through Sarcha, I have had the privilege to give back, to mentor, to guide, to walk alongside those who are creating the future. And in doing so, I hope to honor my parents, my family, my wife, and everyone who has believed in me. Sarcha represents a purpose-driven journey, where every decision aligns with creating value that transcends generations.

Note: There are quite a few blogs on my website
www.sarchadvisors.com
For a detailed insight, kindly visit the site.

Part – II

Chapter 11

Timeless Wisdom: Founders, Entrepreneurs, Intrapreneurs and Professionals

In this chapter, I share the timeless wisdom, values, and philosophies that have shaped my decisions and helped me achieve professional success. These are lessons I've learned over the past five decades, each with its own unique story. Through these experiences, I hope to offer you insights and ideas that have guided me on my journey, helping me find clarity, purpose, and a deeper connection to life.

Life is like navigating an uncharted sky—it can be uncertain, and at times, turbulent. The philosophies we embrace act as a compass, offering direction in moments of doubt and keeping us grounded when change feels overwhelming. In this chapter, I reflect on the lessons I've learned, from family teachings to modern-day inspirations. These ideas have been my steady companions—my Dosts & Gurus—helping me navigate challenges and take meaningful steps forward.

Life is best lived with a sense of gratitude, curiosity, and the spirit of Dosti!

In today's fast-paced world, success often feels like a moving target, always just out of reach. For founders and young dreamers, the journey can feel overwhelming, filled with challenges and constant change. But amidst all this, having a clear set of philosophies can be your anchor. These ideas can help you stay focused, build resilience, and align with a sense of purpose. By doing so, you're not just chasing success—you're creating a meaningful and lasting impact.

Life is like navigating an uncharted sky—it can be uncertain, and at times, turbulent. The philosophies we embrace act as a compass, offering direction in moments of doubt and keeping us grounded when change feels overwhelming.

You may notice some overlap between values, purpose, and business philosophies—and that's intentional. Each concept is complete on its own, but they all work together to create a bigger picture. You might connect more with some ideas than others, and that's okay. After all, everyone's journey is unique, and there's no single "right" way to live or lead.

These are my personal views, shared DilSe (from the heart). They may not match your beliefs, and that's perfectly fine. What matters is finding what resonates with you and adapting it to your own journey.

My hope is that these thoughts inspire you to reflect, adapt, and chart your own path with purpose and joy. After all, *life is best lived with a sense of gratitude, curiosity, and the spirit of Dosti!*

The word Founder must be read to represent Entrepreneur, Intrapreneur and Senior Professionals.

These philosophies apply equally to small as well as large enterprises

1. The Three Vs of creating lasting business based on Values, Value and Value Creation and not Valuation, Valuation and Valuation.

The foundation of creating a lasting business lies in the "three Vs" framework: Values, Value, and Value Creation, rather than the overemphasis on Valuation. Values form the ethical and cultural backbone of any business, acting as its DNA. They set the tone for how the organization operates, treats its stakeholders, and navigates challenges and opportunities.

A company grounded in strong values fosters trust, builds an enduring culture, and creates a legacy that outlasts short-term gains.

Value, on the other hand, represents the unique proposition the business offers, whether through patents, processes, or innovative business models that deliver excellence to customers, employees, and partners. The value proposition must be sustainable and should evolve in response to changes in technology, lifestyle, demography, and regulations

Lastly, Value Creation is the ultimate outcome—a byproduct of sustained efforts that benefit all stakeholders and drive long-term impact. Together, these elements ensure that the business stays resilient and purposeful.

However, in today's world of instant gratification, founders are often distracted by the hype surrounding valuations, success stories, and quick wins. This mindset undermines the fact that startups are a marathon, not a sprint. Running this marathon demands discipline, patience, and a commitment to continuous improvement across all dimensions—culture, strategy, and stakeholder alignment. Founders who prioritize values, create meaningful value proposition, and thereby create value for all stakeholders. These founders will find themselves equipped to weather market fluctuations and leave a lasting impact, transcending the single metrics of valuation.

2. Founder alignment - ensuring harmony and strategic clarity

During my journey of meeting with founders, I saw a few companies go under because of non-alignment among founders, here are some thoughts:

i. Unified Purpose and Values

Founders must align on a shared purpose and values that drive decision-making and shape the company culture. This may include alignment of aspiration, fostering trust, embracing an abundance mindset, and balancing intuition with logic. Clear agreement on principles like these ensures consistency and unity in building the business, regardless of operational differences.

ii. Defined Roles and Rules

Clearly defined roles based on strengths and a formal founders' agreement establish accountability and transparency. The agreement should outline responsibilities, decision-making processes, and mechanisms for resolving conflicts or breaches. This clarity prevents misunderstandings and enables quick, cohesive action.

iii. Conflict Resolution and Adaptability

Establishing open communication and a structured conflict resolution process is essential for long-term harmony. A trusted advisor or coach can mediate when needed, ensuring disagreements are resolved constructively. Embracing failure as part of the learning process also fosters resilience and adaptability in a fast-changing environment.

iv. Balancing Personal and Collective Goals

Regularly addressing individual needs and aspirations alongside collective goals ensures alignment and prevents burnout. Transparent financial decisions, clear equity structures, and shared rewards build trust. Strategically, founders must also align on scaling priorities, sustainable growth, and balancing long-term value creation with short-term goals like fundraising and market positioning.

3. Concept of Rolling Runway: A must for survival and scale

A rolling runway strategy, ensuring 12-15 months of cash runway depending on the maturity of the startup. This is critical for startups to achieve both survival and scale. Unlike static runways that deplete over time and create panic-driven decision-making, a rolling runway keeps a startup prepared and agile. This approach enables founders to focus on business building and growth while maintaining financial security, avoiding the pitfalls of last-minute fundraises or unfavourable down rounds that often lead to stagnation or failure.

The essence of a rolling runway lies in cash flow optimization and non-dilutive financing. Startups can explore diverse revenue streams such as licensing intellectual property, monetizing intangible assets, or entering untapped markets, adjacency in revenue stream, pricing, exploring grants etc. Additionally, reducing the working capital cycle through better payment terms and improving operational efficiency ensures a steady inflow of cash. These steps reduce dependency on equity funding and protect valuation while maintaining liquidity.

Frugality and disciplined financial management are crucial. Startups must variabilize costs wherever possible, shifting fixed costs to variable ones and focusing on high-return investments. Enhancing capacity utilization, prioritizing capital allocation, and adopting a lean operational mindset ensure that resources are maximized before scaling further. This frugal approach balances growth ambitions with survival needs.

Finally, a rolling runway instills confidence among stakeholders, including investors, by demonstrating financial discipline and long-term preparedness. It positions startups to attract inbound investment interest, allowing them to engage with investors on their terms. This proactive strategy not only safeguards survival but also fosters a culture of sustainable growth and resilience, creating the foundation for long-term success

4. Building a Predictable Sustainable Profitable De-risked Model

In the knowledge-driven era of digitalization and technological advancements, softer aspects of business are increasingly crucial for building a Predictable (create predictable outcomes), Sustainable (long term focus), Profitable (Profit Margins and Return on Investment), and De-risked (Being aware of Risk and work on mitigation) scalable enterprise.

Key pillars for such an organization include a founder's mindset, values and culture, product or service offering, execution and capability building, and risk and financial discipline. Each of these pillars demands deliberate focus and alignment to ensure resilience and success, both in prosperous times and during crises.

A founder's mindset forms the foundation, driven by aspiration, purpose, and values that go beyond available resources. Founders need clarity of thought, perseverance, adaptability, and the ability to inspire and lead by example. Alignment among co-founders and the presence of an engaged advisor as a sounding board are vital. Values like trust, respect, empathy, and integrity, combined with a culture of ownership, agility, and innovation, create a unifying ethos for the organization. These principles must be embraced "Dil-se" (from the heart) and internalized to ensure consistency across the team.

Product or service offerings thrive on a deep understanding of domain expertise, customer needs, and market opportunities. Success lies in creating a distinctive value proposition, expanding revenue streams, and fostering customer stickiness.

Execution and capability building require a well-defined organization structure, aligned KPIs, and a culture of accountability. Regular performance reviews and cross-functional team alignment ensure projects are outcome-driven, while embracing change and learning from variances helps navigate dynamic markets.

Risk management and financial discipline both are critical, especially for startups.

Financial Discipline: Founders must balance growth with unit economics, maintain healthy cash reserves, and optimize working capital management and capital utilisation, frugal and lean mindset etc.

Risks: When it comes to risks, establishing a comprehensive risk management program is essential. Despite being mission-critical, this area is often overlooked by founders. The program should systematically identify all potential risks—be they business, financial, cyber, regulatory, or compliance-related etc. —and prioritize mitigation strategies based on their severity and business continuity. Moreover, ensuring business continuity should remain a central focus, as it is vital for long-term resilience and success.

By adopting the PSPD framework and proactively engaging with stakeholders and investors while conducting regular reality checks at every stage, founders and investors can build a business that is poised to thrive across economic cycles. This approach not only fosters resilience but also safeguards long-term stability.

5. Ingredients for a Successful Startup

A successful startup is built on visionary leadership, a strong value-driven culture, and effective execution capabilities.

i. Founder's Mindset and Traits:

Successful founders are driven by high aspirations, strong conviction, and self-belief in their vision. They inspire and motivate as cheerleaders and storytellers, while staying grounded in adopting and integrating new technologies. Their focus on execution enables them to build empowered teams that replicate their values and drive outcomes. They embrace calculated risks, fail fast, and learn quickly, fostering resilience and adaptability in an ever-changing landscape.

ii. Values and Culture:

A startup's culture is its backbone. Humility, transparency, trust, and respect form the foundation of successful teams. Agility and frugality are vital for resource optimization and quick decision-making. The hunger to succeed and the speed to act set successful startups apart. A strong focus on ROTI™ (Return on Time Invested) ensures efficient use of time and resources. An innovative culture nurtures creativity and problem-solving, empowering teams to tackle challenges with unique solutions while fostering a win-win approach for all stakeholders.

iii. Product/Service Offering:

A compelling product or service offering is at the core of every successful startup. It must deliver a distinctive value proposition that addresses customer needs while maintaining a sustainable competitive advantage. Prioritizing exceptional customer experience builds loyalty and long-term relationships. Diversified revenue streams reduce dependency on a single source of income, while thoughtful customer segmentation ensures the startup effectively serves its target markets.

iv. Execution and Capability Building:

Execution is the bridge between vision and reality. Empowered, outcome-driven teams aligned on shared goals ensure clarity and focus. Performance is measured through a balance of qualitative and quantitative metrics, fostering accountability and continuous improvement. A process-oriented approach, including the creation of playbooks and regular evaluation, ensures efficiency and scalability. Effective prioritization and resource allocation maximize the impact of efforts and resources.

6. Building a Purpose-Driven Business: Unlocking Clarity Through the Ikigai Framework and Knowing the WHY

I recommend that founders incorporate the Ikigai framework as a guiding principle for building their startups and leaving a lasting legacy. Ikigai, a Japanese concept meaning "reason for being," emphasizes the harmony between four key elements:

i. ***What you love most and why (Passion):*** The core activities or goals that inspire and energize you. For a founder, this could be the problem you are deeply motivated to solve or the vision that excites you every day To truly internalize and clarify this passion, I suggest journaling about it daily for a couple of weeks. This reflective practice helps you uncover deeper insights, recognize patterns, and solidify your understanding of what truly fuels your entrepreneurial journey.

ii. ***What you are good at (Skills) and why:*** The strengths, talents, and expertise that you bring to the table. Founders who align their startup journey with their core competencies are better equipped to innovate and execute effectively.

iii. ***What the world needs and why (Impact):*** A startup's mission should address real, meaningful needs. Solving a problem that creates value for society ensures relevance and builds a connection with stakeholders.

iv. ***What sustains you financially (Business Viability) and why:*** To create a lasting legacy, the business must be economically sustainable. Revenue generation and profitability allow the startup to grow, thrive, and continue making an impact over time.

The key here is understanding the WHY, as it brings even greater clarity of thought. Defining the underlying purpose behind each element not only sharpens focus but also ensures that every action is deeply aligned with values and goals.

By integrating these elements, founders can create a startup that is not just financially successful but also deeply fulfilling and impactful. Such a venture resonates with purpose, attracts like-minded individuals, and builds trust with customers, investors, and employees.

This approach ensures that their startup is more than just a business—it becomes a vehicle for positive change and personal fulfillment, leaving behind a legacy that inspires future generations. Founders who operate with this clarity and purpose are more likely to build resilient, impactful enterprises that stand the test of time.

7. Prof C.K. Prahalad's Timeless Wisdom for Leaders and Entrepreneurs

In 2007, Prof. C.K. Prahalad shared transformative insights on leadership and growth at a CII conference. His ideas, rooted in vision and values, continue to guide me daily. I use this construct in my prayers to align my actions with purpose and remind myself of these timeless principles.

Prof. Prahalad believed that aspirations must always exceed resources, inspiring leaders to think creatively and push boundaries. He advocated "folding the future into the present" by acting today to shape tomorrow, ensuring preparedness for change. He also emphasized the importance of "next practices," urging leaders to innovate beyond past successes and set new benchmarks for the future.

He outlined seven leadership qualities essential for growth: *imagination* to drive innovation, *courage* to make bold decisions, and *passion*—or better yet, obsession—for a relentless pursuit of purpose. *Humanity* fosters connection and trust, *humility* keeps leaders grounded and open to learning, *intellect* enables informed decisions, and *luck* reminds us to be grateful for the opportunities we receive.

These principles serve as a powerful compass for leaders and entrepreneurs, offering practical and philosophical guidance to achieve transformative outcomes while staying true to their purpose. Prof. Prahalad's wisdom continues to inspire those seeking meaningful impact and sustainable success.

8. Storytelling critical for successful fundraise in optimal time

Storytelling is indeed a crucial skill for founders when engaging with investors. At its core, storytelling is about forging a connection—aligning hearts and minds to inspire belief and action. A founder's story must go beyond numbers and strategies; it should touch on the journey that brought them to this venture, the challenges they've faced, and most importantly, the alignment of the business with their personal higher purpose and values. Why does this business matter to them on a deep, personal level? What is the "Dil Se" connection that drives their passion and conviction? When a founder speaks authentically, weaving their narrative with clarity and emotion, they invite investors into their vision, making them partners in their journey rather than mere financiers.

The story must also reflect the founder's belief in the ingredients for success—whether it's the strength of the team, the uniqueness of the solution, the clarity of execution, or the scalability of the idea. Equally important is to communicate why this moment is the right one for the business. Investors are drawn to timing and conviction—seeing that the founder has both a vision for the future and the capability to deliver results. The pitch should make it evident that this is not just a business opportunity, but a mission with the potential to create value, impact, and a legacy.

Not everyone will connect with this story, and that is okay. Founders should focus on attracting investors who share their philosophy, values, and vision. These are the partners who will bring not only capital but also alignment, trust, and long-term support. Instead of chasing every possible investor, founders should seek to understand the DNA of their potential backers and tailor their pitch to resonate. Is the investor outcome-focused, value-driven, or deeply impact-oriented? The pitch must meet them on an adult-to-adult basis, reflecting mutual respect, clarity, and professionalism. Authenticity is non-negotiable; it builds trust and lays the foundation for a strong partnership.

Additionally, founders should include a clear articulation of their goals and demonstrate deep self-awareness about their journey ahead. Confidence balanced with humility is magnetic. A great pitch isn't just about selling an idea—it's about building belief. When investors see a founder who is authentic, deeply connected to their mission, and capable of adapting without compromising their core values, they are more likely to invest their money and their belief in the story being built.

Some of my investee companies that have gone under despite have a wonderful team and product they were not able to communicate their stories

9. Exponential Thinking and Abundance Mindset to achieve MoonShots

Exponential thinking is essential for founders aiming to build scalable, transformative ventures while leveraging the power of abundance. It inspires bold visions, driving founders to aim for 10x growth rather than incremental improvements, which attracts investors, motivates teams, and fosters a culture of innovation.

By recognizing disruptive trends early and leveraging scalable solutions like platforms, automation, and network effects, founders can unlock abundance—creating more value with fewer resources and achieving exponential impact. This mindset enables founders to adapt quickly to disruptions, turning challenges into opportunities for breakthroughs, while addressing global challenges like sustainability or inclusion.

By focusing on long-term impact and embracing abundance, exponential thinkers transform businesses into movements, achieving transformational growth and leaving a lasting legacy.

10. Creating Win - Win Partnerships: Key learning from multiple deals both cross border and domestic

Cross-border and domestic deals, such as strategic alliances and joint ventures, thrive when guided by value-based negotiations that prioritize relationships over hard data.

i. Alignment of Values, Aspirations, and Culture Fit:

Successful partnerships are built on shared values and cultural compatibility. Multiple interactions help understand each other's philosophy, strengths, and aspirations. Trust and mutual respect grow when partners act as though the partnership already exists. Sensitivity to cultural nuances, including language and body language, enhances communication.

ii. Defining Boundaries and Economics:

Clear goals, decision rights, and economic expectations minimize conflict. Flexibility in refining agreements ensures alignment, and documenting terms fosters mutual understanding. Surprisingly, predefining exit terms can strengthen the partnership's longevity.

iii. Win-Win Mindset:

Fair negotiations that avoid exploiting weaknesses build sustainable relationships. Transparent, value-driven discussions create outcomes that leave all parties feeling valued, ensuring long-term success.

iv. ***Fairness and Transparency:***

Trust is established through openness and collaboration. Transparent communication on aligned areas helps resolve gaps, leaving room to focus on complex issues with mutual respect.

v. ***Solution-Oriented and Closure-Focused Approach:***

Resolving deadlocks requires positivity, perseverance, and face-to-face interactions. A solution-oriented mindset attracts creative energy, while urgency ensures steady progress.

vi. ***Role of the Negotiator:***

A trusted, empowered negotiator drives discussions with humility, energy, and transparency. Effective negotiators manage expectations, take quick decisions, and maintain a focus on deal closure while avoiding ego-driven conflicts.

vii. ***Regulatory Preparedness:***

Regulatory and third-party compliance are critical. Engaging regulators directly provides clarity, enabling smoother transactions.

viii. ***Step-by-Step Process:***

Starting with a term sheet or MOU simplifies the transition to a full agreement, reducing misunderstandings and streamlining negotiations.

ix. ***Monitoring the Process:***

Frequent communication and activity tracking ensure alignment and urgency, helping meet deadlines effectively.

x. ***Independent Perspective:***

External advisors bring objectivity, and seeking multiple opinions clarifies decisions while encouraging innovative solutions.

Ultimately, successful partnerships balance expectations, build trust, and emphasize the softer aspects of collaboration. Transparency, humility, and a focus on solutions drive timely closures and ensure mutually rewarding relationships.

Most of the principles and philosophies will apply to realignments amongst Families as they maintain harmony, and ensure brand and legacy and monetary wealth only enhances

11. Developing Owner's Mindset in Employees

Founders must hire people with an Owners Mindset as it drives passion, commitment to deliver best outcome for the individual and company. Founders must cultivate an owner's mindset within their teams.

Employees with this mindset see themselves as stakeholders, aligning deeply with the company's vision and goals. Their fearlessness, freedom of - speech action, thought, time and choice and ability to say NO fosters innovation, trust, and resilience. They embrace challenges, learn from failures, and prioritize long-term impact over short-term gains, treating company resources as their own.

To nurture this mindset, founders must lead by example, communicate transparently, and empower employees with freedom to act and take ownership. Recognizing contributions, encouraging risk-taking, and fostering a culture that treats failures as learning opportunities create psychological safety and accountability. Equity or profit-sharing can further align incentives with the company's success.

For existing team members, training can instil this mindset, ensuring a culture of ownership that attracts and retains top talent.

12. Clones Concept for the Founder

The concept of a clone is pivotal for founders as it allows them to multiply their energy and time, leading to outcomes that far exceed sum of individual efforts. A clone effectively serves as an extension of the founder, aligned with their aspirations, passion, values, philosophy, and purpose. This alignment ensures that the founder's vision is consistently executed, enabling them to move from a reactive mindset—constantly managing immediate tasks and challenges—to a proactive mindset, where they can focus on strategic leadership and long-term goals. This transition not only enhances the founder's ability to lead with clarity and purpose but also fosters a sense of balance, fulfilment, and well-being.

Importantly, a clone must possess a hunger to profitably scale the business while embracing diverse approaches to achieve shared goals. Diversity in thought and execution enriches the journey, bringing innovative solutions and complementing the founder's perspective.

Building such clones requires a deliberate process: identifying individuals who share the founder's values and vision, investing in their development, and empowering them to operate with autonomy while maintaining clear communication. By nurturing clones who resonate deeply with the founder's purpose and who can scale with agility, organizations can create a sustainable path to growth, harmony, and long-term success.

13. Founder takes all debits and passes credit to team

A founder who takes all debits (responsibility for risks, failures, and challenges) while passing credits (acknowledgment and rewards) to the team fosters an environment of fearlessness and trust. By shielding the team from blame and focusing on their contributions, the founder creates psychological safety, where team members feel secure to experiment, take calculated risks, and innovate without fear of repercussions. This encourages creative problem-solving and unlocks the team's full potential, leading to groundbreaking outcomes.

Such a culture stems from the founder's ability to lead by example, demonstrating humility, accountability, and a deep commitment to collective success. When the team sees their leader owning setbacks yet generously celebrating their contributions, they feel valued and motivated. Over time, this approach nurtures a sense of ownership and loyalty among team members, as they trust that their efforts will be recognized and their mistakes won't lead to punishment. The result is a highly engaged team that works with purpose and fearlessness, driving sustainable innovation and exceptional results.

14. Founders must be authentic while building values driven culture and laying foundation of future

Founders must be authentic while building a values-driven culture because their actions set the tone for the organization, creating trust and alignment among employees and stakeholders. Authenticity ensures that values are not merely aspirational but integral to decision-making and daily operations.

To truly build a values-driven culture, it is essential to walk the talk and internalize the values that define it, rather than letting them remain as mere statements displayed on the walls. This requires identifying and embracing values that can be genuinely practiced and are already aligned with one's habits and behaviors. By integrating these values into daily actions, they become a living part of the organization's culture, fostering authenticity and consistency

One powerful way to drive behavior in alignment with values is to assign weightage to compliance with these values in the appraisal system. For instance, organizations can allocate a percentage of performance evaluations (e.g., 20-40%) to assess how well employees embody core values like integrity, humility, agility, collaboration, customer focus, respect, trust etc. This can be implemented by defining measurable behaviors for each value, using 360-degree feedback from peers and managers, and incorporating these discussions into appraisals. By tying values directly to recognition and rewards, founders emphasize that living by the organization's principles is as critical as achieving results, fostering a culture where actions consistently reflect the company's ethos.

15. Power of Same Page in driving the organisation towards desired outcomes

Leaders must embrace and instil the philosophy of the Power of the Same Page by clearly defining organizational goals and explicitly articulating the meaning of each associated attribute, ensuring no room for individual interpretation based on personal beliefs or perceptions. This clarity eliminates ambiguity and ensures that every team member has a shared understanding of aspirations, values, operating philosophies, and key metrics. By doing so, the organization aligns its collective efforts and energy towards common objectives, fostering consistency in decision-making, seamless collaboration, and a unified culture. This precision not only prevents miscommunication but also empowers teams to act with confidence, driving outcomes that reflect the organization's vision and values

16. Measuring Return On Time Invested (ROTI™) from effort to outcomes

For founders, success isn't about long hours but about delivering outcomes. Return on Time Invested (ROTI™) emphasizes results over effort, ensuring time is spent on high-impact activities aligned with company goals.

Many founders mistake busyness for productivity, spending hours on tasks that feel rewarding but add little value. The lure of instant gratification often drives this behavior, as completing urgent, low-priority activities provides a false sense of accomplishment. However, this focus on immediate rewards frequently overshadows strategic goals, resulting in short-term fixes rather than sustainable progress.

Maximizing ROTI™ (Return on Time Invested) requires a careful balance between immediate wins and long-term goals. While it's easy to get excited about new ideas and jump straight into execution, a more effective approach is to evaluate their potential impact on driving the operating plan. Given the inherent constraints—be it capital, management bandwidth, or energy—it is crucial to prioritize ideas that promise the greatest impact and have a higher likelihood of closure over less significant initiatives.

Some of my founder friends have successfully implemented this framework, emphasizing strategic actions like building partnerships or strengthening leadership. These efforts often deliver far greater results than routine tasks. By consistently evaluating activities based on their contribution to overarching goals, founders can make smarter decisions, sharpen their focus, and significantly improve their chances of at least achieving if not exceeding the desired outcomes.

By setting clear goals, delegating non-critical tasks, and fostering a results-driven culture, founders can allocate their time to achieve meaningful outcomes and avoid NVAs (Non Value Added) activities. This approach enhances productivity, supports sustainable growth, and reduces burnout, making ROTI™ a mindset for long-term success.

I have recently trademarked ROTI™.

17. Founders should believe that the company's Existence is because of ecosystem, leading to long-term partnerships and win-win

Founders who recognize that they exist because of their ecosystem rather than believing the ecosystem exists because of them are more likely to succeed because this mindset fosters humility, empathy, and a collaborative approach. Such founders understand that businesses thrive in interconnected systems involving customers, employees, suppliers, investors, regulators and the broader community. By appreciating the role of each stakeholder, they build trust and respect, laying the foundation for sustainable relationships. This perspective enables them to see partners as extension of their business. This thought also ensures the company to see opportunities and challenges through the lens of others, fostering innovative solutions that create long-term value for all parties.

Empathy for stakeholders leads to a win-win approach, where success is shared and enduring. For example, founders who view employees as partners in growth invest in their well-being and development, ensuring loyalty and productivity. Similarly, by considering the needs of customers, they create products and services that genuinely solve problems, strengthening customer loyalty. This mindset also attracts investors who value integrity and long-term sustainability. Ultimately, businesses led by such founders are more resilient, as their focus on shared value creation enables them to adapt and thrive in changing environments, guided by trust and mutual respect.

18. Overcoming Complexity: Breaking Down Problems for Focused Execution

To tackle a complex problem effectively, we must break it down into smaller, manageable components, assign priorities, and establish clear timelines for each, while identifying interlinked dependencies. This structured approach helps clarify the desired outcomes and keeps the focus on week-by-week progress. By channeling efforts into executing the tasks at hand, we avoid the inefficiency of revisiting activities that are not yet meant to be executed.

This method also helps combat the wandering thoughts and uncertainty that often arise when facing complex challenges. The fear of the unknown can distract us, making it harder to concentrate and stay productive. A clear, step-by-step plan provides a sense of direction and control, enabling us to focus on actionable goals and build momentum. By staying aligned with this process, we cultivate confidence, reduce anxiety, and make consistent progress toward achieving the desired outcomes.

19. Guru Philosophy for current times - 10 % Parent, 70 % Dost (one on one) and 20% Child

In today's fast-changing world, the role of a guru must evolve to stay relevant and impactful. The modern guru in my view must operate as 10% parent, 70% dost, and 20% child, creating a relationship built on complete trust, mutual respect, and a heartfelt connection (DilSe connect). This balanced approach is essential for meaningful collaboration and mutual growth in dynamic times.

As a parent, the guru inspires, energizes, while ensuring the founder stays anchored to their values and purpose. They provide clarity of thought, unconditional support, and acting as a constant source of encouragement while being available 24/7.

This guidance strengthens the founder's moral compass and resilience, especially during challenging times.

As a dost, the guru functions as a trusted and candid advisor, embodying the wisdom of Vidur's. Recognizing that the founder, as the king knows their business best, the guru offers unbiased, thoughtful insights without overstepping boundaries or imposing control. while being clear of their role of being a Mantri and not the king The guru remains clear about their role as a Mantri—a counselor and guide—not the king, respecting the founder's ultimate authority and vision.

Finally, as a child, the guru approaches the relationship with curiosity and a willingness and hunger to learn. By valuing the founder's innovative thinking and real-world insights, the guru fosters a virtuous cycle of mutual growth.

This philosophy ensures the guru inspires, advises, and learns in equal measure, making a profound impact while adapting to the accelerating pace of change. It creates a partnership rooted in trust and respect, enabling both to navigate complexity with clarity, confidence, and purpose.

20. Non experts bring very different perspectives with no biases

Non-experts often bring immense value by offering fresh, unbiased perspectives. Unlike domain experts who may approach problems with established frameworks and assumptions, non-experts operate from a "clean slate," and first principles approach, allowing them to question norms and propose unconventional solutions. Their curiosity, combined with a lack of preconceptions, enables them to view challenges through a broader lens, often identifying overlooked opportunities or alternate pathways. This ability to think "outside the box" is especially valuable in complex or stagnant scenarios where traditional approaches fail to drive innovation or progress.

Moreover, non-experts contribute by sharing insights drawn from diverse experiences and beliefs, enriching the problem-solving process with cross-disciplinary ideas. They may also bring a unique capacity for pattern recognition and adaptability, unburdened by industry-specific constraints. Their openness fosters creative collaboration, helping teams break free from echo chambers and challenge groupthink. In essence, non-experts catalyze innovation by introducing fresh energy, diverse viewpoints, and a beginner's mindset that encourages exploration and discovery.

21. Founders should Reflect and Reach out for guidance as we often undervalue ourselves.

As founders, we often undervalue ourselves because we are deeply immersed in solving problems, focusing on what needs improvement, and constantly chasing the next milestone. This relentless pursuit can overshadow our recognition of the skills, resilience, and vision that have brought us this far.

To realize our strengths, we must step back regularly and reflect on our journey—acknowledging the challenges we've overcome, the value we've created, and the impact we've made. Engaging in constructive self-assessment, seeking honest feedback from trusted peers or mentors, and celebrating small wins can help shift our perspective.

Additionally, practicing gratitude for our own efforts and maintaining a journal to document achievements can reinforce a positive self-view.

By balancing humility with self-appreciation, we empower ourselves to grow and lead with greater confidence.

22. Balancing Personal Gains and Organizational Aspirations

As a species driven by survival, it's natural for us to be tempted by the allure of personal gains. This tendency becomes even more pronounced with newfound freedom, where individuals may unintentionally prioritize self-interest over broader goals. For founders, this dynamic is particularly significant. While rare, complete freedom can sometimes lead to decisions that prioritize personal gains at the expense of collective or organizational progress.

Understanding the distinction between personal gains and company aspirations is crucial to navigating this challenge. A focus on the company's purpose and goals fuels purposeful growth and aligns with long-term success, while prioritizing personal gains often results in short-sighted decisions that can undermine the very foundation of an enterprise. By recognizing this difference, founders can maintain their integrity, make thoughtful decisions, and build a sustainable path toward enduring progress.

Founders with aspirations grounded in purpose prioritize shared success over personal profit. They emphasize building trust, fostering lasting relationships, and creating a collaborative culture. These leaders understand that ethical and sustainable choices not only drive long-term credibility but also inspire innovation and growth within their teams.

The decisions founders make are pivotal. Greed may lure them toward shortcuts and quick wins at the cost of integrity, but aspiration steers them toward ethical, purpose-driven actions that foster trust and lasting success. Aspiration-driven leaders leave behind a legacy of innovation, credibility, and meaningful contributions to the ecosystem, shaping enterprises that benefit all stakeholders.

By aligning ambition with values, founders can avoid the hollow victories of greed and instead create enduring organizations. In this way, aspiration, grounded in purpose and gratitude, serves as a compass for a founder's journey toward meaningful success.

23. Risk Management Framework and Financial Discipline:

Many founders tend to focus heavily on product development or marketing, often overlooking the importance of a robust risk management framework and financial discipline. This could stem from their inherent optimism, which drives them to prioritize growth and innovation. However, while growth is essential, startups thrive on striking a balance between pursuing growth and exercising the prudence needed for survival.

Key pillars of financial discipline include closely monitoring unit economics, managing cash flow effectively, and adopting an asset-light approach to extend the runway and weather uncertainties. Growth cannot come at the cost of financial health; maintaining this balance ensures startups can scale sustainably while protecting themselves against potential downturns.

Founders must also focus on maximizing return on investment—not just in monetary terms but also with regard to their time and energy. Every decision must be evaluated for its potential impact and alignment with long-term goals, ensuring optimal allocation of these limited resources. Time spent on high-impact activities, energy directed towards critical priorities, and money invested wisely all contribute to extending the runway and driving strategic growth.

Proactive risk management is equally vital—this involves identifying potential risks, assessing their severity, and implementing mitigation strategies to ensure business continuity.

Balancing ambition with caution, while being mindful of ROI across money, time, and energy, allows startups to remain agile and resilient. By integrating visionary leadership, a value-driven culture, sharp execution, and disciplined financial management, startups can effectively navigate the tension between growth and prudence. This harmony between innovation, sustainability, and resource optimization is the key to achieving long-term success in today's competitive landscape.

24. Beyond Compliance: Spirit of Law and the Smell Test

In 2007, while exploring a major restructuring initiative, I met Ajay Bahl, founding partner of AZB & Partners, one of India's top law firms. During our discussion, he introduced two profound concepts: the Spirit of the Law and the Smell Test. These principles became pivotal in guiding my decision-making, particularly in areas where legal and ethical considerations intersect.

The Spirit of the Law focuses on interpreting laws in line with the intent behind their creation. Ajay explained that laws are not just rigid rules but frameworks designed to uphold specific values. By aligning decisions with this intent, one not only ensures legal compliance but also minimizes risks of litigation and fosters trust through fairness and transparency. This approach was particularly relevant during restructuring, helping ensure our decisions adhered to both legal requirements and ethical expectations.

The Smell Test, on the other hand, goes beyond legality. It asks whether a decision, even if legally permissible, "smells right" in terms of ethics, integrity, and public perception. Ajay emphasized that true leadership lies in making decisions that withstand scrutiny in the broader court of public opinion, not just the courtroom.

These concepts taught me the importance of balancing legal prudence with moral responsibility. By applying the Spirit of the Law and the Smell Test, I have consistently aimed to uphold values, build trust, and make decisions that create lasting impact.

25. Instant gratification and long term balance

Balancing instant gratification with long-term rewards is essential for building enduring institutions and leaving a meaningful legacy. Short-term wins, such as celebrating milestones or quick achievements, provide motivation, boost team morale, and maintain agility in dynamic environments. However, a focus on long-term thinking ensures sustainability, aligns actions with vision, and creates a lasting impact through ethical practices, innovation, and value-driven decision-making.

The key lies in aligning immediate rewards with broader goals, fostering a culture of learning and adaptability, and prioritizing institutional values. By combining short-term agility with a commitment to long-term purpose, institutions can create both immediate impact and a timeless legacy that resonates with future generations.

26. The Power of 'AND': Balancing Growth, Purpose, and Resilience in Startups

Moving from "OR" to "AND" unlocks a mindset of abundance, enabling founders to embrace complexity and find creative solutions that integrate seemingly opposing priorities. It fosters a culture of balance, resilience, and adaptability, where trade-offs are replaced with synergistic outcomes. This approach leads to better decision-making, as founders can pursue rapid growth AND sustainability, innovation AND market fit, or personal well-being AND business success.

The word "AND" plays a pivotal role in the success of startups, signifying balance, inclusion, and the ability to embrace multiple perspectives simultaneously. In business, it allows startups to focus on growth AND sustainability, ensuring long-term success, as seen in companies like Tesla, which scales production while staying committed to innovation. It bridges innovation AND execution, transforming groundbreaking ideas into reality, as exemplified by SpaceX. Startups can also strive for profitability AND purpose, creating meaningful impacts alongside financial success.

Balancing customer experience AND scalability is critical, as Airbnb has demonstrated by using technology to retain its customer-centric approach.

On the personal front, "AND" fosters work AND life balance, ensuring founders sustain productivity and happiness. It enables vision AND flexibility, allowing leaders to adapt while staying true to their goals, and promotes leadership AND learning, where confidence pairs with a learner's mindset. Balancing risk-taking AND prudence ensures stability amidst uncertainty, while confidence AND humility allow founders to lead effectively while staying open to growth.

Ultimately, "AND" encourages holistic thinking, aligning short-term actions with long-term objectives, fostering innovation, resilience, and sustainability across both business and personal spheres. "AND" mindset empowers startups to thrive in dynamic environments while staying true to their mission and values.

27. Log Kya Kahenge - don't hand over your life's remote to others

Focusing inwards and living consciously frees us from the trap of "log kya kahenge" (what will people say). When we seek external validation, we hand over control of our choices and emotions to others, driven by fear of criticism or rejection. This outward focus disconnects us from our true selves and values.

Living consciously means prioritizing inner peace and self-awareness over societal expectations. It's about asking, "What aligns with my growth and happiness?" rather than worrying about others' opinions.

Most judgments are fleeting, and true freedom comes from living authentically, guided by our own values, not external pressures.

28. The Harmony Framework: Aligning Soul, Heart, Brain, and Body for Purpose-Driven Success

Purpose = soul, core human values = heart, core business value = brain and core operating philosophy with respect to stakeholders = karma/body framework

This philosophy integrates purpose, values, intellect, and action into a cohesive framework. Purpose is the soul, the essence that gives direction and meaning, driving long-term vision and legacy. It ensures that decisions are rooted in a higher intent.

The heart embodies core human values, guiding actions with humility, respect, gratitude, empathy, integrity, compassion, and fairness etc. These values balance ambition with humanity, fostering trust and meaningful relationships.

The brain symbolizes core business values, representing logic, strategy, and innovation. It ensures alignment between purpose, values, and measurable outcomes through focused and sustainable operations.

Finally, the body, or karma, represents action, bringing purpose, values, and strategy to life. It reflects an operating philosophy that honors all stakeholders with accountability and transparency.

This framework harmonizes the soul's vision, the heart's empathy, the brain's strategy, and the body's execution, creating a balanced and holistic approach to life and work.

29. The power of acceptance: Lessons from Anekantavada

A few years ago, I had an insightful conversation with my friend Rakesh Bhutoria on the topic of acceptance. We discussed how people's beliefs, values, and experiences shape their unique perspectives, often leading to conflicting viewpoints. Rather than focusing on disagreements, we explored how these differences could serve as opportunities for deeper understanding.

Rakesh introduced me to the Jain concept of Anekantavada, which suggests that truth is multifaceted and that there is no single "right." Instead, multiple perspectives can coexist, each valid in its own context. This idea shifted my focus from judging perspectives as "right" or "wrong" to appreciating the coexistence of diverse truths.

This learning emphasized the power of acceptance—not as a compromise of values but as an acknowledgment of others' experiences and viewpoints. It fosters empathy and builds bridges of understanding, enabling harmony even amidst differences. The philosophy of Anekantavada has since influenced how I approach relationships and decisions, reminding me to embrace life's complexities with openness and respect.

30. The 4A Principle: A life-changing insight from Edwards Bono

In the early 2000s, I had the privilege of meeting Edward de Bono, the legendary author of Six Thinking Hats. Our conversation took place at the coffee shop of Hyatt Regency, Bhikaji Cama Place, New Delhi. Though it lasted just thirty minutes, the insights he shared have stayed with me ever since.

During our discussion, Edward introduced the "4A principle"—*Attention, Affection, Appreciation, and Achievement.* He explained how these four elements are essential to human motivation and fulfillment. Attention represents our need to be noticed and acknowledged, while Affection speaks to our longing for connection and care. Appreciation emphasizes the recognition of our efforts, and Achievement fulfills our drive to grow and accomplish goals.

This framework resonated deeply with me. Over the years, I have applied it to my personal and professional life, striving to give attention, show affection, express appreciation, and celebrate achievements—both mine and others'. These principles have brought greater depth to my relationships and a stronger sense of purpose.

Though brief, my meeting with Edward de Bono remains a profound memory. The simplicity and universality of the 4A principle continue to guide me, and I share this story with the hope that it inspires others to embrace these values in their lives.

Chapter 12

Winds of Wisdom: Personal Philosophies That Shaped My Journey

As I journeyed through the ever-evolving landscapes of ambition and achievement, it became clear that success is not just built on hard work or talent, but on the deeply rooted philosophies that guide us. These philosophies are the winds that steer our sails, providing direction amidst the uncharted waters of uncertainty and the strength to endure during turbulent times. They are the foundation upon which we build resilience, the compass that helps us navigate life's complexities, and the light that illuminates the path when the way forward seems unclear.

In this chapter, I reflect on the timeless principles and personal philosophies that have not only shaped my decisions but also defined the essence of who I am. These guiding ideals have anchored my values, inspired my aspirations, and influenced the relationships I've built along the way. They are not abstract concepts or distant ideals but living truths—principles that I have lived, breathed, and experienced firsthand. These philosophies have provided me with clarity in moments of doubt, courage in the face of adversity, and the humility to recognize that life's greatest achievements are often born out of the lessons learned in failure.

Through the highs and lows of my journey, these philosophies have served as both a shield and a beacon. They have empowered me to embrace growth, adapt to change, and pursue a vision far greater than myself. Whether it was making a difficult decision, choosing the path less traveled, or standing firm in my values, these principles have always been my steadfast companions.

The philosophies I am about to share are not just reflections of my beliefs but the very fabric of my journey. Each has left an indelible mark on me, shaping my perspective, informing my actions, and influencing the way I approach life, relationships, and work. They are drawn from experiences that tested my resolve, moments of introspection that deepened my understanding, and the wisdom imparted by the mentors, friends, and loved ones who have walked alongside me.

1. Moonshot driven by purpose and devotion attracts cosmic energy for a better world

A moonshot driven by a higher purpose, rooted in values and devotion, aligns individual effort with universal principles, attracting cosmic energy that amplifies its chances of success.

My belief is that God needs people on the ground to lighten its burden in delivering outcomes for humanity and nature. When our actions transcend self-interest and serve a greater good, they resonate deeply with the collective consciousness, drawing resources, opportunities, and like-minded individuals and energies to the cause.

This alignment of purpose, values, and devotion not only fuels resilience but also ensures authenticity and impact, leaving a lasting legacy. Such endeavors become transformative, uplifting individuals and communities while fostering trust and goodwill.

By acting as instruments of a higher power, we contribute meaningfully to a better world, creating outcomes that endure far beyond our own efforts.

2. Rin (debt) framework drives understanding of karmic debt to be repaid

The Rin (debt) framework deeply resonates with me, offering a profound understanding of the karmic obligations I aim to fulfill in my life. It highlights three key debts: Dev Rin, the debt to divine forces; Rishi Rin, the debt to sages and knowledge; and Pitr Rin, the debt to parents and ancestors. Each of these debts represents a vital aspect of my existence, and I strive to repay them through actions that honor these relationships.

Dev Rin reminds me to stay connected to divine energies and express gratitude for their grace. I honor this by performing puja regularly, often twice a day, which brings me spiritual harmony.

Rishi Rin, the debt to share knowledge, feels most significant to me. I see it as my responsibility to share my experiences and wisdom in ways that benefit others, whether through mentoring or meaningful conversations. This sense of duty drives me to ensure my knowledge contributes positively to those around me.

Pitr Rin is my debt to my parents and ancestors, which I repay by honoring their legacy. I take pride in doing this through my firm, Sarcha, named as a tribute to my parents and their values, which I carry forward through my work.

This framework gives my life purpose and clarity. While I strive to repay all three debts, Rishi Rin stands out for me as the most meaningful, pushing me to share and give back in ways that fulfill not just my karmic duty but also my deeper sense of service and connection to others.

3. Definition of wealth - leading to balanced life

To me, wealth is a multi-dimensional concept that goes far beyond material possessions.

It begins with health, both physical and mental, as the foundation for a fulfilling life.

Rishtey and Dosti (Relationships and friendships) are integral, as they provide opportunities for learning, sharing, and creating meaningful connections.

Legacy and reputation ensure that one's impact is authentic and rooted in values, leaving a lasting impression that inspires others.

Spiritual wealth fosters inner calmness and the ability to live in the present.

Intellectual wealth keeps one young and curious, constantly evolving.

Finally, money serves as a practical enabler, meeting daily needs and supporting other forms of wealth.

This holistic definition of wealth reflects my purpose and goals in life. By focusing on each dimension, I align my actions with a deeper sense of success and fulfillment. Health sustains energy, meaningful friendships enrich life, legacy grounds me in authenticity, spirituality nurtures peace and blissfulness, intellectual growth fuels creativity, and money ensures stability.

This approach isn't rigid—it's adaptable to individual needs, but it serves as a guiding framework for living a balanced and purposeful life.

4. Humility defined as Samta, Mamta, Kshama, Namrata - building deeper relationships and dosti

This philosophy took root during my meeting with Brijmohan Ji on January 3, 2010, when I visited him to extend New Year's wishes. During our conversation, I expressed my admiration, telling him, "You are a symbol of humility." To my surprise, he humbly replied that he had only recently understood the true essence of humility through a discourse by Swami Ji a few days earlier. Brijmohan Ji, an embodiment of humility himself, then wrote down four profound words—Samta, Mamta, Kshama, Namrata—on a piece of paper and handed it to me. Inspired by his gesture and these timeless words, I began reflecting on them deeply, seeking to define and internalize their meaning in my own life

I have since been using it in my morning prayers.

Humility, when defined as a harmonious blend of Samta(equanimity), Mamta (affection, love and compassion), Kshmata (respect for who you are and your capabilities), and Namrata (speaking softly), becomes the foundation for building meaningful and enduring dosti (friendship).

Samta ensures that relationships remain balanced and free from ego or judgment, fostering mutual respect and acceptance.

Mamta brings warmth and care, nurturing bonds with genuine affection and selflessness.

Kshmata reflects a deep appreciation for the other person's unique qualities and abilities, reinforcing trust and admiration.

Namrata, with its emphasis on gentle and thoughtful communication, creates an atmosphere of emotional safety and openness.

Together, these qualities shape friendships that are profound, respectful, and filled with compassion.

5. Swasth, Vyast and Mast approach to channelise energy in right direction

Swasth (Health), Vyast (Engagement), and Mast (Joy) are three key ingredients that help channel our energy positively and create a balanced, fulfilling life.

Swasth refers to physical and mental well-being, as a healthy body and mind are the foundation for sustained energy and focus.

Vyast signifies purposeful engagement or being productively occupied, ensuring that our time and efforts are directed towards meaningful pursuits rather than distractions.

Mast embodies a joyful and contented state of mind, fostering optimism and gratitude, which act as catalysts for resilience and creativity.

Together, these attributes form a powerful triad: health provides the strength, engagement gives direction, and joy sustains motivation, enabling us to live a life of positive impact and inner peace.

This philosophy is key learning from my guru Deep Prakash Bhatt and I expanded these into defining as follows and practice it in my morning prayers -

Swasth – Strive to live for 150 years with robust health and resilience, embodying the strength of lakkad hazam, pathar hazam. Sadbudhi or vivek bana rahe (Prioritize physical and mental well-being to sustain a vibrant, enduring life)

Vyast – Cultivate consistency of will and thought, singleness of purpose, and unwavering resolve in facing life's situations and self-control. (Practice self-control and discipline to channel your energy effectively)

Mast – Embrace the present moment fully. Let go of worries about the past and anxieties about the future. If the present is a continuum, staying happy now leaves no space for unhappiness. empty mind, forgiving and forgetting. (Allows peace and joy to flow naturally)

6. **Jo mera hai wo koi le nahi sakta and jo mera nahi hai wo koi de nahin sakta**

This philosophy reflects a profound understanding of contentment, self-awareness, and the nature of destiny. It helps in reinforcing surrender & acceptance.

It teaches us that what truly belongs to us—be it opportunities, relationships, or outcomes—will find its way into our lives, and no external force can take it away. Conversely, what is not inherently ours cannot be bestowed upon us by anyone.

It invites us to embrace life with faith and detachment, focusing on our efforts while surrendering to the larger flow of the universe.

By internalizing this perspective, we can cultivate inner peace, reduce desires, and trust in the fairness of life's unfolding.

7. **Go for higher Gratitude to Desire ratio- leads to inner peace**

The balance between gratitude and desire can be thought of as a ratio that defines our state of mind—whether we feel calm or restless.

A higher gratitude-to-desire ratio signifies a mindset anchored in appreciation, where we value what we have over what we lack. Gratitude, in this context, acts as a stabilizer, grounding us in the present and fostering inner peace. It reduces the noise of constant striving and helps us feel content and fulfilled.

Conversely, a higher desire-to-gratitude ratio reflects a state dominated by longing and dissatisfaction. While desires can inspire ambition and progress, an overwhelming focus on what is missing creates restlessness, anxiety, and a sense of never being "enough." This imbalance often pulls us into a cycle of chasing goals that rarely bring lasting satisfaction.

The ratio serves as a compass for our emotional state: the closer it is to gratitude, the more calm and centered we feel. A shift toward desire tilts us toward restlessness. To manage this balance, we can consciously cultivate gratitude by reflecting on our blessings, achievements, and the meaningful relationships in our lives. When desires are grounded in gratitude and aligned with our values, they can fuel purposeful action without disrupting our peace.

Ultimately, striving for a gratitude-to-desire ratio that leans toward gratitude can lead to a life of greater fulfillment and serenity.

8. Gratitude and Sabr for blissful happiness

Gratitude and Sabr (patience) are twin virtues that create a foundation for meaningful and blissful happiness.

Gratitude shifts our focus from what we lack to what we have, fostering a sense of contentment and appreciation for life's blessings. It rewires our mindset to celebrate even the smallest joys, making us more resilient in facing challenges. Sabr, on the other hand, teaches us to endure difficulties with grace, recognizing that struggles are temporary and often lead to growth.

Together, gratitude and patience create a powerful balance—gratitude fills our hearts with bliss and peace in the present, while sabr prepares us for a better tomorrow. This combination nurtures an inner strength that transcends fleeting pleasures, paving the way for a deeply fulfilling, harmonious, and blissful life.

9. Dil Se connect - building long term bonds in any relationship

In any relationship, Dil Se Connect fosters authenticity and trust, creating a strong foundation for lasting connections. Bonds formed through the heart go beyond superficial interactions, focusing on empathy and shared values, which are essential for long-term sustenance.

i. The Heart as a Guide

When exploring relationships, the heart often senses alignment that the brain may overlook. While the brain analyzes logic and tangible benefits, the heart evaluates trust, values, and emotional connection. If your heart encourages you to proceed, even when the brain hesitates, it may indicate potential for a meaningful bond.

ii. Balancing Heart and Mind

The brain focuses on measurable aspects, while the heart seeks alignment in vision and intentions. When they conflict, reflecting on the heart's instincts can lead to deeper, more fulfilling relationships. Trusting the heart often opens doors to connections that enrich your journey in unforeseen ways.

iii. Enduring Relationships

Bonds formed with Dil Se Connect are transformative, thriving on trust and care. These connections endure challenges and grow stronger over time, as they are nurtured by mutual respect and emotional integrity.

Letting the heart guide relationships ensures authenticity, creating bonds that are meaningful, fulfilling, and built to last.

10. Dil Se investing using framework of Biology, Chemistry, Physics and Maths

As an angel investor in the pre-Series A stage, my Dil Se investing philosophy blends Biology, Chemistry, Physics, and Maths to assess both the business and the founders.

Biology (60%) is central, focusing on the founder's DNA—their values, experiences, and purpose. By connecting emotionally, I evaluate their alignment with my values and their team's complementary skills. These connections often lead to shared trust and understanding.

Chemistry validates this by assessing how others perceive the founder—their strengths, weaknesses, and ability to build relationships and inspire confidence.

Physics involves questioning the venture's assumptions using first principles, ensuring it's built on a solid foundation.

Maths checks the cash flows and commercials, ensuring financial viability while remaining secondary to the human aspects.

Post-investment, I monitor energy levels of the founders and a positive interaction is enough for me to gauge the sense of the status of the firm. In case they need any bouncing of ideas, I spend time sharing my thoughts and perspectives to solve the issues

11. Respect yourself first to earn respect from others

Respecting yourself is the foundation of earning respect from others.

When you value yourself—your time, boundaries, and principles—you project confidence and integrity. Self-respect comes from living in alignment with your values, being honest with yourself, and acknowledging your worth without seeking external validation.

When you embody self-respect, it becomes a mirror that invites mutual respect in relationships, creating a cycle of positivity and trust.

12. Harnessing Power of Subconscious mind - to achieve impossible

The power of the subconscious mind lies in its ability to shape our reality by turning thoughts, beliefs, and emotions into actions and outcomes.

It operates like a vast reservoir of potential, influencing our decisions and behaviors in ways that often bypass conscious awareness.

When harnessed effectively, the subconscious mind can help achieve seemingly impossible goals by aligning our inner thoughts with our outer actions, fostering creativity, perseverance, and resilience. By feeding it positive and clear intentions, it becomes a powerful ally in breaking through limitations.

To leverage this power, focus on positive affirmations, clear visualization of success, and consistent belief in achieving your goals. Focus on gratitude for what you have and optimism for the future. Eliminate negative self-talk and doubts, and consciously choose empowering thoughts and language.

Avoid practices like "touch wood," which often stems from fear or superstition and implies the possibility of loss—this can subtly reinforce negative outcomes, similarly I do not watch live debates or breaking news on TV as it only drives negativity. I have been in an environment in my city where using abusive words/slangs is a part of daily conversation. However, I made a conscious decision to harness my mind to not use abusing language and voila, it has been more than 20 years since I have used any single such word. That is the power of subconscious mind.

By creating a supportive mental environment, the subconscious mind becomes a relentless force in turning dreams into reality

13. Karma centred living: embracing the journey and learning from the outcomes

This philosophy emphasizes focusing on effort over outcome, finding joy in the journey rather than being overly attached to results. While goals provide direction, the process of working towards them is where true growth and satisfaction lie. Results are often influenced by external factors beyond our control, and obsessing over them can lead to stress and disappointment.

The key is to focus on what is within one's control—delivering the best effort with sincerity and purpose. This approach aligns with the concept of karma, where the emphasis is on performing one's duties without attachment to the fruits of the labor. By doing so, one remains resilient and open to learning from every outcome, whether it meets, exceeds, or falls short of expectations.

Viewing each result as a learning opportunity fosters a growth mindset and keeps one centered in the present. Staying in the "now" avoids distractions from past regrets or future anxieties, enabling clarity and adaptability. This mindset not only reduces stress but also helps maintain emotional equilibrium, even in challenging circumstances.

Ultimately, this philosophy encourages us to stay present, adapt to change, and trust the journey. By focusing on the process, we can navigate life's uncertainties with grace, celebrate

14. Be aware that 5 units of Positive energy is required in certain situations to neutralise 1 unit of negativity

A positive mindset is crucial to neutralize negative energy because negativity has a disproportionate impact on our thoughts, emotions, and decisions. According to the Gottman Ratio, it takes at least five positive interactions to counterbalance one negative interaction, demonstrating how much more powerful negativity can be in shaping outcomes. This principle can be extended to various aspects of life, including personal relationships, workplace dynamics, and financial decisions. Negativity tends to drain mental energy, stifle creativity, and reduce productivity. When negativity dominates, it also affects health—leading to stress, anxiety, or even physical ailments.

For example, in financial terms, if the price of a share drops by 80%, you would need a 5x gain (500%) just to return to the original value. This illustrates the asymmetry of recovery: losses require far more effort and positivity to overcome than maintaining an even or upward trajectory. Similarly, a negative event or setback in life can create a significant dent in morale and confidence, making it essential to cultivate a robust positive mindset. Positivity not only neutralizes negativity but also creates the momentum needed for recovery, allowing creativity and productivity to flourish.

To achieve this, awareness is key. Practicing gratitude, focusing on solutions rather than problems, and surrounding oneself with supportive environments are ways to counterbalance negativity. Without intentional efforts to generate positivity, the drag of negativity can spiral, compromising not just outcomes but also emotional well-being and long-term growth. Understanding the effort required to overcome negativity highlights the importance of minimizing it wherever possible and proactively nurturing positivity as a daily practice.

I have been able to stay close to the center by being aware and practicing gratitude. progress, and build long-term resilience, regardless of the outcome.

15. Wisdom can come from the youngest teachers - My 4 years old grandson Rihaan's leadership skills -

Leadership often seems tied to experience, yet my 4-year-old grandson naturally exhibits traits that define great leaders. His ability to live in the moment, enjoying life without attachment to outcomes, mirrors the resilience of effective leaders. When he stumbles, he takes ownership, learns from his mistakes, and moves forward with fearless enthusiasm—an essential quality for navigating challenges.

Humility shines in his actions, whether he's apologizing for mistakes or respecting elders. These values-driven behaviors remind us that great leaders balance confidence with humility and foster trust and inclusion. His curiosity and creativity, paired with agility and adaptability, reflect traits vital for thriving in a fast-changing world. Even his habit of keeping his belongings organized demonstrates the discipline leaders need to achieve their goals.

What stands out most is his authenticity. His hearty laugh and unfiltered emotions highlight the power of vulnerability, helping leaders connect deeply with others. His natural charisma draws people toward him, much like a great leader who inspires teams. And, like any leader, he leans on all of us as his "Chief of Staff".

In his simplicity, my grandson offers profound leadership lessons: resilience, humility, creativity, authenticity, and connection. Interestingly, I treat him as a dost, he calls my wife by her first name and believes my daughter Ishani is his buddy. It's a reminder that leadership is as much about being as it is about doing—and wisdom often comes from the youngest teachers.

16. Dosti Banana (Building Bonds of Friendship)

Twenty years ago, when a friend asked me, "What's your role in the company?" I instantly replied, "Dosti Banana" (building bonds of friendships). At first, it felt like an offhand answer, but when I reflected, I realized it captured who I am. I've always seen relationships as opportunities to connect with sincerity and compassion, whether at work or in life.

For me, building friendships is about more than being friendly—it's about trust, understanding, and mutual respect. It's also about genuinely celebrating my friends' successes as if they were my own and being a true partner in their joys and sorrows. This deeper connection has strengthened the bonds I've created, making them more meaningful and lasting.

Over the years, this simple philosophy has shaped my journey, helping me foster deep, lasting relationships that span decades. These friendships have been the foundation of partnerships, shared successes, and personal growth.

There is no age for dosti. My father-in-law became my dost at the age of 85, even though our relationship had existed for years before. Every evening around 9, we would eagerly wait for our daily 5–10 minutes of conversation, a ritual that became a cherished part of our lives. He passed away a couple of years ago, and though he's no longer here, I often find myself missing those heartfelt conversations and the bond we shared. Looking back, "Dosti Banana" isn't just something I do—it's who I am. It's a belief that relationships thrive on care, empathy, and shared experiences. Living by this philosophy has brought immense meaning and fulfillment to my life, and it's one I'll continue to uphold, creating connections that truly matter.

17. The Durga Maa - Lord Ganesh - Saraswati Maa - Lakshmi Maa (The Supreme Power) Framework: A cosmic approach to guided wisdom

When founders or individuals seek my guidance, they are often surprised by the depth and clarity of my questions or the solutions I propose. I attribute this not to my individual capacity but to a framework inspired by the divine energies of Durga Maa, Lord Ganesh, Saraswati Maa, and Lakshmi Maa. In this process, I see myself as a channel for universal wisdom rather than its source.

Durga Maa, embodying strength and determination, inspires thoughts in binary clarity—zeroes and ones—representing the foundation of structured and decisive thinking. These thoughts are then processed by Lord Ganesh, the harbinger of wisdom and intellect, who computes and organizes them into actionable insights. Saraswati Maa, the goddess of knowledge and expression, articulates these thoughts in a way that resonates and adds value to the conversation. All of this happens under the graceful management of Lakshmi Maa, who ensures that this exchange brings not just clarity and solutions but also harmony and abundance to everyone involved.

This framework allows me to stay fully present and in the "now" during these conversations, removing ego from the process. The guidance I provide is not a reflection of my persona as Rohit but an outcome of cosmic energy and universal alignment working through me. This mindset enables me to approach each interaction with humility, gratitude, and a sense of higher purpose, creating a space where genuine learning and value creation can occur.

18. Only sins are acquired during our life journey and that's all that belongs to me, as all gunas (virtues) are given at birth

I believe that all virtues (gunas) are given to me at birth, while sins are the only things I acquire during my life journey. These sins—my mistakes, shortcomings, and negative actions—are entirely self-acquired and are the only things that truly belong to me. When I offer prayers, I do so with the awareness that I can only offer what is mine: my sins.

By offering my sins in prayer, I acknowledge my imperfections and surrender them to a higher power. This act is not just about seeking forgiveness but about freeing myself from the burden of my mistakes and opening the door to transformation and growth. It is a reminder of my accountability for my actions and a practice of humility, allowing me to come closer to my true nature, which is inherently virtuous.

This perspective keeps me grounded and helps me stay aware of my actions, inspiring me to strive for a life that reflects the virtues I was gifted with at birth. It is through this surrender and self-awareness that I seek to purify my journey and grow spiritually.

19. Bridging hierarchy Gaps

When I was entrusted with turning around a struggling call center where average age was just 23. I knew success required more than operational fixes—it needed trust, respect, and camaraderie. I decided to see myself as a dost (friend) to everyone, fostering closeness across all levels.

One day, while having chai at a roadside dhaba with some of the team members, a customer service representative asked, "How can you be our dost when you are the president of the company ?"

I replied, "Titles like President or CSR are just labels. At our core, we're all human—we face challenges, seek connection, and enjoy life. The only difference is our badges. Because we are equals, we can absolutely be dosts."

This conversation reinforced my belief that respect and humility are vital. Seeing myself as a dost helped create a culture of openness and collaboration, where people felt valued and empowered. This principle has stayed with me, guiding my leadership approach throughout my career.

20. You can write your own destiny empowered by gratitude, faith, purpose and resilience

"Write Your Own Destiny" is a powerful call to action, rooted in gratitude, driven by purpose, strengthened by faith in God and oneself, and sustained by resilience. It emphasizes that life's challenges are stepping stones to growth, and with gratitude, one can find peace and abundance in every moment. Purpose serves as the guiding compass, faith provides unwavering strength in the face of uncertainty, and resilience ensures the ability to rise stronger after every setback.

Together, these principles empower individuals to take ownership of their journey, craft meaningful lives, and leave a legacy of inspiration and impact.

21. Definition of Happiness

When my late friend Amit Chaturvedi asked me to define happiness, my instinctive response was "an empty mind." On reflection, I realized it reflects the state of being fully present—free from past regrets and future worries. In this state, happiness emerges naturally, alongside a sense of calm and balance.

An "empty mind" is not passive; it promotes learning, curiosity, and creativity. By being in the now, we become open to new ideas and experiences, unclouded by distractions. This presence reduces emotional ups and downs, allowing for quicker recovery from negativity and a steady sense of inner peace.

Detachment is also key—not apathy, but freedom from overattachment to outcomes. It's about embracing life as it flows, finding joy in the process rather than the results. This perspective fosters resilience and contentment, unlocking both peace and growth. To me, happiness is living in the present, with gratitude, mindfulness, and the openness to learn and create.

22. Beyond Valuations: Measuring Success in Lives, Not Dollars

I was a speaker at a conference and moderator asked me a question what is the likely highest valuation a startup from India will achieve in ten years

When the moderator asked me about the highest valuation an Indian startup might achieve in ten years, my instant response was "8 billion lives." At that moment, I realized how deeply I'm driven by the idea of creating a positive impact and spreading happiness across humanity. While Prashant Tandon CEO of TATA 1mg spoke about a trillion-dollar valuation, my perspective naturally leaned toward the value of human lives—something far beyond monetary measures. The moderator insisted that I say a number, I hesitantly said you can write any number from 10 billion to one trillion

I was curious why this instant response was 8 billion lives, as this equals the number of people on the planet. But when I sought guidance from Durga Maa, the answer came: life is far more expansive than humanity, and 8 billion may represent less than 10% of all living beings. This revelation humbled me and reinforced my belief that there is so much more to Mother

Nature than we often acknowledge. It was a reminder of my responsibility to contribute meaningfully to this vast web of existence through my interactions with entrepreneurs

My response reflects my values—seeing wealth not just in financial terms but in the positive impact we can create for people, nature, and the interconnected systems that sustain us. It also reaffirmed my purpose: to do even more than I am currently doing and to approach life and work with a deeper sense of gratitude and responsibility. For me, true value lies in spreading happiness and preserving the harmony of the world around us.

23. Forgive and Forget: unlocking the next level of my journey of Samarpan (surrender)

Meeting my long-time guru few months ago, Mr. Arun Maira—former member of the Planning Commission—was a deeply transformative moment. It was my first meeting with him since moving on from the Hero Group, and I was eager to share my journey. As I narrated my story with pride and passion, I spoke about the joys and challenges I had faced, and the guiding principles of samarpan (surrender), gratitude, and sabr (patience) that had shaped my path.

Mr. Maira listened with his characteristic wisdom and warmth. While he appreciated the positivity in my story, he gently pointed out something I hadn't fully acknowledged: there were lingering emotions tied to certain people from my past that I hadn't forgiven or fully let go of. His observation struck a chord. I realized he was right—despite my growth, I was still carrying unresolved feelings.

Immediately after our meeting, I reflected deeply on his words. I sought forgiveness from those individuals in my heart and sent them my blessings. In doing so, I felt an immense sense of relief, as though a heavy, invisible weight had been lifted. This simple yet powerful act helped me truly let go and brought me to a deeper level of samarpan.

That meeting with Mr. Maira reminded me of the power of forgiveness—not just as a gift to others, but as a profound liberation for myself. It marked a new milestone in my journey of surrender, allowing me to move forward with an even lighter and freer spirit.

24. Lessons in humility and warmth from Global leaders - Nikolaus Von Bomhard and Paul Pollman

In 2008, during discussions for a potential joint venture between Hero Group and Munich Re, I had the privilege of meeting Nikolaus von Bomhard, then CEO of Munich Re. His humility and simplicity stood out, creating a lasting impression. Though the venture was dissolved in 2009, his ability to treat every interaction with respect, regardless of outcomes, left me inspired.

In 2013, I briefly interacted with Paul Polman, then CEO of Unilever, during a Formula 1 event in Noida, India. Despite the informal setting, Mr. Polman's warmth and genuine interest made our 30-minute conversation memorable. He demonstrated how even short exchanges can leave a lasting impact when approached with authenticity.

Over the years, both leaders have consistently maintained contact—Dr. Bomhard through emails and Mr. Polman via WhatsApp—responding promptly despite their demanding schedules. On the rare occasion Dr. Bomhard took longer, he sent an apology for the delay, further highlighting his thoughtfulness.

These interactions have taught me invaluable lessons: humility, respect, and responsiveness are hallmarks of true leadership. Their actions show that great leaders connect as individuals, valuing people over positions, and leaving an enduring impact through their authenticity and grace.

25. Philosophy of Personal balance sheet - A holistic view of wealth and accountability

The personal balance sheet is a tool for self-reflection, capturing life's wealth, responsibilities, and inner strength. It aligns actions with values, fostering a purposeful existence.

Assets reflect true wealth beyond material possessions. Health is the foundation of vitality, while relationships (Rishtey and Dosti) bring emotional richness. Legacy and reputation ensure a lasting impact through values and authenticity. Spiritual wealth provides inner peace and resilience, and intellectual growth fosters curiosity and lifelong learning. Financial stability supports freedom and the ability to fulfill responsibilities.

Liabilities represent duties and obligations. Financial debt requires accountability, while *Dev Rin* (debt to divine forces) is fulfilled through gratitude and prayer. *Rishi Rin* calls for sharing knowledge to honor sages, and *Pitr Rin* involves upholding parents' values and legacy.

Reserves and surplus symbolize inner strength. Durga Maa's blessings offer protection, while surplus wisdom from life's experiences provides clarity and guidance.

This framework nurtures gratitude and accountability, promoting harmony and fulfillment by balancing wealth, responsibilities, and inner strength.

26. Clear Definition of Purpose minimises friction both in Personal and Professional life

A clearly defined purpose acts as a guiding compass, minimizing friction in both personal and professional life by aligning actions, decisions, and priorities with a meaningful direction. It reduces ambiguity, eliminates distractions, and fosters clarity, enabling individuals to focus their energy on what truly matters.

In personal life, it strengthens relationships and builds inner peace by creating a sense of fulfillment. Professionally, it enhances productivity, teamwork, and resilience by providing a shared vision and motivating people to overcome challenges.

With purpose as a foundation, conflicts and indecision diminish, leaving room for growth, harmony, and sustained progress.

27. Definition of Spirituality

- *Humility:* Recognizing our place in the larger scheme of existence and approaching life with modesty and openness.
- *Acceptance:* Embracing life as it is, without resistance or judgment, and finding peace in the present moment.
- *Gratitude:* Acknowledging and appreciating the blessings and lessons life offers, big or small.
- *Love:* Unconditional care and compassion that connects us with others and the world around us.
- *Empathy:* Understanding and sharing the feelings of others, fostering connection and kindness.

Spirituality, for me, is the harmonious integration of humility, acceptance, gratitude, love, and empathy. It is about living with awareness, embracing the present, and connecting deeply with oneself and others. This perspective guides my actions and fuels a sense of purpose, enabling me to contribute meaningfully to the world around me.

28. The Essence of a Dost: Building Bonds Beyond Time

A dost is not just a friend but someone who fosters enduring and meaningful relationships (dosti) built on a foundation of shared values, mutual trust, and respect. This connection transcends transactional interactions and evolves into a lifelong bond.

i. ***Alignment of Values and Chemistry***

At the heart of a true dost relationship is a complete alignment of values. This ensures that both parties operate from the same ethical and emotional foundation. Chemistry—the natural ease and connection between individuals—strengthens this alignment, making interactions effortless and authentic.

ii. ***Trust and Respect***

The pillars of any strong bond, trust and respect, enable the relationship to flourish. Trust comes from reliability and consistency, while respect acknowledges each other's unique contributions and perspectives. Together, they create an environment of psychological safety and mutual admiration.

iii. ***Open and Transparent Communication***

A dost relationship thrives on honesty and vulnerability. Open communication allows for the free flow of thoughts, ideas, and feedback, while transparency ensures there are no hidden agendas. This openness eliminates misunderstandings and fosters deeper connections.

iv. ***Learning and Deepening the Bond***

A dost relationship values continuous growth—both individually and collectively. By engaging in meaningful experiences, sharing insights, and navigating challenges together, the bond deepens over time. Each interaction becomes an opportunity to strengthen the connection and enrich the relationship.

By nurturing these principles, a dost ensures that the relationship is not only enduring but also fulfilling for everyone involved. It's a connection that grows stronger with time, bringing meaning, joy, and shared success.

29. Gratitude to Maa Durga, Gods and Goddesses, (The Higher Power/The Supreme Power) and my parents: I practice thankfulness and affirmations in my meditation

I consciously practice gratitude and positive affirmations by thanking Maa Durga, parents and the divine energies for the many blessings and attributes I already possess. This daily practice anchors me in the present and fills my heart with humility and positivity.

Here's what I express my gratitude for:

Thanks for who I am and what I have.

Thanks for making me smile all the time.

Thanks for your blessings and help me live in the now.

Thanks for the gift of a wonderful, happy, and healthy family, friends, teams, gurus, and the amazing people around me.

Thank you for making me caring, loving, happy, healthy, wealthy and wise.

Thank you for giving me belief in myself and my dreams, the ability to count my blessings, and the unwavering faith to stay confident.

Thank you for helping me make a huge impact in lives of others.

Thank you for making me fearless and granting me the freedom of speech, action, and thought.

Thanks for giving me the power to say NO.

Thanks for giving mc thc wisdom to bc fair and transparent.

Thanks for being born in one of the best times in the world.

Thank you for teaching me the power of acceptance and the grace to go with the flow.

Thank you for making me imaginative and creative, energetic and hardworking, disciplined and focused. perseverance and wisdom, passionate and courageous, flexibility and inflexibility, agility, obsession and resolve, the dedication of Riyaz (practice) and Tapasya (penance), a sense of urgency and the grace of tolerance. Thank You for instilling the value of trust in people, teaching me to share the fruits of growth, and enabling me to deliver excellence and remarkable outcomes while staying true to my values and higher purpose.

Lastly, I thank you for accepting my sins—Kaam (Desire), Krodh (anger), Lobh (Greed), Moh (Attachment), Maya (Illusion), Ahankar (Ego), Irshya (Envy), Bhay (Fear), Bhookh (Hunger), Alasya (Laziness), Amanavta (Inhumanity), Anyay (Injustice), Ghrina (Hatred), and Jhoot (Falsehood).

This daily acknowledgment not only deepens my connection with the divine but also helps me embrace my imperfections and strive for a better self. It's my way of aligning with gratitude, positivity, and the grace of the divine.

30. Early morning Affirmations

I normally wake up for a few minutes between 3.30-5.30 am, this is the most purest time, I do my prayers for 5 minutes which is as under:

Hey Durga Maa aapne itni khusiyan di kamaal hi kar diya, what a wonderful day, giving me unwavering faith and stay confident.

Here are the words which all have a deep meaning that I say in the morning more as a realisation and also positive affirmations:

- Samarpan, Prerna, Dhairya, Urja
- Blessings, Gratitude, Forgiveness, Acceptance, Love
- Durga ki Razaa, Aazmaish, Apni dua mein rakhna, Shukrana, Sabr
- Shraddha, Tyag, Vishwas, Rin, Niswarth
- Fairness, Acceptance, Imagination, Trust and Humility

I seek from Durga Maa:

- Forgive me, bless me, love me, thank you
- Mere ko Swasth, Vyasth and Mast Rakhna
- Mere ko sadbudhi dena aur sadmarg dikhana

31. Bhabha Bhala, Bhool, Bhana: A Daily Prayer of Acceptance

The phrase Bhabha Bhala, Bhool, Bhana from Gurbani is a cornerstone of my daily prayers and a guiding philosophy in my life. It encapsulates the essence of spiritual wisdom: to accept God's will (Bhana) with trust and faith, to believe that everything ultimately happens for the greater good (Bhala), and to humbly acknowledge and seek forgiveness for our mistakes (Bhool).

Reciting this as part of my daily prayers instills a sense of humility, resilience, and gratitude, reminding me to embrace life's challenges and blessings as part of a divine plan. It is a constant source of strength and a reminder to live with grace, faith, and surrender to the Almighty's infinite wisdom.

My Parting thoughts as the journey continues

As I conclude this labor of love, I carry the hope that these words will spark curiosity, evoke gratitude, and inspire resilience in the hearts of those who read them—just as my journey has shaped and inspired me. My story, I believe, is not very different from yours. We all share the drive to deliver on our potential, fueled by purpose and an obsession to make a significant positive impact on millions of lives. Staying focused on core human and business values is what brings meaning and authenticity to this journey.

The stories I have shared are not universal truths but reflections of my lifelong interactions and experiences. My hope is that they encourage you to think deeply about what you want to become and why. These philosophies apply universally to leaders of both small enterprises and large organizations. Anchored in values, driven by meaningful contributions, and focused on inclusive growth, leadership becomes about uplifting others and honoring the world we share.

Although I discovered my purpose at 61, this book marks a milestone in my journey at 66. It has been nothing short of embarking on a second startup. Just as a 21-year-old, full of energy and optimism, explores the unknown with enthusiasm, I approached this endeavor as a student of philosophy, psychology, and digital technologies. It is a testament to the belief that age is but a number and that the spirit of curiosity and the drive to create something meaningful can be evergreen. This project has rekindled in me the excitement of creation, the joy of learning, and the hope of contributing to a better world.

I encourage you to start your journey of discovery sooner by exploring the Ikigai framework. This powerful tool helps you integrate four essential elements: what you love and why, what the world needs and why, what you're good at and why, and what you can be rewarded for and why. Once you discover your purpose, define your values and seek a true Guru who resonates with you and connects dil se. A Guru will guide you to live a life of purpose, joy, and fulfillment.

My purpose is deeply rooted in a devotion to impacting lives and nurturing Mother Nature. Guided by the timeless principles of Values, Value, and Value Creation, I strive to respect every stakeholder as an extension of myself and my enterprise, fostering harmony, shared prosperity, and sustainable growth. These values have been my guiding light as I wrote this book, and they will continue to shape my actions as I pursue my dream of positively impacting at least a million lives, directly or indirectly, over the next 7-10 years.

Some of you may have a question mark about the audacity of this dream, but I believe in its power and will continue to thrive toward this goal with unwavering determination. Writing this book has been one of the most fulfilling experiences of my life, an opportunity to reflect, learn, and share. It has been a journey filled with moments of introspection, gratitude, and the joy of storytelling—much like a startup navigating through challenges and triumphs.

Your contribution to making this dream a reality is invaluable. As you carry forward the lessons, reflections, and stories shared in this book, I humbly ask for your blessings and best wishes. Every kind thought, every word of encouragement, and every act inspired by this book strengthens my resolve and brings us closer to spreading happiness, purpose, and positivity across the world.

This book is not just my story—it is a shared journey. It is a testament to the strength of human connection, the beauty of purpose, and the boundless potential we all have to create meaningful impact. Thank you for being a part of this journey and for allowing me to be a part of yours. Together, let us nurture a world filled with joy, gratitude, and the spirit of giving. From the depths of my heart, I send you my love, my prayers, and my gratitude. May you always thrive and find your own purpose, spreading happiness wherever you go.

NOTES

NOTES

NOTES

NOTES

www.ingramcontent.com/pod-product-compliance
Lightning Source LLC
Chambersburg PA
CBHW062308240926
51846CB00013B/676
9789360702625